STAR SHROUD

KEN LOZITO

ACOUSTICAL BOOKS LLC

Published by Acoustical Books, LLC

KenLozito.com

IF YOU WOULD LIKE TO BE NOTIFIED WHEN MY NEXT BOOK IS RELEASED VISIT -
WWW.KENLOZITO.COM

ISBN: 978-0-9899319-9-1

Chapter One

Fort Meade, Maryland, 1986

Bruce glanced toward the window where dark skies peeked in along the edges of the blinds and didn't know whether it was late in the evening or early in the morning. Either way he was in deep shit with Kathryn. Late nights spent reviewing reports and attending last-minute meetings were becoming a common occurrence in this line of work—not something the mother of his three young children wanted to hear.

He glanced at the picture of his family that took up prime real estate on his desk. It had been taken when they were on vacation in the Florida Keys. Kathryn loved the beach. The children missed him, and the thought of his constant absence from their lives hit him like a blow to his gut. Perhaps he would take off work tomorrow. Shoulders hunched, he stiffly rose out of the chair and switched off the lamp.

As he slipped on his gray suit jacket, the desk phone rang.

The special line was flashing red, indicating that the call was coming from the pit. Eric was on duty and wouldn't call if it weren't important. He had probably called the house first, waking Kathryn and the children. Maybe those damn pagers hadn't been such a bad idea, but security protocols for Dux Corp mandated that the use of pagers was forbidden because they left more of a trail than using the telephone.

He strode back to his desk and picked up the phone.

"Bruce, thank god you haven't left yet. You need to come to the pit right away. We have an incident."

Incident was code for "get down here now," and this was all that could safely be mentioned on a phone.

"I'll be right there," Bruce said.

In the late seventies the U.S. Army had commissioned an intelligence-gathering project to test the validity of the "psychic warrior." These specialists were used to spy on enemy installations and provide preliminary reconnaissance deep in hostile territory. Bruce Matherson was a project-lead contractor for Dux Corporation, and at thirty years old he had a proven track record for getting solid results. At this point, the project only received laughable support from the U.S. military, but Bruce didn't care. The brass didn't know the team had stumbled upon a veritable goldmine in intelligence gathering, but they wouldn't have been able to see beyond its militaristic application. There was more to do than spy on enemy nations. Research institutions—both domestic and abroad—warranted closer scrutiny, and the insights gained were truly enlightening.

Bruce was using the program to test subjects who showed an inclination toward a sixth sense, with none of the hokey, new-age bullshit that went with it. The program fed the army some useable intelligence reports with a marginal rate of error. But Bruce, along with his partners, Eric Bridges and Jeffry Radford— the rising stars at Dux Corp—had agreed that in order to maintain the most influential role in the project, they couldn't be completely honest with their findings. Intelligence was the world's currency, and Bruce knew the Russians had similar programs running.

The pit, where the magic with monitoring and reconnaissance happened, was located in the old wooden barracks, well away from the real action at Fort Meade. Housing them there had been intended as an insult, but it suited their needs quite well and was far away from prying eyes. Bruce hopped in an old army Jeep they used to get around the base and drove down to the barracks.

It was a cool fall evening with a hint of moisture in the air. Through slightly foggy windows, Bruce noted the vacant buildings lining the road. They were old and hadn't been used since the seventies. The glowing lights of the barracks were the only indication that anyone was working at this part of the base.

Eric was outside waiting for him, waving excitedly as Bruce parked the Jeep and got out.

"You're not going to believe what's happening," Eric said, holding the door for him.

"It must be important, since we're not supposed to leave the pit until we've been relieved," Bruce mildly chided.

"Radford is there. I had to call him in too," Eric said, leading him down the hallway and into the pit, where a grouping of eight reclining seats was equipped with leads that attached to the viewers who occupied them.

Remote viewing enjoyed a time-honored status that lingered

between "ridiculous" and "flights of fantasy." Most people confused a sixth sense with deductive reasoning, but Bruce's team had been able to demonstrate a way to delve deeper into the capabilities of the human brain. Although shamans used hallucinogens to reach a receptive state and eastern monks spent years meditating to achieve it, with the help of the army, the team had been able to run a series of tests on candidates to determine how receptive a person was without those practices. If the candidate qualified, they were brought into the program for more training. Bruce's work focused on bringing non-military personnel into the training program.

They normally ran sessions with three viewers at a time, tasked by various intelligence agencies to observe and report on assigned targets. Usually by the time the requests came to them, the investigators had exhausted all other avenues. Coming to them was, in essence, a Hail Mary pass at the end of the fourth quarter, and the clock had already expired.

The viewer's vitals were constantly monitored while they were in the "cradle," which was a reference to the recliners the viewers sat in during a session. Monitoring vitals was essential to the validation of the viewer's report. This kept both the viewers and trainees honest. Even the best liars had a "tell" of some sort, be it an elevated heart rate, a twitch, or some other physical movement.

Bruce entered the pit. The viewers all had their eyes squeezed shut. Their heart rates were elevated, and beads of sweat dotted their foreheads. Bruce bent over one of them and snapped his fingers in front of their face, but there was no response. He checked their vitals again, but they hadn't changed. It was as if the viewers weren't aware of their physical surroundings.

"What happened? How long have they been like this?" Bruce asked.

"They started the session normally, studying this evening's targets. About fifteen minutes into the session, Lewis began muttering about space and something called "the nine." Started saying all kinds of strange things. We're still recording, but we can see a video of it in Observation," Eric said.

"Have you tried to wake them?"

"They've been unresponsive to all attempts so far."

Bruce frowned, studying the viewers. "Call the nurse in here to start IV bags with saline for each of them. That should prevent dehydration."

Observation was a room away from the pit where they could monitor the viewers without causing distraction. Jeffry Radford was standing to the side as they entered, speaking to three young men in army fatigues. Each had a notebook out, recording the time and instrument readings.

"Great, you found him," Radford said when he saw them.

Bruce took in the room for a few seconds. There was a quiet flurry of activity as each person focused on their assigned task. The readings from the instrumentation for monitoring the magnetic field in the room were erratic, as if something was upsetting the field.

"What's causing all this disruption?" Bruce asked.

"You got me. This all started about an hour ago—the same time the viewers in the pit became unresponsive," Radford said.

The phone rang, and Eric went to answer it.

Radford waved Bruce over to the TV with a video player. He pushed in the VHS tape and pressed the play button.

"This is from earlier," Radford said.

Bruce watched as the viewers got in the cradles and had the electrodes connected to them. Each of the viewers used their own techniques for achieving the state of what the project team called the "observant mind," and Radford fast-forwarded through this process, slowing the tape as one of the viewers—Lewis—started shaking his head back and forth. As he did this, the lighting dimmed and there was momentary interference with the video. When it cleared up, Lewis's mouth was moving, but Bruce couldn't hear him. He raised the volume.

"… so much space. The void is empty. The cold burns. The nine is the key … we must get to the nine…"

Lewis suddenly started spewing random numbers. At this point the viewers all sat up with their backs arched and their chins raised toward the ceiling. After a few moments they laid back down as if whatever held them had eased its hold.

"They've been like that ever since. Sometimes the others speak, but it sounds like gibberish," Radford said.

Eric came over to him. "It gets better. Eight other viewers are in the same state as the ones on duty. We're checking on the rest."

Bruce turned toward the monitor showing the pit. "Is everything being recorded that can be?"

Eric nodded.

"We need to bring in the other viewers. I don't care if we have to pull them from hospitals," Bruce said.

Eric headed back to the phone and started dialing.

"This is going to bring us a lot of attention," Radford said.

"We have to risk it," Bruce answered.

"What do you think this is?"

Bruce chewed on the inside of his lip. "It's like someone is trying to tell us something, but we can't get the full picture. We'll observe and record like usual. Then we'll compile all the data and see what we've got."

"But Bruce, how long can we let them stay like this?"

"Let's get the on-call MD in here," Bruce said.

He took off his jacket and tie, placing them on the hangar by the door. *So much for going home tonight.* Bruce promised himself that he'd make it up to his family as he pulled on his lab coat and headed back out to the pit. Entering the room, the hair on his arms stood up as if there was a lot of static electricity in the area. He went over to Lewis, who was among the most gifted viewers the program had ever produced. Lewis was whispering, and Bruce brought over a stool and sat on it.

"They are coming … they are coming … must go … go," Lewis whispered.

The nurses quietly checked vitals but couldn't wait to put as much distance between themselves and the viewers as possible. Bruce stayed by the viewers. As hard as he had tried in the past, he didn't have the inclination they had. His talents lay with disseminating the information the viewers produced.

The hours went by like quicksand, and the pit filled as eight other viewers were brought in. All of them were in a state of unresponsiveness. Five of the viewers were connected to the open cradles, and cots were set up for the rest. Bruce and the team ran out of equipment and had to borrow some.

The doctor on call tried a few different ways to get the viewers to wake up, but not even adrenaline or smelling salts worked. Whenever one of the viewers did speak, it was mostly gibberish that they couldn't make heads or tails of.

They brought in transcribers who would review the recent

video tapes and record each and every word spoken. The gibberish was subject to interpretation. Bruce retrieved a few pages of it and pressed his lips together as he studied the data. Not having any luck looking at individual pages, he grabbed some Scotch tape and fastened a few pieces of the transcribed notes together, sticking them to the wall. Before long he had a ten-foot section of wall filled floor-to-ceiling with them. Bruce rubbed his eyes and rolled his shoulders, trying to keep exhaustion at bay for a little while longer. He cocked his head to the side and studied the meaningless jumble of numbers and symbols.

Eric came out of Observation and glanced at the wall of paper. "I like what you've done with the place."

Bruce forced his tired mind to focus on the papers, looking for some pattern. "It's like some kind of code. Do you think this is all some sort of message?"

Eric frowned, taking a closer look. "You might be onto something here, but doing it this way is going to take forever. We need access to a mainframe."

Bruce nodded. "We need a search algorithm that can identify patterns at the highest level, and then we can work our way deeper."

Radford stuck his head out of Observation and shouted, "They're waking up!"

Bruce and Eric ran to the pit. All of the viewers appeared slightly disoriented. The nurses and doctor kept telling them to remain seated while they went around to check them. More than one had to be told where they were.

Bruce and Eric went over to Lewis, who was sipping some

water. He kept looking around as if he didn't trust what he was seeing.

"How are you feeling?" Bruce asked.

Lewis set his cup down. His hands were shaky, and they all saw it. His breath began coming in gasps, and the monitor showed his blood pressure spiking.

"Lewis, look at me," Bruce said, squatting down and placing his hand on the viewer's shoulder. "You're all right. We're here at the base."

It took Lewis a few seconds to process what Bruce was telling him, and after a few moments he calmed down.

"Can you tell us what you saw?" Bruce asked.

Lewis cleared his throat. "It was all black, like something grabbed hold of me and pulled me down," he said, and closed his eyes. "Space. It was so vast and cold, but ... not quiet."

Bruce shared a glance with Eric. They both knew that the most vibrant viewings affected all five senses.

"It took control of me," Lewis said, his eyes darting around, looking for some nameless threat.

"It's not here. We've been at your side this whole time. Can you tell us anything else?" Bruce asked.

"Regret. There was regret and desperation. I'm sorry. I just need some time," Lewis replied.

"Just take it easy for a few minutes. The nurse will be coming around with the standard questionnaire. I know it seems routine, but tonight was definitely different. Don't hold back any detail, even if it seems insignificant," Bruce said.

Lewis nodded, and Bruce and Eric stepped away from the pit.

"This is huge. They can't possibly pull our funding now," Eric said.

They were both tired, but the relief of having their viewers return from whatever had held them pushed the exhaustion back.

"We can't tell them," Bruce replied.

Eric's brows shot up his forehead. "What do you mean we can't tell them? Bruce, this is too much to cover up. We need more resources to run analysis on all this data we're collecting."

"If the brass catches wind of this, they'll take the project away from us. Then they'll likely misinterpret the data and keep it locked away somewhere to be forgotten. We know something extraordinary just happened, but we need time to run our own analysis. I'm not just going to give this up," Bruce said.

"If we get caught, then all of us could be brought up on charges of treason. Do you understand what treason means? It's when they either lock you away and tell your family you've had an accident, or death by firing squad, which amounts to the same thing minus the rotting-away-in-jail part," Eric said, trying to speak in hushed tones and failing miserably at it.

Bruce held his hands up in front of his chest. "Listen to me. Our deal with the military was never going to last. There are rumblings that the project is being transferred to the jurisdiction of the CIA. It would be treason to hand this over to them. They're bogged down in more politics than the military. I won't let this become another black ops program."

Eric sighed. "I just don't want to end up in jail, or worse."

Bruce smiled. "We won't. We'll take the data and leverage our connections to piecemeal the analysis. This is going to take a while—years, in fact—but it'll be worth it. The viewers kept talking about space. We've only sent out a few probes and been to the moon. If whatever the viewers saw pertains to some kind of threat in space, then we're not ready to deal with that. Not by a long shot."

Eric frowned. "Aliens?" he asked with a half-committed chuckle.

Bruce shrugged. He didn't want to venture any guesses at this point. His gut instinct was to get this program out of government hands, and the sooner that happened, the better, even at the expense of reputations. Their work had just begun, but it might be his grandkids who would deal with the brunt of it.

"Come on. Let's get back inside. I need to give Kathryn a call to tell her I'll be a while," Bruce said.

"She'll understand, even if she doesn't like it," Eric said.

Bruce nodded and made a mental note that he needed to make up these more frequent absences to his family.

Chapter Two

Chicago, Illinois, 2046

Illusions. Everyone had them. Some people needed them to get through the day and others needed them to wake up. The world was an infinitely less friendly place once awakened. That had happened for Zack nearly nine years ago in 2037 when he dropped out of MIT, despite being only a few credits short of getting his Ph.D. He was nineteen then and part of the Gifted Prodigies Program. He was lumped in with a small group of twelve other prodigies. All of them had demonstrated exceptional aptitude toward hard sciences and engineering disciplines. Everything had a pattern, and one of Zack's talents was deciphering those patterns.

He'd performed his first computer hack at age ten. His teacher had had it coming to her. She'd cheated on her husband and used social media to meet with the other guy, not to mention the pictures she'd posted. The school district's homepage had never been so popular. Zack smiled at the innocence of that first hack. With a few keystrokes, he had slain the beast. Ms. Harding had been no one's favorite teacher, and Zack had almost gotten away with it, but the local cyber crimes unit, or CCU, had traced the change back to his house. Even with the police in their living room, which was enough to scare a boy of ten, Zack could tell that his father wasn't mad at him. The crime, as it were, hit close to home. After the police left, Zack's father hugged him and said he was proud of him. A cheating spouse was a sore point for his father as well. It had been just Zack and his dad for a long time. He could barely remember his mother.

Zack's exploit caught the attention of one of his favorite teachers—Mr. Hammond of the Computer Engineering Department. Zack learned that despite breaking the law, which he had ultimately done, there was such a thing as social justice that people respected, even if they weren't allowed to say it openly. Mr. Hammond had taken Zack's hobby to a whole new level, and Zack had become much better at covering his tracks.

Zack's attention was pulled from this reverie as the coffee-timer in his kitchen blared its golden herald that the brew was done. Some people used supplements to get that early jump in the mornings or to burn the midnight oil, but Zack enjoyed coffee. The aroma of freshly brewed coffee filled the bare walls of his apartment, pulling him back to the past and Saturday mornings with his father. They'd never been rich by anyone's standards. His father had worked as an auto tech, repairing computer systems that ran in cars. Cars used to need just mechanics, but the smarter they got, the more attention they needed to keep them in good working order. One of his father's few indulgences had been gourmet coffee, which they ground themselves.

Zack poured his cup of ambition and added cream and sugar. Not real sugar. God no. Heaven forbid. Sugar was poison; everyone knew that. Even though it seemed that his wiry frame should be able to handle sugar, his bio chip said otherwise. His genes indicated a tendency toward diabetes and obesity, so he avoided most sugars. He supposed that twenty or thirty years ago he would have been the fat kid diagnosed with diabetes and put on medicine that might have caused more harm than good. Not even he could argue with his own genome. Maybe he would hack that someday.

He went over to his makeshift work area. Most people had living rooms, but Zack's apartment was a jungle of electronics. Some things he had built himself and others he had purchased. He sold some of the things he made to amateur hackers. The money was enough to get by on and didn't garner much attention, which he avoided in his line of work.

The two-dimensional holographic display showed multiple bronze-colored flat screens that were slightly transparent. Each window had data streams running the various tasks and traces he had going. Zack stared at the screen without really registering what he was looking at. He had been feeling a bit nostalgic lately. This tended to happen when he approached the anniversary of his father's death. He'd been away at MIT at the time, almost on the eve of getting his Ph.D. on Adaptive Systems and Artificial Intelligence. The accident report had said an electrical short stemming from a faulty battery stopped his father's heart while he was running diagnostics on someone's Ford. Despite the EMTs' best efforts, they couldn't revive him. Zack felt a slight flutter deep in his stomach. It had been over ten years, and it still got to him. Every September. He raised his cup of coffee and nodded to the sky.

Zack had done his own investigation into the flaw that had taken his father away from him. The faulty wiring had been due to a manufacturing defect. At first he'd thought it was the fault of the car company cutting corners and saving money, but he'd been wrong. While there were different automakers out there, the principles for battery technology used in all of them were the same. The source for such principles led back to DARPA, but it was the battery maker that was responsible for the defect—something Zack exposed despite that corporation's best efforts.

Between big corporations and the military, MIT was a place for both recruitment and monitoring. When Zack had found out how much people like himself were being monitored, he began poking around at how deep the rabbit hole went, and he hadn't liked what he'd found. Freedom was an illusion. He, in essence, woke up. Everyone was a prisoner of some sort—imprisoned either by crushing debt, a thankless job, or some other marketing that told them to want something they didn't need. The rich weren't any freer than the poor. It was then that he decided to walk away from everything he'd ever known and become anonymous. In ten years, he'd never owned any property other than the clothes on his back. The lease he had on his apartment was sublet, which he paid for in cash. He moved around a lot. What had started out as an investigation into the death of his father had turned into a crusade against the people who were in control. He took his time, gathered information, and uncovered enough dirt to bring those running the corporations and banks to their knees. No system was totally secure, and no one had been able to trace what he'd done back to him. Kick enough rocks over and you'd be sure to find something. The code he'd written during his time at MIT was still being used for securing anything from bank transactions to a Fortune 100 company's crown jewels.

His computer chimed, driving the remnant morning fog from him. One of his traces had finished running its subroutine, and the window was brought into prominence onscreen.

"All right, let's see what we've got here," Zack said, and sipped his coffee.

He'd been poking around companies that specialized in disaster recovery and data backups. He pulled up the directory of a storage array and went to work. He didn't open any files, as that would trigger an alert that would appear in some security operations center, which may or may not be ignored. A couple of directories held file types he hadn't seen in a long time. The FITS file type had been used by NASA to store images, as well as scientific data. It was positively ancient by current standards, but the names of the files intrigued him. There were directories for pre- and post-processing, along with one for shared. The name New Horizons kept popping up. He executed some code that would break the data down and encrypt the bits. The data would then be copied to multiple public mirrors used for storage. Then, later on, one of his other bots would collect it. The mirrors were located throughout the world, and his program would literally break the files apart, sending the pieces in all directions. Nothing would be able to trace them, and the partial data would appear as junk on the mirrors. Junk data would be deleted as part of normal operating procedures, and, let's face it, no one really secured the trash. It was likely that whatever security operations center was monitoring this company's data would never even sense the breach.

Since he had time, he made himself some breakfast. Eggs and bacon. If there was a god, surely bacon was one of mankind's most precious gifts. Chocolate for women, bacon for men.

Zack piped through his news feeds, on which the spaceship called Athena kept appearing in the headlines. Athena was the result of a multinational, joint space agency project to build a long-range ship constructed and fabricated entirely in space. Robots and drones did most of the work. Athena was slated to go to Titan, one of Saturn's moons, in the next few months. While Zack could appreciate the engineering that went into the construction of such a massive effort, he had no desire to leave Earth. Space was a one-way trip to a quick death as far as he was concerned.

Zack checked his watch. It had been about an hour, more than enough for his latest data dump to process. He logged into the remote systems he used to retrieve data. A quick glance at his connection told him this system was located somewhere in Australia. Someone would have to back-trace him through so many nodes that only an actual machine could disseminate the pattern of where he was operating from. Even then, most security firms didn't have access to comms satellites.

Zack spent the next few hours going through the data he found. One of those things was New Horizons, a spacecraft that gained some notoriety in 2015 for being the first to fly near the planet Pluto. Nine years to get there. No wonder the program quickly faded to obscurity, which explained why he'd never heard of it. The manned mission to Mars was on everyone's mental road map as one of mankind's pivotal achievements, right up there with the lunar landings of the Apollo program of the 1960s.

The raw preprocessing files were encrypted at a level for the truly paranoid at the time, something grade school kids could crack as part of their school project by today's standards. Algorithmic encryption was a thing of the past. The directory held more image files. Once again, the names of the files caught his attention. There were numerous Pre-NASA and Scrubbed NASA references. Whoever had named these files hadn't thought they would be accessed by an unauthorized user. Oh well, that was where the secrets were.

Zack brought up one of the preprocessed image files, and his mouth fell open. The image was a close-up of a region just south of Pluto's equator. Nestled between two icy peaks was some type of structure. The image was tagged to bring attention to it, and the grainy structure was circled. Along the top of the image was a faint word for the software used to process the image. Zack expected it to say NASA, but instead it read Dux Corporation.

Oh crap!

Zack surged to his feet. Dux Corporation was a military contractor that had its fingers dipped into everything. He'd come across multiple references to them over the years, and he knew enough to avoid them. They didn't own New Horizons or the satellite that had sent the images back to Earth. What they did own was the software that processed the image. Zack brought up the image NASA had released to the public and compared it with the Pre-NASA marked image. Those sneaky, manipulative bastards. Dux Corporation had been sitting on the biggest discovery in the history of mankind for the past thirty-one years: proof of an alien structure on Pluto. Zack's brain raced, thinking of the implications. The space agencies of the world pushed farther and farther into space, from mining asteroids to experimenting with maneuvering asteroids onto Mars. No one really cared if they miscalculated and sent a mineral-rich asteroid into the lifeless planet. They had even brought one near the moon. But no one had gone back to study Pluto. He did a few quick checks. After New Horizons, it was as if all the space agencies had begun focusing elsewhere.

They didn't know.

Someone at Dux Corp must have decided the world wasn't ready. Zack glanced out the window, expecting heavily armed men to come busting through. While a normal security firm wouldn't be able to trace him back through satellite channels, a military contractor would have no issue doing so. He needed to move fast. His location was compromised, and they were probably already on his trail. A blast to major news outlets should help. He did a quick write-up for the images. There were more files in other directories, some referencing events from much earlier—all the way back to the 1980s. There was more to this than an alien structure on Pluto. There was a pattern here, and he almost kicked himself for not seeing it on his own. Humanity was being pushed to travel farther into space, but why? Space travel was a societal obsession fueled by a marketing machine that used every angle from scientific research to entertainment.

After he uploaded the images, the information would spread like wildfire. The news media would have no choice but to give it attention. Likely they would try to spin it as the latest in conspiracy theory. But the right people would learn of this and know he had their secrets. He had to run.

Zack sent the upload. Then all the data windows came down

at once as his purge routine ran its course, deleting everything and overwriting whatever was left. Nothing would be recoverable, but the important data was still out there. He had to move. He walked out of his apartment with just a backpack loaded with the clothes he could carry and untraceable credit chits. There was a bus station nearby. He'd head there.

Zack exited the building and came onto the busy streets where something immediately felt off. There was "normal" and then there was "too normal." Delivery bots flew overhead, racing to their next delivery. He had picked this neighborhood because of the high traffic, be it on foot or in a car. He glanced around, but couldn't pinpoint what was wrong. No one gave him a passing glance. Zack pulled the hood of his sweatshirt over his head and started at a brisk pace down the street. The bus station was only a few blocks away. Despite his own self-assurances, he started to jog.

Overhead he heard the high-pitched whine of a rotorless chopper heading in his direction. Zack turned to go back the way he'd come, and another chopper was hovering in that direction. Black unmarked cars appeared out of nowhere, and hardened men exited the vehicles with their weapons pointed at him. They didn't close in. Just waited.

That's it, I'm dead, Zack thought. The breath caught in his chest. A large man dressed in black detached himself from the group. He removed his sunglasses, revealing intense dark eyes. The man looked as if he could snap Zack in half merely by thinking about it.

"Mr. Quick, we'd like to have a word with you," he said.

Zack looked at him and back at the men surrounding him. Part of him wanted to run for it, but there was no way he could escape. Their muscles showed through their clothing. Any one of them could end him if they chose to do so. While he was wiry and enjoyed the occasional run, he knew he was no match for them. *This is what I get for being careless.*

"Zack, calm down. We just want to talk. Let's do this the easy way," the man said.

People were starting to gather on the sidewalks to see what was happening. They weren't going to kill him, not in front of all these people. Would they kill him if he went with them?

Zack pressed his lips together. "If I go with you, I'll never be free again."

The man held his hands up in a nonthreatening gesture. "As I said, we just want to talk. My orders are to bring you in unharmed. Please don't make a scene."

"Who are you?" Zack asked, and immediately regretted it. Any second now they would rush him, and it wouldn't be gentle. Zack shook his head. He had no choice. They could have taken him by force if they'd wanted, and yet here they were asking him to come with them. *What have I gotten myself into now?*

Chapter Three

Kaylan couldn't believe she was here, piloting a new TX301 and cruising at forty-one thousand feet. She had so many other things that had to get done, but Nana was sick and had asked for her. Initially she had doubted she'd get clearance to leave the mission prep for Athena, but a request from the wife of the late great Bruce Matherson carried a significant amount of weight at NASA. Even Michael Hunsicker, the mission commander, was surprised but wished her well. Michael would have told her to go anyway.

She needed so many hours in the cockpit to maintain her astronaut status, which she had in abundance, but the TX301 was the Porsche of the skies. She had only flown the prototype as a test pilot prior to joining NASA almost four years ago. The prototype TX was completely devoid of comfort, but the production model had a smooth, comfortable interior. This model's sleek design, barely more than a wing with a cockpit, allowed for only two passengers. The smart HUD display actually increased visibility. The speed that could be achieved approached that of some military jets. This was the toy for the ultra rich pilot enthusiast. The net worth of the extended Matherson family rivaled most small countries. She might have been one of the many granddaughters of Bruce and Kathryn Matherson, but she had definitely never followed in the footsteps her sisters or cousins had. Namely, she wasn't a lawyer or running one of the many corporations that were part of the Matherson conglomerate. She held her Ph.D. in Aeronautical Engineering. That, along with her time working on the TX project, had gained her admittance to the NASA Astronaut Program. She was pretty much the black sheep of the family.

The Manhattan skyline was rapidly approaching. Special clearance had been given to enable her to fly through the no-fly zone. Her home was near Houston now, and she hadn't been to the city in years. She passed the infamous skyline and headed straight for the Gold Coast. Nana's home was on the north shore of Long Island.

The trip had taken about an hour. Kaylan was sure she could have shaved more off that time. Perhaps a different route home. She circled the lush estate and hovered over the old helicopter pad. The HUD confirmed the landing gear was ready and she set it down. She killed the engines and the landing gear lowered the craft to a meter off the ground. The canopy opened, and she breathed in the salty sea air. She unzipped her flight suit and pulled it off, noting the gentle sounds of a nearby fountain and music playing in the distance. She checked her appearance against the TX's smooth silver sides. Kaylan undid her bun and allowed her dark hair to fall past her neck. Her white cotton button-down shirt and jeans would stick out in the sea of silk shirts and black dresses she was sure to find inside.

Looking at her reflection, she pressed her lips together and reached inside her pocket for her lipstick. The kiosk she had gotten it from indicated it was a perfect match for her tanned skin tone. Nana often said a girl could always use a little lipstick if she didn't have time for anything else. She blew herself a kiss and headed up the path to the main part of the property.

The estate was a vision of well-manicured gardens maintained by a crew of gardeners who were masters of their craft. The pathway led to a stone stairway. She'd had the run of the place when she was little and her parents had taken her to visit on the weekends. She'd explored every nook and cranny of the estate. Now that she was here, the reason for this impromptu trip pushed down on her. This was it. After today she would likely never see her Nana again. Her throat swelled at the bittersweet thought. Nana was well into her nineties and had lived a very full life. It was easy for Kaylan to bury herself in her work and forget that life was still going on for the family she more or less ignored.

"Just had to make an entrance, didn't you?"

Her sister Iris stood at the top of the stone staircase, smiling widely and looking as if she had just come from the catwalk. Iris was three years older than Kaylan and blessed with a body that just wouldn't quit, as her husband liked to joke. Kaylan was more athletic.

"Still crushing men's hearts and making married men cry?" Kaylan asked.

"Only when they find out I'm happily married. Still single?"

There it was. Not even here for a minute and the question had already come up. "We eloped."

Iris laughed. "Yeah right. I figured I'd get that question out of the way."

After a quick embrace, the two sisters headed toward the butler's entry. Iris guessed correctly that Kaylan really just wanted to see their grandmother.

"Are you really going into space?" Iris asked.

"Yes, in less than two months."

"And how long will you be gone?"

"About a year," Kaylan answered.

Iris looked as if she'd been about to say something but decided against it. "It's what you've always wanted. I don't know how you do it, but do me a favor," Iris said, and placed her hand on Kaylan's arm.

"What's that?"

"Stay safe. I know you don't see eye to eye with most of the family, but you are missed."

Kaylan placed her hand over her sister's and gave it a gentle squeeze. "I will. I promise."

Iris nodded and they headed up the narrow staircase to the second level.

"Where are you going?" Iris asked

"Has it been that long since we spoke? I would have thought Mom would have told you. I'm going to Titan. It's one of—"

"Saturn's moons," Iris finished. "See, I know more than just corporate law and running a company. Why go to Titan?"

"There's a lot we can learn by going there. It's the only moon in the solar system with clouds and a planet-like atmosphere. Titan is one of the most Earth-like worlds we've ever found. There is a strong possibility that there's life there."

Iris looked at her. "You're such a nerd."

Kaylan laughed as they emerged onto a small landing near her grandmother's rooms.

A butler approached Iris. "Pardon me, Mrs. Barrett. You have a call."

Iris thanked him and nodded for Kaylan to go on without her.

The brightly lit hall with its smells of polished wood greeted her. Kaylan sighed. Perhaps she should have visited more, but with the visits came the questions and general disapproval of how she lived her life. There had been very few men in her life, and none since she'd joined NASA.

The door to Nana's room was open. The "room" had cathedral-high ceilings and a four-poster bed that wouldn't fit in Kaylan's apartment. The bed was empty.

"Come in, dear," Nana's soft voice called from the open terrace.

Kaylan walked over, her eyes taking in the sight of her grandmother. She sat propped up in a padded chair, from which the oxygen tanks were hardly visible. Her thin gray hair barely kissed the nape of her neck.

The hospice nurse standing with her grandmother gave her a simple nod before stepping away to give them some privacy.

Kaylan felt the guilt of not coming to visit more often drag down in the pit of her stomach. She should have made time.

"Hello, Nana," Kaylan whispered, her eyes brimming with tears. Oh, why hadn't she made time to visit more?

Nana held up her arms, and Kaylan gave her a gentle hug. She felt so frail.

Seeing the look on her face, her grandmother smiled. "Time

catches up to us all, my dear. Please just stand there and let me take a look at you."

Kaylan stood and smiled as her grandmother took in the sight of her.

"So beautiful. You always were. Any man would be lucky to have you," Nana said.

Kaylan felt her cheeks warm. Getting a man's attention had never been her problem. It was finding the right one that was the real challenge.

"Bruce always thought the world of you, even if the rest of them didn't understand."

"I'm sorry I didn't come sooner. I'm sorry you had to ask me to come," Kaylan said.

Her grandmother smiled and her eyes grew distant for a moment, chasing a memory. "You're just like him, you know. Bruce always worked hard—so hard that he often missed everything going on around him. When your mother was very young, she hardly saw your grandfather because he was working so much. It wasn't until much later that I understood why Bruce worked so hard."

"Some would say it paid off," Kaylan said, and gestured around her.

Her grandmother eyed her, some of the old spark back in her eyes. "Guilt built this place. At least that was what I used to think. Now I think it was necessary to achieve the goals we had. The grandness of this place holds little sway with you, just as it did with him," her grandmother said as she looked at a portrait of Kaylan's grandfather. He wore a dark gray suit and seemed to be lost in thought when the picture was taken. "Bruce loved all of his children and grandchildren very much. Most play a vital role in the companies they're involved in. But none of their jobs are as important as yours."

"Mine? What do you mean? Nana, I'm an astronaut. A scientist. I don't run a global enterprise. I'm not responsible for thousands of employees," Kaylan said.

Her grandmother started to cough, and the nurse came over to adjust the level of oxygen. After a few moments her grandmother began to breathe easier.

"He always wanted to go there, you know," Nana said, and nodded toward the sky.

Kaylan smiled and knelt down next to her grandmother's chair, taking her hand. She looked so tired. "I remember using the telescope with him when we came here. He was always trying to get me to look at Pluto by tapping into the deep space telescopes, but Jupiter and Saturn were my favorites."

The nurse gave her a meaningful look that said her grandmother needed to rest. Nana closed her eyes and seemed to drift off to sleep. Kaylan knelt there holding her grandmother's hand, remembering the last time she'd been here. She had just been accepted into NASA and was excited to tell her family the good news. Most of them had been in a state of shock and couldn't believe she was pressing on with scientific research.

Her grandmother squeezed her hand. "It's no accident that you're the one to go into space."

Something in her voice tugged at Kaylan's curiosity. "What do you mean?"

"You were meant for this trip. I will miss you," she said, and sank back into the chair.

Kaylan waited a few moments to see if she would wake again.

"She'll sleep for a while now. You were lucky. She's usually not this active," the nurse said. She adjusted the chair's controls so it reclined more.

Kaylan thanked the nurse and silently left the room. She'd earned her place on the Athena Mission. It had been her goal since NASA first announced a deep space ship being built in space. It was a revolutionary concept. Most of the materials used to construct the ship were made on the lunar surface. A joint venture between different countries' space agencies had guided a mineral-rich asteroid into a soft landing on the moon, then built a base around it. Very few people were actually stationed there, with the bulk of the work being done by robots.

Meant for this … The way her grandmother had said it was as if she had always known Kaylan would be going on the Athena Mission.

She headed down the hallway that led to the central staircase in the middle of the house. Iris was at the bottom of the stairs and waved her over excitedly.

"You're not going to believe this," Iris said.

There was a group of people gathered around a large holo-screen. The larger-than-life newscaster's head dominated most of it, with a heading that read "Aliens on Pluto?"

"Trending on the internet are these pictures taken from a NASA spacecraft that passed by Pluto in 2015. These photos were allegedly taken from the New Horizons spacecraft that was launched in 2006. As you can see, there is some kind of structure on the surface. We've had to dig into the old news archives for the photos broadcast on this network."

The report went on about how authentic these pictures were, but Kaylan couldn't keep herself from laughing, which drew the attention of others around her.

"You don't think this is real, do you?" Kaylan asked.

Some muttered that it could be real.

Janet Williamson, a NASA spokesperson, came on-screen and reported that they would be analyzing the photos and would release an update later in the week.

"Are you sure you're still going to Titan?" Iris asked quietly at her side.

"Of course. They're not going to change what's been planned for the past four years because of what could be a hoax," Kaylan said.

Iris shrugged her shoulders, and at the same moment a text message registered with Kaylan's internal HUD. The comms implants were made of small nanobots that worked like traditional contact lenses, except she never had to remove them and they would never be rejected by her body. The movement of her eyes actually powered the nanobots that worked with the small implant located at the base of her skull. Implants like these were pretty much standard at NASA and were becoming more available to the public. There were some purists who would never trust technology near their brains. These were the same people who used older cellular phones that could cause tumors to grow on the hip or brain, depending upon where the phone was most often. She'd take an implant any day.

With that thought, Kaylan brought up the message.

Return to Houston ASAP. M. Hunsicker.

Kaylan glanced at the holoscreen, whose broadcast still held the attention of those around her.

"I have to go," Kaylan said to her sister.

"You've only just arrived," Iris said, looking disappointed.

"I know. Perhaps you could come down to Houston before I leave?" Kaylan asked.

A wide smile lit up her sister's face. "I would love to. I mean it. I would love to see what keeps you away from all this."

"I'll call you in a few days," Kaylan said. After a brief hug, she headed back to her plane.

Chapter Four

Kaylan didn't see a single soul on her way back to the helipad, which was how she preferred it because her swollen eyes bore the telltale signs of the tears she'd shed on the way. She kept turning back to the house, where the blaze of ceramic Spanish roof tiles basked in the September sun. She wished things had been different. Deep down she knew she wouldn't be coming back here for a long time. Possibly ever. Without her grandmother here, there would be no reason.

Kaylan approached the TX301, which she had left waiting on standby. No one else could sneak in and take off. A soft ping registered with her neural implant and the cockpit opened. The landing gear lowered to her specifications so she could easily climb inside. After running a few preflight checks, she engaged the engines and hovered in the air just above the tree line. Kaylan took one long last look at the estate, then swung the plane around and sped south.

She felt better once she was on her way, and kept the controls on manual. The TX hit twenty thousand feet in hardly any time at all. Against her better judgment, she gave in to her urge to punch it and see if the TX was as fast as she remembered. She skirted west of Philadelphia and then turned southwest near Harrisburg, Pennsylvania. This route would take her over the George Washington and Jefferson National Forests, which were part of the Appalachian Mountains. It was a scenic route to travel either by car or by plane. Most commercial aircraft took a more direct path south, so she didn't anticipate much air traffic flying this route at all. She should have sent her updated flight plan to the Air Traffic Control Network, but the TX was too small to be picked up by anything out here. Had she flown one of the commercial routes, the ATC would have been all over her.

The sprawling national forest whipped past below. A few minutes after crossing the North Carolina state line, the HUD brought the plane's radar system to prominence on the display. There were two flashing dots approaching from the southwest. Kaylan frowned. Normally there would be a flight number to identify the plane, but these were unmarked, and they were approaching fast. Kaylan altered her course, and her two unknowns immediately changed course to intercept.

Kaylan brought up the comms. "This is flight Z3014 en route to Houston. Unidentified aircraft south of my position on intercept course. Please respond."

Kaylan waited a moment, but there was no response.

She maintained her airspeed and heading and repeated herself over comms. The two jets were closing in on her now. They buzzed past her in a black blur. Kaylan sucked in a breath. *That was too close.*

"Who the hell do you think you are!" she shouted into comms.

Kaylan turned to get a better look at them. The black jets were small, one-man fighters. Stinger class S93s, designed for quick response. *Military.*

The radar showed that the two Stingers had circled and were closing in fast on her position.

"Civilian Flight Z3014, you've deviated from your flight plan and are in a no-fly zone. You will be escorted away," a male voice said over comms.

One of the Stingers pulled alongside her. Kaylan looked over but couldn't see anything through the dark canopy. The other Stinger stayed on her six.

"Your no-fly zone isn't registered. With whom am I speaking?" Kaylan asked.

"This is Major Dale Hicks, United States Air Force. Ms. Farrow, you will comply with my instructions."

They knew her name. His smug southern accent sent her hackles rising. Kaylan adjusted her hands on the stick.

"Ms. Farrow, Lieutenant Garcia is going to ease up in front of you—"

She hated the way he said her name. The Stinger alongside eased up in front of her craft.

"Major Hicks, if that's your real name, I don't have to follow you anywhere since there is no military base in the vicinity. You have no authority over me."

Kaylan pressed her lips together in a thin smile and engaged the supersonic protocols. She swung out from behind the Stinger and punched it. The TX shot ahead. Traditionally, pilots going this speed had to wear a mask to keep from passing out, but that was a thing of the past. The ceramic poly alloys used in her jet's construction were extremely high heat resistant. At twenty-two hundred miles per hour, she was at Mach 3 and couldn't feel the slightest bit of pressure.

A muffled curse sounded over comms. Her TX was as close to a military jet as a civilian could get. The Stingers caught up to her. Kaylan put on more speed and banked to the right, then made a beeline for the misty mountaintops ahead. Hicks kept calling for her to stop, but there was no way she was going to do that. She didn't know who they were, and they didn't have proper authorization. That made them black ops. Kaylan had never been in the military, but she had spent a fair amount of time as a test pilot re-enacting aerial combat scenarios. The clouds would give her cover.

Kaylan's mind raced. What was she going to do? They weren't going to shoot her down—at least she didn't think so. She'd lead them to a public place and land. At this speed she was about fifteen minutes from Houston, and she came out of the clouds to clear skies. All at once her HUD turned red with the words: **Override. Pilot lockout.**

"Wouldn't want you to wreck such a nice jet, darling," Hicks said.

She'd lost control of the TX, which was now being remote-piloted. Kaylan released the stick and cursed. Civilian aircraft all had remote override as part of their autopilot systems. The TX slowed down and headed east, back toward the mountains.

"Just sit back and relax. Enjoy the flight, Ms. Farrow," Hicks said.

Kaylan bit back her response and reached down to open the access panel on her right. One of the black Stingers coasted up next to her. The autopilot system was in the rear of the jet where she couldn't reach, but if she could sever the link, then she could take back control. The system used for the autopilot was taken from missile comms that allowed for ongoing control despite the range. They relied on satellite communications.

"Ms. Farrow, I'd like to know what you think you're doing." Hicks said.

"Oh, I'm just enjoying the flight, Mr. Hicks," Kaylan replied innocently.

She reached past the wires to the redundant sat controller beyond. Her fingers found purchase where the wires met the controller board.

"Although, I think I'd rather fly myself," Kaylan said, and she yanked back the connections.

The sudden surge caused the HUD to black out, and when it came back on it was green. Kaylan grabbed the stick and darted ahead of her Stinger escorts. Hicks's garbled reply was lost as Kaylan streaked away again. Surging the system gained her control because the autopilot systems were shorted out and couldn't be reset from the air.

Kaylan let out a small laugh. This was the most fun she'd had in a long time. The comms channel on the HUD flashed, drawing her attention, and Kaylan answered it.

"Kaylan, this is Ed Johnson from Dux Corp. We met prior to you leaving to go to NASA. Do you remember me?" Ed asked.

Kaylan eased back on the throttle. Ed was a director of special projects at Dux Corp. He pretty much moved wherever he was needed. He was an older man who had a calm, let's-roll-up-the-sleeves-and-get-to-work mindset that she liked. "What's all this about, Ed? I was on my way back to Houston before Major Ramjet here tried to take control of my plane."

The Stingers had caught up to her again but were staying back, giving her some room.

"I'm sorry Major Hicks wasn't more tactful. I've been in contact with NASA, and they are aware of your delayed arrival. I need to speak to you about recent events and your mission to Titan," Ed said.

As Ed finished speaking, a text message came up on the HUD from Michael Hunsicker, Commander of the Athena Mission, confirming that NASA was indeed aware of the current situation.

"Okay, Ed. I'll come in. Tell the pilots of those two Stingers to hang back."

"Will do. We have a small hangar just south of Asheville. Sending the coordinates now," Ed said.

A few minutes later she found the hangar. It was so well concealed that it blended in with the foothills surrounding it. There were no roads in or out. Without the coordinates, she never would have spotted it. There was one large hangar in the middle of two smaller ones. The hangars were unmarked. Kaylan brought the TX down toward the center hangar, hovering a few feet over the ground, and the ground controller waved her inside. The hangar was empty except for one other plane. She eased past the doors and deployed the landing gear. Another ground controller directed her to an open area, and she touched down.

Kaylan killed the engine and shut down the systems. The canopy opened as the landing gear lowered to her predefined preferences. She stepped out and watched the two black Stingers fly in and land near her. Each had a blue stripe that ran the length of the wings with the USAF designation.

The two pilots exited their planes and removed their helmets. The shorter pilot was a woman who had pinned-up, jet-black hair and must be Lieutenant Garcia. As Garcia turned in her direction, Kaylan noticed just how full-figured she was and was willing to bet Garcia turned more than a few heads.

The second pilot removed his helmet and scowled in Kaylan's direction. Major Dale Hicks was tall and lean with short-cropped brown hair. He stormed over to her, his blue eyes ablaze with fury.

"What the hell, lady! Your little stunt put us all at risk."

"Then perhaps you shouldn't have been all over my ass out there," Kaylan replied, and heard the lieutenant stifle a laugh.

Hicks sent a withering glance over to Garcia.

"I should ask *you* who you think *you* are. You're a military officer. You have no authority over a civilian aircraft, and yet you tried to lock me out of my own plane. I should have you brought up on charges," Kaylan said.

Hicks's mouth hung open. "Do you believe this one?"

"Oh, I like her. Anyone who can get the jump on you is all right in my book," the lieutenant said, and stuck out her hand to Kaylan. "Lieutenant Katie Garcia, ma'am."

Kaylan shook Garcia's hand. Ed Johnson came out of one of the rooms off to the side and jogged over to them, calling out as he came.

"Why don't we all calm down and brush this unfortunate incident aside," Ed said, dividing his gaze between Hicks and Kaylan.

Kaylan looked over at Ed. "What's this about? You wanted to

speak to me about the Athena Mission, and you sent the military to bring me in?"

Ed's brows drew down. "I'm sorry, Kaylan. It was a simple miscommunication. We're on high alert. Hicks and Garcia were patrolling around DC airspace when they picked up your signal. Things were happening fast, and I needed to get you here as quickly as possible."

"I'm here, Ed. I even got a message from NASA."

"Oh good. Michael got ahold of you," Ed said, sounding relieved.

"You know Michael Hunsicker?"

"Oh yes, he and I have been acquaintances for over twenty years. We worked together for a time during the Orion missions to Mars," Ed said, and waved for them to follow him.

Hicks looked like he had more to say but kept his mouth shut. He held up his hand, inviting Kaylan to go ahead of him. She heard Garcia chuckle as she went ahead, and Kaylan felt her own lips curve in response.

Ed stopped outside a small, empty conference room and turned to face them. "Hicks, Garcia, could you please wait outside for a minute, while I bring Kaylan up to speed? Don't go far because I'll need the both of you in a few minutes."

Kaylan walked into the conference room. The old gray linoleum floor was swept but retained a permanent film of grit that rubbed the bottom of her shoes as she walked in. She picked one of the sparsely padded chairs toward the middle of the table and sat. Ed closed the door behind them and sat across from her.

"Do you know a person named Zackary Quick?"

Kaylan frowned in thought. "Zack? Yes, I knew Zack. He and I were at MIT together."

"Gifted Prodigies Program?" Ed asked with a raised brow.

"Yeah. You know, none of us in the program appreciated that name. Kinda singled us out."

"But you knew him."

"Yes, we were friends. Zack was into computer engineering. He did research into data security and adaptive systems. He worked from a grant, and quite a few companies used Zack's research, including Dux Corp. Is something wrong? I haven't seen Zack in a very long time. Is he in some kind of trouble?" Kaylan asked.

Truth be told, she hadn't seen him in over ten years. Zack had dropped off the map, saying he couldn't take all the Big Brother stuff going on. At the time she'd thought he'd snap out of it, but his father's death had hit him hard, and he wasn't quite the same after that.

"We've had a data breach," Ed said solemnly.

Kaylan's brow shot up. "You think Zack's responsible?"

"Oh, we know he's responsible." Ed snorted.

"What did he do?" Kaylan asked. She remembered Zack as always pushing the boundaries, particularly with secure systems. He'd hack MIT's campus media controls and change the pitch of the professors' microphones so they sounded like they'd just inhaled helium, or he'd raise the heat in select offices. They had always been harmless pranks. She glanced at Ed. His watery eyes had hints of red around the edges, and she wondered when he'd last slept. Whatever Zack had done must have been something serious.

"Have you seen the news?" Ed asked.

"Just some half-baked story about an alien structure on Pluto

—" Kaylan started to say but stopped when Ed nodded. "Are you telling me that story is true?"

Ed sighed. "This company and many others we're partnered with was conceived by your grandfather. He took over Dux Corp in the early nineties and had one vision he was working toward: the betterment of mankind. Your friend stumbled upon an old storage array and was able to decrypt the files. Something that was supposed to be impossible. He then broke them down and copied them out to the internet."

Kaylan held up her hands. "Are you saying there is, in fact, an unknown alien structure on Pluto?"

"We've known about it since 2015 when the spacecraft New Horizons first beamed its data back to Earth."

Kaylan's mouth hung open, her mind racing to come to grips with the moment. "This doesn't make any sense. How could Dux Corp have done this? They weren't even involved with that mission."

"We don't have a lot of time, but to put it as simply as possible, Dux Corp made it their mission to monitor all Earth-bound transmissions from all the space agencies of the world. If not us, then it would have been one of our other corporations that worked with a foreign government entity. In some instances we were able to analyze the data prior to releasing it to the intended recipient—in this case, NASA."

Kaylan stood up and paced a few steps, shaking her head. "I don't believe this. You're telling me that the Matherson conglomerate has been spying on the world's space exploration efforts for the past sixty years?"

Ed got to his feet and came around the conference table. "I

know this is a lot to take in, but just hear me out before you judge too harshly."

After a few seconds, Kaylan nodded.

"There was an incident that occurred during the eighties where an entity not of this Earth contacted a select group of individuals specially trained in remote reconnaissance. The contact lasted for hours, during which time they were completely incapacitated. Within the data we collected, we learned there was an encoded message. We later learned that the incident had occurred globally at exactly the same time. It even spread to coma patients at nearby hospitals. We collected all the data we could and were even able to decode some of the message. There is a theory that the message was meant to be decoded in parts. As we made scientific advancements, other parts of the message became clearer. In 2015, when we first saw that alien structure, we knew there was intelligent life out there," Ed said.

"Why wouldn't you have shared this discovery? Ed, this is huge."

"We weren't ready. Pluto was nowhere near within our grasp. We'd just managed to get the US government to allow private companies a crack at offering services dealing with space. To unveil that discovery then would have led to an arms race that would have made the Cold War look like a summer vacation."

"You don't know that. What if it had brought us together?" Kaylan asked.

"The people who know about this have debated that very subject ever since we first saw those images. We're not going to sort that out now in the next few minutes. It was decided that it was better to push scientific research to support space explo-ration. Now, that doesn't mean that all our efforts went into building a big spaceship. As you know, there are a lot of different technologies that go into anything having to do with space, from robotics to special alloys and fusion technology. None of those were developed quickly. It happened over a long period of time," Ed said, and stopped to take a sip of water.

"I'm still having trouble believing any of this. Are you saying our scientific achievements over the past sixty years have been because of the content in an alien message?" Kaylan asked.

"Not even close. Whoever sent the message went to great pains to ensure that we earned the knowledge for ourselves. For example, we'd find a reference to certain chemical compounds. We'd offer grants to universities to research these compounds to see how they worked and what their application could be. So the message functioned as a guide in certain respects, but it didn't take us anywhere scientifically that we wouldn't go ourselves," Ed said.

"It sounds like we were being nudged."

Ed's eyes lit up. "That's an excellent way to put it."

"But aliens, Ed? Really?" Kaylan said, and then held up her hands. "Never mind that. So Zack opened the lid on the discovery from 2015. Most people are skeptical at best when it comes to alien contact."

"We were hoping for another ten years before this knowledge was released, or at least "discovered" by another robotic probe. With the amount of work going on in the asteroid belt, we felt a serious mission to Pluto would be feasible by then."

"Where is Zack now?" Kaylan asked.

Ed gave her a long look before answering. "He's here. We've been questioning him, but he's been uncooperative."

Kaylan's lips curved slightly into a small smile. She remembered how stubborn Zack could be.

"Is this why you brought me here?"

"I'm not going to lie to you—it is part of the reason. Mostly it was to tell you about what we've just discussed. Zack is in real trouble. He's upset a lot of powerful people," Ed said quietly.

Kaylan swallowed while meeting Ed's gaze. Zack's life might be in danger.

"You need his cooperation," Kaylan said.

"Not just us. All of humanity needs it. If he's capable of what many of us suspect he is, then humanity's future may depend on it. That message contained a warning," Ed said.

"Bring him in here, then. I'd like to hear what he has to say about all this," Kaylan said.

Ed nodded and went over to the door. He stuck his head out, spoke quietly to whoever was outside, and then returned.

"They're getting him," Ed said.

They waited in silence. One thing Ed excelled at was reading people, or a situation, and he instinctively knew when to take action or let someone absorb the information he had given them. Kaylan was still coming to grips with it, and after a few minutes' contemplation, another question was brought to the forefront of her mind. What did this have to do with her? Why ask her about the Athena Mission? NASA and the other space agencies had invested too much in that mission to simply scrub it. It was less than six weeks away.

The door opened and a much older-than-she-remembered Zack Quick entered the room. Zack had always been wiry, but the ten years since she had last seen him had hardened him. He still had those deep, penetrating dark eyes, and his short black hair had a slight curl to it. His face lit up with an unexpected smile at the sight of her.

"Zack," Kaylan greeted, coming over to him. Then she saw that he had handcuffs on and looked back at Ed. "Really? Can you take the handcuffs off?"

Ed nodded to the two armed men who had followed Zack into the room. They removed his handcuffs, and Ed asked them to wait outside.

"Are you all right?" Kaylan asked.

"Kaylan—" Zack began and stopped. "It's really good to see you," he said, and glanced at Ed.

Kaylan smiled. "I hear you've been busy."

Zack shrugged. "To be honest I didn't know what I'd stumbled onto at the time."

Ed's feet slid across the floor as he sat up in his chair. "Then why did you send those images to multiple news media agencies around the globe?"

Zack's gaze hardened. "What's the matter? Don't like having your secrets brought into the light?"

"If it had been a simple data breach, then it wouldn't be so bad. Your actions will have repercussions felt around the world," Ed said.

"I could say the same thing for the actions of Dux Corporation."

Kaylan agreed with Zack, but now was the time for caution. Having someone here like Ed Johnson was Dux Corporation's way of playing nice.

"Take it easy, Zack," Kaylan said.

Zack's gaze softened for a moment before it reclaimed its

guarded expression. "What are you doing here? I thought you were with NASA."

"I am with NASA. I've only been here for about twenty minutes. Ed was just telling me about the alien structure on Pluto and the data you found," Kaylan said.

"It's really something. I was only able to scratch the surface, and there's a lot more where that came from," Zack said.

"And we'd like the data back," Ed said.

"If I turn the data over to you, I'll be locked away for who knows how long, or worse," Zack said.

"The authorities haven't been alerted … yet."

Kaylan watched as Zack weighed his options.

"Ed," Kaylan said, "wouldn't there have been copies or backups made of this data?"

"There are. What your friend stumbled upon were the digitized recordings and data sets going back all the way to the eighties. In essence, they were originals," Ed said.

"What happens if I return your data?" Zack asked.

Ed's mouth twitched, confirming for Kaylan that this was exactly where Ed wanted the conversation to go.

"We'd like your help deciphering it," Ed said.

Zack blinked his eyes a few times, looking surprised, and then shook his head. "Most people think Big Brother is the government, but Dux Corp has proven to be the ultimate Big Brother. The Matherson conglomerate has an intricate web that ties into everything. I've spent the last ten years of my life bringing that company's dirty secrets out into the public, and now you want me to help an organization such as yours? No way."

Ed put his elbows on the conference table and bridged his

hands in front of his face. "Mr. Quick, let me tell you a couple of possible ways this could play out. Then I'll let you decide which one works best for you. First, you could persist in withholding the data you stole or destroyed, which could spell certain doom for humanity. The message contained a warning that will affect all of us. This is much bigger than you or me. Second, you could help us. You could help Kaylan. She is going to need your help."

"Me? What do you mean?" Kaylan asked.

"Do you honestly think the mission parameters for Athena aren't going to change?" Ed countered.

"We're going to Titan."

Ed shook his head. "Not anymore. The countries that funded the Athena Mission will push to send you to Pluto. It comes down to cost and benefit. It's true we can learn a lot going to Titan. It would be the deepest of any manned missions to space to date. But now that people know about Pluto, they will demand that we go see it for ourselves."

"They would send a probe to Pluto first. That takes time to set up. Pluto is over six billion kilometers from Earth," Kaylan said.

"Not necessarily. One second," Ed said.

He leaned over to press a button. A panel in the center of the conference table lowered and withdrew. The tip of a holoprojector rose several inches and came on. The lights in the room dimmed automatically. The projector showed the solar system and kept the display the length of the conference table.

"Here is Pluto. It has a different orbit relative to the other planets," Ed said.

Pluto's orbital path became more prominent in the display, and then several blinking dots with Russian names appeared.

"The Russians have had two space vehicles operating in the Kuiper belt for studying comets that pass through the area," Ed said.

Kaylan studied the position of the Russian spacecraft. Relatively speaking, they were within the vicinity of Pluto. "It would still take those machines months to get close enough."

"What good would that do? Wouldn't we only get more pictures?" Zack asked.

Kaylan shook her head. "If I'm remembering this correctly, this was a joint venture between Russian and Chinese space agencies."

"NASA was involved as well. We provided the specs for the miniaturized rovers they were using to land on asteroids as they passed by," Ed said.

"Even if they had a rover left over, it couldn't get to Pluto before the Athena Mission is set to depart," Kaylan said.

Ed calmly looked at her. "Work the problem. How could this work?"

"I would be basing it off assumptions."

"Indulge me," Ed replied.

Kaylan frowned. "In space, it's always an issue of resources. And the thrust required for either of those two vehicles would be …" Kaylan stopped and let out an exasperated smile. "The two vehicles working together could make it. The shared resources would give them the power they need to make the journey. Were these produced at Titus Station?"

"What's that?" Zack asked.

"It's part of the mining exploration missions in the asteroid belt. It's a robotic station that can construct the probes we have studying the asteroids there," Kaylan answered.

"A robotic station? Are there really no astronauts there?" Zack asked.

"It started out that way, but now there is a small crew stationed there," Ed said.

"So if they are able to link the two craft together, then they might make it in time," Kaylan said.

"I'm glad you think so, because that's exactly what's happening right now. We've wanted another look at Pluto for some time now and were working toward this," Ed said.

"Who's we?" Zack asked.

"If you help us, then I'll tell you that and more."

Zack glanced at Kaylan.

"Why do you think Zack could help?" Kaylan asked.

"Because you're going to Pluto. If you don't believe me, then you'll find out when you get back to Houston. The reason I know Zack can help you is because of his expertise. He has repeatedly proven that he can break into countless systems and manipulate data on a structural level, and he sees the patterns that most of us miss. There is a lot we don't know about the message. There will be intelligence that you'll need," Ed said.

Kaylan knew Zack liked a challenge and saw the hunger in his eyes for this. "Let's say for the sake of argument that what you claim is true. The further away from Earth, the more the communications gap widens. How much help would he be?"

"That's why we're proposing that Mr. Quick be added to the Athena Mission."

"What!" Zack and Kaylan said at the same time.

"He'll never get clearance," Kaylan said.

"He would if you helped him," Ed countered.

"Uh, I didn't say I would go," Zack quickly added.

The door to the conference room opened, and Major Hicks and Lieutenant Garcia entered the room.

"We need to be wheels-up in fifteen minutes," Hicks said.

Ed nodded and killed the holoprojection of the solar system. The harsh fluorescent lighting came back on.

"You can always rot in a cell, or you can get out there and do some good. The choice is yours," Ed said, and left the room.

"Ms. Farrow," Hicks said, "will you please join us in the hangar in five minutes?"

Kaylan nodded, and they left the room. She and Zack were alone. Zack faced the wall, looking at nothing in particular, and shook his head.

"They can't do this," Kaylan said.

"Yes they can, and you know it."

"They can't force you to do this."

"I want to help you. I've only seen part of the data, and it's like nothing I've ever seen before. If half of what that guy said is true, then this could be the challenge of a lifetime, but … space … I'm no astronaut," Zack said.

"We can't do anything from here. Come with me to Houston and we can get this sorted there."

"What do you know about that guy?" Zack asked.

"Ed is a straight shooter. He doesn't beat around the bush. Even knowing this, I'm having trouble believing everything he just said. But you know what's even scarier than that? What if everything he said is completely true?"

"Humanity in danger? Come on," Zack said. "I'll go with you to Houston, and that's it. I'm not going into outer space."

Chapter Five

Zack was trying to keep it together as he followed Kaylan down the hall at Dux Corporation's secret mountain base. When they'd taken him into custody, he'd thought it was the FBI or CIA. He remembered getting into the car and then he blacked out. When he'd awakened, he was here, only he didn't know where "here" was. They'd had him locked in a room. Someone had come in and asked him a few questions, but the questions were so idiotic that he now thought it had been some type of assessment. Whatever it was, he must have passed.

Seeing Kaylan was a surprise. Her fine brown hair had reddish highlights from the sun. She always had liked being outside. He had forgotten how beautiful she was. Most of the boys in the Gifted Prodigies Program at MIT had known who Kaylan was. Those honey brown eyes could melt even the most stalwart of egos. They'd been friends and could have been something more, but he had left. Walking down the hallway with her now, he kept her within his line of sight, and she turned to give him a reassuring smile.

Edward Johnson was someone he hadn't expected. He *had* expected to be threatened and hoped he could bargain his way out of trouble. Not this time, it seemed.

They emerged into the pungent smell of the hangar, where they were joined by a man and woman in uniform. The man gave him a look that said, "Don't mess with me, and I won't end you," which was fine with Zack. The woman, however, had a slight playfulness in her eyes. Zack could tell she liked to flirt. With a shapely body that her flight suit only hinted at, who wouldn't want her attention? She noticed him watching, and he looked away quickly.

There were armed guards everywhere. Zack had spent a fair amount of time assessing the physical security of corporate crown jewels around the world, and he had to tip his hat to Dux Corp. They only hired professionals, at least the ones who carried guns. They were all focused and watchful.

Zack leaned up to Kaylan, who walked in front of him. "Where are we?"

"We're in North Carolina, south of Asheville."

Zack shook his head. They had knocked him out and flown him hundreds of miles away, and now they were heading to a small passenger jet. "Why are they so on edge? Who's gonna attack us here?"

Kaylan was about to answer when the man in uniform stopped and turned around. Zack let out a soft chuckle when Kaylan scowled at the man, then she headed toward the jet.

"I'm Major Dale Hicks," he said, sticking out his beefy hand to Zack.

Zack looked at the hand for a second before deciding to shake it. He thought it best not to piss off everyone who could break him in half. Hicks was a good five inches taller than him.

"Zack Quick."

"Nice to meet you, Zack. We're flying to Houston to meet with NASA, and from there I'm not sure," Hicks said.

Zack nodded. "Got your marching orders, soldier." Right after he said it, his stomach turned to ice at the glare Hicks gave him.

"They tell me you're needed. You'll be watched by me or Lieutenant Garcia until we reach Houston. If you don't give us any trouble, then everything will be fine," Hicks said.

Zack looked at Garcia, and there wasn't any flirtation in her eyes now. She was all business just like Hicks, and judging by her bearing, Zack would bet she could take him down just as easily as Major Hicks.

"I won't be any trouble," Zack promised.

Part of him expected Hicks to threaten him. It's what a lesser person would do, but Hicks just nodded. Zack climbed up the steps and into the small jet. He was greeted by aged leather furnishings and a sparkling brilliance that stank of money and power. Kaylan sat near the cockpit, and Zack decided to sit across from her. He thought he would try and say something witty, but everything that came to mind made him feel stupid, so he just sat down.

A small holoscreen was showing the news next to him. They were still flashing up pictures of the alien structure on Pluto. Every now and then they would change to a correspondent who would weigh in. Mostly it was just the news station's attempt to sound as if they had half a clue.

"Let me get this straight," Kaylan began. "You broke into Dux Corporation's data center, found these files, and thought, 'Oh goody, I'll broadcast this to the world?'"

"I was just poking around on some old storage networks. I didn't even know the data belonged to them. I broadcast it to the world so they wouldn't ... you know. Off me or something," Zack said.

Kaylan stared at him for a moment and burst out laughing. "Off you? No one is going to kill you."

Zack leaned in. "You don't know what these guys are capable of."

"You're in trouble. There's no doubt about that. Why don't you tell me about what you found?" Kaylan said, then changed her mind. "Hold that thought. Why not start with telling me what happened to *you*. You just up and left MIT, and no one has heard a word from you since then."

The door to the jet shut, and they taxied out of the hangar. He could barely hear the engines as the jet left the ground, hovered in the air for a moment, and then eased forward.

"It was my father. He died in some crappy accident, so I started looking into who was responsible. He was just running a simple diagnostic and there was an overload. The electricity stopped his heart. I traced the design back to the car manufacturer. I even found the quality and control people involved with testing that model automobile. After that I went to the people who designed the battery and circuitry that should have had the fail-safes to prevent an accident like this from occurring in the first place. I later learned *that* company was under consultation by one of Dux Corporation's subsidiaries. I knew I couldn't take them on directly or openly, so I started going after heads of R&D, CEOs, and all other forms of corporate leadership."

"How come I've never heard of this?" Kaylan asked.

"You did. You just don't know it. Major scandals about cover-ups? I was especially good at finding where they cut corners. It was obvious. Accidents like what happened to my dad were deemed an acceptable loss to those idiots. Most of the time they established an insurance fund where they collected dividends that were quadruple the amount paid in any lawsuit," Zack said.

"You're right. It's unacceptable that they did this. Why didn't you bring your findings to the FBI or something?"

"I tried. These people operate above the law, and they have deep pockets. So I decided to hit them where it hurts."

"What do you think about what Ed said?"

"The part about sending me into space? Or the part where there is some alien outpost on Pluto?"

"Don't worry about the space part. I meant the other one," Kaylan said.

"As far as I can tell, the image from 2015 is genuine. They said they recorded some of this stuff in the eighties, if you can believe that. I would need to take a closer look. I planned to, actually, before I realized they were onto me. What I would like to know is who is really calling the shots? Ed was pretty insistent that the mission parameters were going to change. Who would have the clout to do that?"

"NASA is a civilian entity that works hand in hand with different agencies, including the military."

Zack wasn't convinced. There was a difference between suspecting something to be true and knowing it was true.

Edward Johnson knew that the Athena Mission was going to Pluto. The question for him was whether they would make an untrained civilian go along for the ride.

A short while later they landed in Houston at a small airport and a car took them to the Space Center. They were assigned three protective details, which further confirmed Zack's suspicions. These guys weren't messing around. Perhaps he should just hand over the data and try to get out with some community service. He didn't have much of a chance to speak to Kaylan because there was always someone around, so they both stayed quiet. It was satisfying to watch Kaylan's frosty attitude when it came to dealing with Major Hicks. He didn't know what Hicks had done to earn the ire of one Kaylan Farrow, but he was glad it wasn't him.

At the Space Center, Kaylan led them through the building, which was full of scientist types. There were those who appeared to only be interested in their intellectual pursuits. They were roaming around, hardly noticing anyone around them at all. Then there were groups that were collaborating. They were the problem-solvers and the part of NASA that Zack most respected. He tipped his proverbial hat to them. Then there were the weasels. Some would call the men and women who wore suits "sharks," but he found that weasel was a more apt description for them and their kind. Some may look cute and cuddly, but they were fierce killing machines that had to feed every day. Weasels did a fair amount of posturing, and they would kill more than what they needed, whereas a shark could never do either of those things. To top it off, if weasels were cornered, they could blast a stink bomb just like their cousin the skunk. He would challenge anyone to find a more apt description for a "suit" than a weasel.

Even the most idiotic of them could make shit stick to an explanation that was an outright lie and magically convince people to believe them.

A group of three people waited for them at the security checkpoint beyond the atrium. One of them was an older woman who appeared to know Kaylan. She handed them each a thin, clear visitor's badge and asked that they all place their thumbs on them to confirm their identification.

"These badges will get you into any designated area marked blue. The red areas will require an escort," the lady said, and proceeded to lead them into the maze of hallways that led to the Space Center's interior.

The other two people in the threesome that had greeted them were men who wore dark suits and had the same bearing as the men at Dux Corporation's secret base. Zack guessed they were his very own escorts.

They stopped outside a large conference room where continuous murmuring escaped through the closed doors. Kaylan, Hicks, and Garcia proceeded inside, but Zack's two new escorts stopped him. The older lady said she was to take him to a waiting area while the meeting was in session. Kaylan nodded to him that it would be fine.

Zack was led a short distance away. Along the walls were large pictures of different NASA missions that proceeded like a timeline. Seeing all the different types of rockets and capsules pulled at the heartstrings of the young boy inside him. Who hadn't dreamed of becoming an astronaut as a child? They stopped at an open door. Inside was a small office that didn't look to be in use.

"You can wait in here," the lady said, and left. His two

escorts positioned themselves outside the office on either side of the doorway, and he estimated his chances of escape in the negative numerical range.

Zack sat down at the desk and looked up at the digital pictures on the wall. These were cycling through different men and women, and it took him a few moments to realize that these were people who had died while on a mission. The boyish dreams of space travel gave way to the harsh reality that going into space was dangerous. He could only imagine what was being discussed wherever Kaylan was, but he was pretty sure they wouldn't get approval to send someone like him on this crazy mission. Why would they? All he'd proven was that he had stumbled onto something … amazing. It truly was. Whenever he thought about seeing those images for the first time, it got his heart going. But going into space was death, and he didn't want to die. He also didn't want to go to jail. Zack's thoughts drifted to Edward Johnson and the things he'd said. Ed had made it sound like Kaylan personally would need his help. Was it just a ploy to use a personal attachment to get him to cooperate? Zack's lips curved as he thought of Kaylan. It was really good to see her. Before his father died, Zack had been working up the courage to ask her out on a real date.

Zack tapped his fist on the desk and was surprised when the wood finish faded to become an actual screen. A true desktop. Zack looked up at the door to see if anyone had noticed. They'd left him in here with an active connection. He sat poised, unsure of what to do. The memory of Kaylan's honey brown eyes stared back at him. No, there was no way they would take him on this mission *or* let him go home. Not right now, unless he proved himself. Zack scanned the doorway again. This was too convenient. They must be watching him. The two goons outside the room were just for show. This was a test of some sort. He was being tested. There were so many things in the data he'd seen from his hack that had been tugging at his curiosity, and he yearned to scratch that mental itch. Perhaps if he just took a quick look and poked around a bit. Give them enough information and they would just let him go home. With another glance at the closed door, Zack brought up the interface and got to work.

Chapter Six

Kaylan entered the Big Room. This was the second most important place at Space Center Houston, with the first being mission control. Missions were planned elsewhere, but it was in the Big Room that decisions were made, projects were prioritized, and scientific research was weighed and measured to determine feasibility. It used to be much more difficult for universities around the world to send their experiments into space, but not anymore. Even the average high school science class could send an experiment beyond Earth's atmosphere. It was all part of the initiative to get the next generation interested in science and exploring beyond our planet. Experiments that needed to run on other planets were a different story.

Kaylan had only been in the Big Room one time before, and that was to confirm her selection for the Athena Mission to Titan. Department heads sat on the panel on the far side of the room. To the left were holodisplays that connected to other space agencies throughout the world. They must have thrown this together quickly for the Russian and Chinese representatives not to be physically in attendance.

She spotted Michael Hunsicker and headed over to him. Hicks and Garcia followed. When she gave them a questioning look, Hicks replied that they had been told to stick around. He seemed sincere, and he was making small attempts to soften her anger towards him. If he could play nice, then so could she.

At fifty-three years of age, Michael Hunsicker was trim and in excellent shape. All astronauts had to be. His short-cropped gunmetal hair hugged his scalp and had been the same since his time as an officer in the military. When Kaylan stopped, Hicks and Garcia both snapped a salute.

"Colonel," Hicks said. "It's an honor to meet a member of the Pytheas mission, sir."

Michael returned the salute and shook both Hicks and Garcia's hands. "I haven't been an officer in a long time."

"Once an officer, always an officer, sir," Hicks replied.

Kaylan had long gotten used to people coming up to Michael this way. He had been part of the first manned mission to Mars under the Pytheas program.

Michael nodded and looked at Kaylan. "I'm glad you're back. Everything go okay visiting your grandmother?"

Kaylan's insides clenched for a second. She appreciated Michael's old-school mentality that people came first, but her visit was still raw. She nodded. "What's all this?"

"Craziness in a nutshell. They've been analyzing those images that have been on the news at JPL. Whoever leaked them to the world sent us a copy as well," Michael said.

Given Zack's situation, she couldn't see what else he could

have done, other than not poking around places he shouldn't have been.

Kaylan was about to tell Michael about Zack, but there was a call for quiet by the panel. Standing at the centermost podium was Dr. Jonah Redford. He was a brilliant astrophysicist and part of the Athena Mission. While he was a genius, he lacked certain people skills.

"Thank you all for coming," Dr. Redford said. "We've analyzed the images that were released late last night, and it is the opinion of the team that they are genuine. After this meeting we will announce our findings to the world."

Vladimir Cherkovski, who was a director of the Russian Space Academy, came to prominence on the holodisplays.

"We would like to formally submit our vote to change the Athena Mission parameters to go to Pluto instead of Titan."

Many of those in the room voiced their support. Kaylan glanced at Michael, but he was watching the panel at the front of the room.

Vladimir cleared his throat and continued. "We've run preliminary numbers and know that this is possible with the Athena spaceship."

"They've already run numbers?" Kaylan asked.

"You can bet we have too. With a stop at Titus Station for resources, the Athena can reach Pluto," Michael said.

"Do we know who released these images?" Vladimir asked.

"I'll take this one."

The holodisplay shifted to Edward Johnson. "We know who the person is, but as of right now we're not convinced of any wrongdoing. The person in question stumbled upon the images and released them to the public."

Michael glanced at her. "They know who it is?"

Kaylan nodded. "It's why Ed wanted me to stop near Asheville on the way here."

"We've done some analysis ourselves and have a recommendation," Ed said.

It was a testament to Dux Corporation's reputation that the various space agencies, including NASA, gave their assent to hear what Ed had to say.

"I'm sure most people here are in the process of proposing something similar to what I'm about to say. We would recommend taking a two-pronged approach to this." Holding up an index finger, Ed said, "Have the Titan mission team continue their preparations for what could be an accelerated launch window." Holding up a second finger, he continued, "Have their respective teams consider changing the mission to go to Pluto instead. Given the nature of Pluto and the very real possibility of working with alien technology, this will necessitate an additional specialist for the mission."

There were some hushed comments made, and Ed waited for them to quiet down before continuing. At first, Kaylan hadn't wanted to believe Ed seriously wanted Zack on this mission, but the fact that he was already pushing for it changed her thinking.

"The second prong, and one that could give us an answer in a few days, would require the cooperation of the Russian and Chinese space agencies. The Putin and Hu deep space probes in the Kuiper belt have the resources to be at Pluto in the next forty-eight hours. It's just dumb luck that Pluto is in the right position in its orbit at this time. The probes may even be able to send their last rover onto the surface to take a closer look at the alien structure," Ed said.

The meeting went on for a short while, but Kaylan was still coming to grips with the possibility of them going to Pluto. If NASA was willing to alter the current Athena Mission, would they make changes to the crew? She needed some time to work the problem.

Dr. Redford left the podium and headed their way.

"Anyone fancy a trip to Pluto instead of Titan?" Redford asked.

"We need Efren so we can all sit down and talk about this," Michael said.

"They have him running power consumption projections in the lab," Redford replied.

They left the Big Room and Michael noticed that Hicks and Garcia were following them. "What's this?"

"Ed wanted us to be a part of mission discussions from here on out," Hicks answered.

Redford's dark, beady eyes gave Hicks and Garcia an appraising look. "So we're bringing military personnel on this mission now?"

"Our authorization should have gone through by now. You can check it if you want," Hicks answered.

Redford brought up his tablet and keyed through the options. After a few seconds, he nodded and they kept going.

Kaylan looked at Hicks. "Where did they take Zack?"

"He's being tested," Hicks answered.

Kaylan explained who Zack was and what he had done.

"So he's the one Ed wants put on this mission," Michael said.

"He does, but Zack's had no training. We can't expect him to be ready for this," Kaylan said.

"I think I'd like to meet this Mr. Quick," Redford said.

"Me too," Michael agreed, and looked at Hicks. "Where is he being tested?"

Hicks shook his head. "I'm not sure. I just know they were taking him to an office close by."

They heard a slight commotion down the hallway nearest them, and Kaylan heard Zack's voice.

"I was just having a look around. I wasn't doing anything wrong."

Kaylan rounded the corner and saw Zack pinned against the wall with his arms pressed firmly into his back.

"Kaylan! You're not going to believe what I've found. Can you get these guys to let me go?" Zack asked.

Hicks went over to them and told them he would take it from here. The two guards let Zack go. "I thought you said you wouldn't be any trouble," Hicks said to Zack.

"They left me alone with an active internet connection. It's like you and flybys. Sometimes you can't resist," Zack said, and Hicks grinned.

"What did you find?" Kaylan asked.

"Ed was right. The data is amazing. I was just getting started when they came in," Zack said, rubbing his wrists. He stopped when he noticed them all watching him. "What is it?"

Redford looked at Kaylan. "He's your friend?"

Kaylan nodded.

Redford keyed a few commands into his tablet and a profile of Zack appeared on the desktop nearest them. Zack's profile listed his credentials, research at MIT, awards he had earned, and his last known address.

"Very impressive," Redford said. "Mr. Quick, why don't you enlighten us as to what you've found?"

Zack killed his profile. "You mean the part about Dux Corp keeping the public in the dark about an alien structure on Pluto? Or the fact that they had some kind of contact with them in the nineteen-eighties?"

Michael Hunsicker glanced around to make sure they weren't being overheard. Kaylan noted that Michael didn't appear to be surprised by what Zack was saying.

"Why don't you show us what you've found?" Michael said.

Zack went around to the other side of the desktop and cleared the display. "I started from the beginning, using what Dux Corp researchers were able to translate to form the beginning of a cypher. And there is a reference to signal acquisition from the ninth orbital body. I think it's safe to say they're referring to Pluto."

"Let me get this straight," Michael began. "You stumbled onto this data set and were able to decode some of it in about an hour?"

Zack shrugged. "It's not that hard if you know what to look for, but this will only work for the first part of the message. The other stuff is way more complex. I would need more time with it."

"How much time?" Michael asked.

"I don't know, a few weeks maybe, possibly longer," Zack said.

"That's too much time," Redford said.

Kaylan frowned. "What do you mean? We have six weeks to launch the Athena."

Redford rolled his eyes, and it raised Kaylan's hackles.

"I think we as a crew need to come to grips with two soon-to-be facts. One, we're going to Pluto instead of Titan.

Two, we will be launching a lot sooner than expected," Redford said.

"He's right," Michael said, and glanced at Hicks and Garcia. "And I'm willing to wager we'll be taking a few extra people with us."

"You can't mean me, right?" Zack said.

"Of course he means you. You seem to be the only one of us who can translate the bloody thing," Redford said.

"Yeah, but I'm not an astronaut," Zack said.

"Well neither are they," Redford said, gesturing to Hicks and Garcia.

"It's true we're not in an astronaut training program for NASA, but we've been training at Sacramento Bay," Hicks replied.

Redford frowned. "What's that?"

"It's the training facility for the United States Space Military Corps," Michael said.

Redford stifled a laugh. "A Space Marine. Two of them. Wonderful. I thought we would be bringing more people who could be of use." Dr. Redford shook his head and left the office.

"Garcia and I are trained in salvage and worked on the comms space program," Hicks said.

"What's that?" Zack asked.

"Rather than let old satellites burn up in the atmosphere, we've been salvaging them for parts. It was primarily a robotic probe duty to clean up the debris field, but someone thought it was a good idea to have us get actual training in the upper atmosphere," Hicks said.

Michael nodded. "Well, we have two days. Kaylan, I'd like you to run your own numbers on a course to Pluto. We don't have a lot of time. If they want to move as fast as Jonah thinks they are, then we could be leaving very soon."

Zack's brows drew up in alarm. "I thought if I worked on the data they would let me go home, not sign me up for a mission."

"Up there things are different. We need to depend upon each other. Normally I wouldn't want to bring an untrained astronaut into space, but we've done accelerated training for specialists in the past. One thing Ed told me about the data you've seen is that they've been working on it for more than sixty years. He said you were able to spin circles around his best people in a limited amount of time. Having you with us could save lives. The key to any successful mission into space requires having the right people with you," Michael said.

Zack glanced at Kaylan, and she could tell he was torn. She knew Michael was right, but she didn't want to put extra pressure on Zack.

"I don't even know how to work in space," Zack said.

Michael chuckled. "We'll help you. The Athena is a one-of-a-kind ship, unlike anything we've built before."

"He's right, Zack. I'll help you," Kaylan said, and looked at Michael. "You don't seem too shocked about any of this."

"I've been here since I got Ed's call last night. The shock is wearing off a bit. Let's take them over to JPL and get them fitted for what they'll need. I'm guessing they'll want us to finish the mission prep on board the Athena," Michael said.

Kaylan walked next to Zack, and she could tell he was scared. He had every right to be. "The Athena really is a miraculous ship."

"Why don't you tell me about it then?" Zack said.

"Well, for one, it's the first manned ship with a fusion reactor core," Kaylan said.

"Runs on water?"

Kaylan grinned. "A little more complicated than that. In order for missions to go beyond Mars, we needed to be able to scavenge for resources ourselves. It's not like we have a fleet of ships and someone to come rescue us if we get into trouble."

Zack leaned in. "They're not telling us everything," he whispered.

"Who?"

"Dux Corp. That data contains a warning. It was one of the first things I saw because it wasn't encrypted."

"What was the message?"

"It's a warning not to trust the Xiiginn."

Kaylan frowned. "That doesn't make any sense. Who are the Xiiginn?"

"There's something else that looks like a timer, but I didn't want to say anything."

Kaylan nodded.

They left the Space Center and were shuttled over to JPL. A few hours later, they got the call. They were heading to the Athena a lot sooner than expected.

Chapter Seven

Edward Johnson dimmed the lights in his office. The twinkling lights of Washington D.C. spread out into the distance, and crickets blared their song with a constant vigilance that would go long into the night. He was well past exhaustion but not quite to total collapse. He opened the desk drawer and poured himself a glass of cask strength Kentucky Straight Bourbon Whiskey. He brought the glass up to his nose, and faint hints of cherries and cinnamon entwined to make his mouth water.

Bruce Matherson had recruited him into Dux Corporation more than thirty years ago, but he'd only been brought into the inner circle less than ten years ago. Bruce had given him this bottle of bourbon and told him to keep it in his desk for one of *those* days. Ed held up his glass in salute to his long-deceased friend and took a sip. Notes of caramel and toasted nuts coated his tongue, and a slow burn blazed a path down his throat when he swallowed. He added a cube of ice and a splash of water to cut down on the burn.

The screen on his desk flashed with an incoming call, and Ed answered it.

"This is David. Things are set in motion," said a person through a voice changer.

David wasn't the caller's real name.

"I think I've cashed in all our chips on this one," Ed answered.

The inner circle was comprised of very few people. The influence that Dux Corporation had was maintained through a cell network much like terrorists had used for years. It was effective at keeping the entire operation from being compromised. It had worked since the nineties, and here they were in 2046.

"There has been concern raised by the others about Zack Quick being added to the Athena crew," David said.

Ed had been anticipating this, but he had to follow his gut on this one. "We need him, even if he isn't one of us."

"A hacktivist will not follow protocol if the outpost turns out to be more than what's been theorized."

"My main concern is for the Athena crew to not only survive the encounter with an alien structure, but to gain entry so the rest of the message can be deciphered. Mr. Quick got further in a few hours than we've ever been able to do. There is a reason why so many different agencies tried to recruit him. If his father hadn't died, they might have been successful. Regardless, we can't pull him out now," Ed said.

The truth was they could pull Zack out easily, but it would raise a lot of questions. Zack's replacement could be someone who was completely beyond their control. There was history between Kaylan and Zack that Ed was counting on.

The silence on the call dragged on, and Ed knew he had to say something before the rest of the inner circle decided to take matters into their own hands. "Look, this is the best we're going to get. Truth be told, this mission is coming at least ten years too early. The fail-safe was for us to maintain our influence over manned missions to space. Out of a crew of twelve, we have three members we know are definitely loyal to the cause. I think when push comes to shove we can trust that Kaylan and Zack will have humanity's best interests at heart," Ed said.

"What about Jonah Redford? He has some awareness of the cause, but he's never fully committed to us."

Ed took another swallow from his glass, draining it. "Dr. Redford is extremely intelligent and has proven to be ruthless on occasion to achieve his goals."

"There is still time to issue a kill order for Redford," David said.

"Tensions are high enough as it is. If we do that, we could lose the chance to get to Pluto for years to come. The Russians and Chinese are already upset by the fact that our people outnumber theirs on this mission. Neither one of them are changing their candidates. Redford is dangerous and would throw his own mother under the bus for a scientific break-through, but we need his expertise as well. Talk like this is the reason I want them on the Athena and away from Earth as soon as possible. The longer that takes, the more chance of things unraveling that could shoot us in the foot before the mission really begins," Ed said.

They had tried to have Dr. Jonah Redford removed from the

Athena Mission, but there was only so much influence they could exert without drawing attention to themselves.

Bruce Matherson himself had assigned Ed the task of guiding Kaylan in her pursuit of becoming an astronaut. She had a hell of a resume, and NASA was lucky to have her. If Kaylan had a shortcoming, it was a tendency to be a tad rash at times. This wasn't a trait NASA looked for in their second in command.

The call closed and Ed checked the time. They still had twenty-four hours until the probes reached the outpost. The researchers at Dux Corp had decided long ago that the structure on Pluto was some type of alien outpost. They assumed its function was to observe them here on Earth. It was anyone's guess as to why they had built it so far away. Surely they could have put it closer and it wouldn't have been noticed. It was dumb luck that the New Horizons spacecraft had gotten a picture of the damn thing.

Ed leaned back in his chair and chewed on the last bits of bourbon-covered ice. He wished he were twenty years younger. Then he would have put his own name in the hat for a bid to make this journey. What would they discover out there? The warning was always there. Bruce hadn't let any of them forget it, and ran this operation as if they were on borrowed time.

Ed blew out a breath and initiated a call to Moscow. It would be the first of many he would have to make in his push to get the Athena Mission away weeks earlier than they had expected.

Chapter Eight

"What did they inoculate us for?" Zack asked. He shifted in his new flight suit and kept looking at the fiery wings of a phoenix on the Athena Mission patch.

Kaylan had one foot on the bench next to him and was waiting for him.

"Really Zack, we've been over this. The inoculations are so we don't infect each other with anything that could be detrimental to the mission," Kaylan said.

He and the rest of the crew had been kept in isolation. All of them had been inoculated. No one could come near them without being covered from head to toe in heavy rubbery plastic armor. Zack knew it wasn't really made of plastic, but they made him feel as if he were some type of quarantine victim. He didn't feel sick, and everyone else appeared to be healthy.

The past thirty-six hours had gone by in a whirlwind. Kaylan had taken it upon herself to spend a few hours with him to go over the Athena systems, and Zack felt fairly confident that he wouldn't blow himself out of an airlock. She had drilled into him that red buttons required caution. Other than that, he hadn't seen too much of Kaylan. She was going over the mission prep adjustments. Dr. Redford cornered him a few times, expressing particular interest in how Zack had decoded the alien data. Zack gave him his preliminary analysis but kept what he considered "trade secrets" to himself. He suspected Redford wasn't fooled, but he didn't press the issue. Why would he? They would be on board a spaceship together for who knew how long.

Zack spent much of his time with Dale Hicks and Katie Garcia. Each of the Athena's crew had given them an overview of their specialties and advice on how to function on the spacecraft. In a nutshell it boiled down to the following: Don't be a jerk, always be willing to help someone out, and the most important thing to remember was not to do anything stupid. In Zack's mind that last one was the most important for his ultimate goal of staying alive.

"How you holding up?" Hicks asked.

"Pretty well for never being this scared in my entire life," Zack said.

Hicks couldn't be more opposite from Zack. Where Zack was wiry and quick with a snarky remark, Hicks was muscular and had a quiet air of confidence that people responded to. Despite the way he sometimes glanced at Kaylan, Zack decided that he liked the guy. Katie Garcia was an enigma to him, which wasn't a surprise. She was a woman. Underneath her flirtatious dark eyes and shapely figure was a person of shrewd intelligence. She looked as if she lived for the chase. She also looked gorgeous. Her long dark hair curled naturally and fell in waves past her shoulders. Zack had caught himself staring a few times and wondered how Hicks could seem so completely oblivious to working closely with such a beautiful woman.

Emma Roberson was a bit on the shy side, as if NASA had plucked her from a lab at Oxford University. Her specialties were xenobiology and botany. She would be their resident expert on understanding any alien life form they might encounter, as well as overseeing the hydroponics lab. Zack hoped the food grown in the lab would taste good.

Efren Burdock was a nuclear physicist whose specialty was the fusion reactor that powered the ship. His presentation was among the briefest because mission prep took precedence over an introductory session for them. Zack didn't mind and could only imagine the pressure Efren was under. The fusion reactor was one of the crowning achievements of the twenty-first century, having been proven as a viable replacement for the more common nuclear fission reactor fifteen years before. The world was slowly migrating away from the toxic waste model of producing power.

"You should embrace this," Hicks continued. "We're heading into outer space, going farther than any human being has ever been."

"Yeah, we can probably get there, but there hasn't been too much talk about a return trip back to Earth," Zack said.

"They'll come up with something. There are multiple options, but none of them would prevent us from leaving," Hicks answered.

"Why is leaving so soon important? Those Russian probes won't even be near Pluto for another eight hours, and then it will be another four hours before we get any more information," Zack said.

Hicks glanced around them. They were standing apart from the others for the moment, waiting for clearance to board the Boeing Space Plane that would take them to the International Space Station.

"The sooner we leave the better it will be for everyone," Hicks said.

"Why? This is what I don't understand."

"Tensions among the different governments are rising because of this. Our crew is predominantly American, and we're heading to an alien structure. We'll see technology that no one has ever been exposed to before."

Zack shrugged. "Since this is a joint mission, wouldn't we just share it?"

"Of course we would, but some in the military would see this as a way to shift the balance in their country's favor."

Zack shook his head. "That's just great. You know, we'd be able to accomplish so much more if people weren't so preoccupied with trying to get the best over each other."

Hicks smiled and was about to respond when Commander Hunsicker called for their attention.

"We've got clearance to leave. We'll be heading to the International Space Station, and from there we'll go to the Athena," Hunsicker said.

"Sir," Hicks said, "have the other payloads been cleared as well?"

Hunsicker nodded. "They're on the way. They will be guided right to the ship along with additional supplies."

They filed out, heading out to the tarmac, where they would board the space plane. They would suit up and then the space plane would be mounted on top of a Boeing 777 that they would use to take them to the upper atmosphere.

"What other payload?" Zack asked.

"Two smaller surface-to-air ships called the Beagle 4S. They're based on the Stinger-class jet. They've been adapted and tested for space. They're used for scouting and salvage. They only seat one person, so they're meant to augment Athena's shuttle capabilities," Hicks said.

Kaylan walked next to them, and Hicks quickened his pace to talk to Commander Hunsicker.

"I can't believe we're doing this," Zack said.

Kaylan smiled. "I'm glad you're coming."

Zack felt his pulse begin to race. His other option was rotting in jail. He'd rather take his chances in space. "How could I say no? Besides, we've got the best pilot in NASA."

"Damn right we do," Kaylan said.

Zack's flight status had bounced between being canceled and restored more than a few times. At one point he thought the FBI was there to arrest him. He wasn't sure how Dux Corp pulled it off, but they'd gotten him on the mission.

Most of the Athena's crew treated him with a reserved manner and probably viewed him as a necessary evil they had to deal with. The exceptions were Kaylan and Michael Hunsicker. He'd known he would get along with Kaylan just fine, but it was Commander Hunsicker who surprised him. The space veteran was as even-tempered as they came and was able to process the changing conditions of the mission with practiced ease. It was no wonder to Zack that Hunsicker had been picked to lead the mission.

The space plane had a hawk-like nose and smallish stub

wings. The ship name on the tail read *Endeavor*. A landing ramp lowered to the runway, and the eight crew members climbed aboard. They strapped themselves in and were checked by ground-based mission specialists. Zack wanted to remember their faces, but they all wore the same bland, white hazmat suits that covered them from head to toe. These would be the last people he would see on Earth for a long time, but moments after they left, he found that he couldn't remember what any of them had looked like.

The landing gear shut, and Zack swallowed back some of his angst. Kaylan sat in the front with Commander Hunsicker. They proceeded through preflight checks for the space plane's systems. Zack felt a slight shudder as the engines roared to life, and the space plane gradually lifted into the air. There was no wobbling at all, for which Zack was thankful. They eased over to the docking clamps on top of the Boeing 777. There was an audible clang as the clamps engaged, and a voice over the speakers confirmed a good dock. Zack released the breath he had been holding and chided himself for doing so. This was the easiest part of the trip. If he couldn't keep it together now, what would he do later on?

To distract himself, Zack started thinking about the encrypted code in the alien message. The data was multilayered in such a way that he suspected it would require the expertise of a group of people to decipher. There had been no time for him to delve further into it as they'd devoted every minute to preparing him for the Athena. Well, perhaps "preparing" was really too strong a word. His training would continue once on board. Zack suspected that he was being kept busy and out of the way. NASA had outright refused to let him bring any of his own equipment with him, but he had a tiny storage device that he kept in the golden cross that hung on a thin chain around his neck. His father had been a religious man and had raised him in the Catholic faith. Zack had never been one for blindly following any doctrine, whether it be on faith or someone else's facts, but the cross had been important to his father, who had worn it for many years. Zack wore it so he could imagine that part of his father was still with him.

The latest version of Boeing's 777 was too big an aircraft for vertical takeoff, especially with the additional load of the space plane. They taxied to the runway to the high-pitched whine of the engines. The runway was extremely long by current standards, but they would need more time to get into the air. The plane lurched forward, slowly increasing speed until they were finally up. Zack peered out of the small round window nearest him. The ground continued to fall away as they rose higher and higher. Zack started to bounce his knee and felt his palms become sweaty inside his thick, insulated gloves.

The ride to the upper atmosphere took less than an hour.

"Preparing for main booster ignition," Kaylan said.

Houston acknowledged.

"We're hot, Houston. Detach docking clamps on my mark. Three, two, one, mark," Kaylan said.

"Confirm good separation. Thanks for the ride," Hunsicker said.

The Boeing 777 started its descent.

"Main engine fire," Kaylan said, and counted down.

When the main engines fired, it felt as if an elephant had decided to step on Zack's chest. They were all pushed back into their seats. The space plane had to maintain its current burn for a precise amount of time in order to leave the Earth's atmosphere. Zack squeezed his eyes shut and just wanted it all to be over. His whole body clenched.

"Zack, just take a breath," Hicks called to him.

Zack opened his eyes and turned to Hicks.

"Can you feel it?" Hicks asked, smiling.

After a second, Zack realized the crushing pressure was gone. He seemed to have risen up into his spacesuit.

"Yeah," Zack said with half a laugh. "This is cool."

He heard Redford mutter something from behind him about prodigies.

"Congratulations, folks. We made it. We'll dock with the ISS in just under an hour. From there we'll get on our ship. Time to stow your gear," Commander Hunsicker said.

Zack unbuckled his seatbelt and floated into the air. It was like swimming underwater except without the water or the resistance. The spacesuits they wore were much less bulky than the ones they'd seen during their classes. Zack couldn't imagine wearing the ones from the Apollo program. These suits were several versions better than what the astronauts had worn to Mars. He'd spent so much time learning how to get in and out of the spacesuit in the past thirty-six hours that he could almost do it blindfolded. Like everything else in space, anything to do with life-support was of the utmost importance.

Zack removed his helmet and compressed his spacesuit while hovering near his chair. He stowed the suit in the storage compartment off to the side. The suits would go back with the space plane, but the ones they would use on the Athena were already on board. Katie floated next to him and stowed her gear as well.

"You know this is actually the third version of the ISS," Katie said.

"Really? What happened to the other two?" Zack asked.

"They got old, basically. They salvaged parts of the original ISS to become part of the new one when they could. Did you know that there are over a thousand robots working in space?" Katie said, her eyes alight with excitement.

"I had no idea you were into all this stuff," Zack said with a slight wave of his hand.

"Look sharp, Casanova, your Venus approaches," Katie said with a teasing smile before moving away.

Kaylan made her way to the storage compartment across from him. "Pretty cool, right?"

"It was a rush," Zack answered. "Katie was just telling me that there are thousands of robots working in space."

"That's right. Some were launched from Earth, but many of them were made at the moon base using resources from the asteroid Z6260. Easier to assign certain tasks to the robots and maintain minimal human presence," Kaylan said.

"Are you saying these robots were programmed to build the Athena?" Zack asked, struggling to keep the panic from his voice.

"Only parts of it. Some things could only be made on Earth, and those were sent up over the course of two years," Kaylan said.

"Can you give me an example of what had to be made on Earth?"

"Pieces of the reactor core and the primary engines were made on Earth. The secondary and navigational engines were constructed on the moon."

"That's amazing. I can't wait to see it," Zack said. His gaze lingered for longer than it should have, and then he hastily looked away.

Kaylan came closer to him. "We need to focus on the mission."

Zack closed his eyes and nodded his head. "I know. Believe me, I know. I just couldn't …" Zack opened his eyes. "For a second there it felt just like old times."

Kaylan's lips curved into a small smile. "I'm glad you're here."

Hicks came over to them. "It's time for us to strap back in."

"Impeccable timing, as always," Zack said as Kaylan headed for the front of the ship.

Hicks shrugged and Katie cleared her throat. "Let's settle down, boys. We've got a long trip ahead of us."

They returned to their seats and strapped themselves in. Hunsicker was confirming Houston's last message.

"We have a change in plans," Hunsicker said. "Houston wants us to dock directly with the Athena rather than the ISS."

Zack leaned over to Hicks. "Can we do that?"

Hicks nodded. "All space-bound ships are equipped with a universal docking connection. This way they can all work together, regardless of which space agency we're dealing with."

Zack felt foolish asking the question, but Hicks had assured him earlier that it was better if he asked those questions. No one expected him to know everything. This was on-the-job training at its best, or worst, depending upon your perspective. Zack had read about the ISS and would have liked to have gone on board.

Hicks nodded toward the windows. "We'll still get to see it. The Athena is waiting for us there. Can you believe astronauts used to live in zero gravity on the older stations?"

"Artificial gravity has only been around for the past five years," Katie said.

"Yeah, but still. They had to exercise at least two hours a day just to keep their bone density," Hicks replied.

"How does the artificial gravity work?" Zack asked.

Katie shrugged. "I only know the theory. There are multiple gravity fields maintained throughout the ship, but they can be compartmentalized if we need to."

"So you could turn off the gravity in one part of the ship but not affect other parts?" Zack asked.

"That's right," Katie answered.

Zack couldn't help but feel a bit overwhelmed. In his own crusade against global corporations, he'd let his own scientific curiosity go by the wayside. If anything, this journey was awakening the youthful curiosity he'd once had. What surprised him was how much he'd missed that sense of wonder.

He brought up the interface on his PDA and looked up the ISS. At six hundred meters, the structure was huge. There were fifty people on the station at any given time. Redford tapped him lightly on the shoulder and told him to look out the window. Six hundred meters sounded big, and the closer they got to the ISS, the more it dwarfed their tiny space plane. Zack's heart pumped with excitement as his eyes drank in the sight of one of mankind's greatest achievements. If the ISS were stretched out in a single line, it would be six football fields long; however, it was broken up into sections. The older sections were made up of rounded compartments, while the newer sections had more square proportions. It was like a small town in space. All sections were built around a central globe structure that housed the fusion reactor to power it all.

"ISS, this is Commander Hunsicker. We're on approach. Sorry we can't come in and chat. We've been ordered to dock directly with the Athena."

"Hi, Michael, Ted Carr here. Your approach is good. Would have liked to have had a chance to catch up, especially since some of us have been watching the Athena for a good long while up here."

"It's good to hear your voice, Ted. How was the last run of diagnostics on it?" Hunsicker asked.

"She passed all the stress tests we gave her with flying colors. Would have liked to have taken her for a spin though. Hey, do you know anything about the lockout?" Ted asked.

"Wasn't aware of any lockout."

"About twenty-four hours ago we were locked out of the Athena systems. It made quite a few people up here nervous. The lockout was highly irregular, not to mention dangerous. Anyway, the last thing we did was offload some additional supplies."

"Thanks, Ted."

They maneuvered the space plane around the ISS so it was between Earth and them. As they passed the last part of the ISS, they saw the Athena. Zack's mouth hung open. All of them were silent as they took in the sight of what would be their home for a while. The ship had a half-moon, saucer-shaped front with a cavity rising off the top that looked like the bridge. The markings of each of the world's space agencies adorned the white hull of the ship. Emblazoned on the side were the fiery wings of a phoenix with an astronaut standing in the middle. The bridge connected to a much larger cylinder shape that Zack knew contained various living quarters, one of four different lab areas, a mess hall, and a living area. There were four more large cylinders connected to the main body, with two on each side. There were differences between them, but Zack couldn't remember what purpose they served. Along the bottom, there was a small shuttle-type craft that was bigger than the space plane they now flew in. The main body of the ship extended about eighty yards to the reactor core and the main engines.

They slowed their approach and came to a stop over the pod-like structure that connected to the airlock. There was a twin pod located beneath the ship. Zack watched the screen nearest him, waiting for the green light to appear to indicate that they had successfully docked. After a moment they were green across the board, and Zack followed the others' examples and unbuckled himself from his seat. All of them were eager to get on board.

Hicks went to the airlock at the back of the space plane and opened it. There was a small hiss of air as the two atmospheres equalized. When it was his turn, Zack pulled himself along and down into the airlock along with everyone else. Commander Hunsicker closed the airlock to the plane and followed.

Kaylan waved him over. Zack clumsily pulled his way to her, and she led him over to a couple of panels on the walls. These opened up to become seats with belts to strap themselves in.

"We won't engage the artificial gravity until everyone is in position," Kaylan said.

Zack nodded. He kept looking all around and tried to brace himself for the sudden shift that was sure to come when the artificial gravity was engaged. Kaylan opened her PDA and sent out the warning to the crew. After about a minute, Zack felt the gradual increase of his weight into his chair.

"The slow increase of gravity is done to help reduce nausea," Kaylan said.

Zack felt as if he had been spinning around for a while and suddenly stopped. He focused on a point on the wall and kept his gaze fixed on that spot. After a few moments, his head stopped spinning.

"Not too bad," Zack said, and stood up. "I'm supposed to work with Jonah to run diagnostics on Athena's computer systems."

"You guys are buddies now?" Kaylan asked, the hint of a smile tugging at her lips.

"If he thinks I'll be calling him Dr. Redford, then he's got another thing coming."

"Go on. I'll be on the bridge. If you need me, you can reach me through your PDA."

Zack walked in the opposite direction. It felt good to have his feet on solid ground again, or at least the illusion of it. Zero gravity had been fun for a while, but it was definitely not how he wanted to spend the next few months in space. A few minutes later he was lost. If they had let him bring his tablet, he wouldn't have needed to go to a terminal to do his job.

Some of these corridors looked the same. He ended up by the crew quarters and decided to take a look at his room. He opened the door and thought he had found a closet. He checked the name on the outside and, sure enough, it said Crewman Quarters - Zack Quick. His room couldn't have been more than six feet across and maybe eight feet long. He squeezed through the door and the motion sensor turned the lights on. There was a bed that was more like a cot and a small table that looked as if it could fold up and be clipped to the wall.

A soft knock snagged his attention, and Zack saw Hicks standing just outside the doorway. "Astronauts used to sleep standing up. They would strap in to keep from floating around while they slept. This is much better."

"If you say so. Still kinda cramped in here. What's up?"

"Redford is looking for you. I also came to bring you this," Hicks said, and handed him a metal briefcase.

Zack took the case. "Thanks. If you see Redford, tell him I'll be right there."

"You can tell him yourself. Just use your PDA or the ship's comms system," Hicks replied and left him.

Zack put the metal case on the table and pressed his thumb on the scanner. The case opened, revealing a tablet computer. *Finally something I can use!*

Zack took it out and booted it up. Lines of code referring to a temporary boot startup process flicked past the screen.

"Hello, Zack," Edward Johnson said on screen. "I recorded this just before your computer was added to the last-minute supply run to the Athena. I think we got off on the wrong foot, but it doesn't matter how we got here. What matters is that you're there, and you can help. I've uploaded everything we have since the event that took place in 1986. I've included all the research and conclusions we came to throughout the years. The data in its entirety has only been entrusted to a handful of people, and you've been brought into the fold. I was very good friends with Bruce Matherson, who is the reason we're where we are today. His granddaughter is on board the Athena with you. Trust me when I say that she is vitally important to the mission. Please use every means at your disposal to help her. I know you think Dux Corp is the enemy, but believe me when I say we're working for the betterment of mankind. One thing that is abundantly clear is that the data contains a warning of some kind. The alien entity that sent the message must have gone to great lengths to give us this information, which helped speed up our advances. The question is why. Why would they do that? It's the question you should be asking yourself as you delve deeper into this information—further than anyone else before. Good luck and Godspeed."

The video ended, and his tablet booted normally.

"No pressure," Zack sighed. He started a few tasks to go through his entire machine just to be sure there were no hidden bugs in it, courtesy of Dux Corp or anyone else. He didn't trust anyone. After setting that up, he left his room to find Jonah and begin running diagnostics on Athena's computer systems.

Chapter Nine

Kaylan was at the rear of the ship, checking the reactor systems. They were in the final leg of their mission prep and the Athena had performed beautifully. They were still orbiting the Earth but had moved the ship away from the International Space Station. The fusion reactor was Efren's area of expertise, and she was his backup. Every system on the Athena had a complete mockup back on Earth that they had used to train on for the past two years, and major cities around the world were switching over to power provided by fusion reactors. It was thanks to this piece of equipment that they could reach out into the solar system as far as they had.

"It's amazing isn't it?" Hicks said, coming to stand beside her.

"We'd be dead in the water without it," Kaylan replied.

"I was thinking," Hicks said, moving in closer. "The Beagle's flight systems aren't all that different from the shuttle we have. If you want, I can run through some simulations with you some-time. Couldn't hurt to have a backup."

Kaylan heard everything Hicks had just said but couldn't help focusing on the blue of his eyes and the shape of his mouth. "That sounds like a good idea. I can show you and Katie the shuttle systems as well."

Hicks smiled, showing a perfect set of pearly whites. "That might get kinda crowded. Besides, Katie is already shadowing Emma in the Bio lab."

He moved in closer, until his lips were only inches from hers.

"Getting kinda close there, aren't you, cowboy? I don't know if my heart can take it," Kaylan said, while gently pushing him back. She wanted to leave her hand against his chiseled chest but pulled it away as she stepped passed him.

"Sorry, ma'am, we Texans wear our heart right there on our sleeve."

Kaylan grinned. "I'm sure this humble country-boy thing works wonders with the ladies in some bar, but we're not in a bar now, are we?"

Hicks laughed, and just then Hunsicker called for their attention over the comms system.

"The surveyor probes have reached Pluto, and we're minutes away from getting their first data burst."

Kaylan shrugged and headed up toward the bridge, while Hicks grinned behind her. They were soon joined by the others. Last to arrive were Zack and Jonah. Zack gave a slight roll of his eyes in Jonah's direction. She could only imagine how Zack's snarky demeanor played on Jonah Redford's prickly personality. They were both brilliant, and she had no doubts that Zack would prove his worth to the team as time went on.

"Isn't it time for us to initiate the first burn now that the engines have been tested?" Redford asked.

"Soon. Our first stop is Titus Station in the asteroid belt," Hunsicker said.

Zack held up his hand, and Hunsicker nodded for him to speak.

"Why are we stopping at the station?"

"Two reasons. First is to resupply. We won't make it to Pluto otherwise. Second is to pick up Cosmonaut Nikolai Vratowski and the Lenoy Salvage System. Nikolai is one of the foremost experts on its use. For those of you who are not aware, the Lenoy Salvage System, or LSS, is used in the asteroid retrieval mission. It's capable of landing on the surface of larger asteroids and drilling into their surface to collect samples. It's mainly used for bagging and tagging. It's equipped with a composite diamond-tipped head that is capable of cutting into all known substances.

"Major Hicks, I would like you to begin familiarizing yourself with the LSS. I want you to be Nikolai's backup," Hunsicker said, and paused for a moment, his eyes sweeping past them. "Some of us have been training for this mission for over two years. The mission parameters have changed, but our jobs haven't. We're still going farther away from our planet than anyone else in history. You were picked for this because NASA believes you are the best suited for it. I consider it an honor to fly with each and every one of you, including those of you who arrived just a few days ago. I think we can all agree that there are parts of our mission that are unorthodox. Our chances of discovering alien technology within our solar system surpass that of any mission that's gone before us. We go out there, do our jobs, and return home safely. That's what I want for all of us. Some of you have worked in space before. Some of you haven't. For those of you who have, please help those who haven't whenever possible. NASA picked me for this mission because I went to Mars and returned. This journey will test all of us, so be ready for it. In a few minutes we'll get the data burst from the surveyor probes on Pluto. After that we'll get underway."

Zack went over to the main table on the bridge and brought up the holodisplay. There was a deep-space communications satellite whose sole purpose was to relay the information sent to it from anything they had out in the solar system.

Kaylan went to Zack and leaned down. "Are we getting the raw data burst, or has this been through one of Dux Corp's filters?"

"It's the real deal. That was one of the things I checked shortly after we got on board," Zack said.

The holodisplay flickered and a message appeared: *Signal Acquired — Standby.*

An image of Pluto's icy surface began to build piece by piece. Putin-1 displayed in the lower left side. Zack keyed in a few commands, and the original grainy image of the alien structure was brought up on a secondary display.

"I thought it would be good for comparison," Zack said.

Kaylan nodded. "Good idea."

The others joined them around the table.

The more recent surveyor photographs were much more detailed. The structure nestled in the icy mountains was dome-shaped, with dark spires at four different points. There were smaller buildings extending on the east and west planes. The structure appeared to be made from a dark metallic substance.

Kaylan couldn't tell if it was because of a shadow or something else. The dome was a lighter color.

"There's more. Looks like a video feed from the rover," Zack said.

Another holowindow opened and a video started. The perspective was perhaps a foot off the icy surface. They caught sight of the rover wheel for a moment, but it was definitely moving. When the rover stopped and panned the camera around, Kaylan gasped. The alien structure was huge. Toward the middle of the dome was another smaller building they hadn't seen from the surveyor photograph. Flashes from a pulsating light were coming from somewhere off screen. In the next moment, the rover video became lopsided, as if something had knocked it over, and then the video cut out.

"What happened?" Efren asked. He was first to break the silence.

"We lost the feed," Jonah said. "Zack, is there any more?"

Zack shook his head. Just then the comms channel lit up.

Hunsicker clicked his PDA. "This is Athena."

"Hello, Athena. This is Houston. Robert Baker. We've just reviewed the data burst from Putin-1."

"So have we. We're still trying to figure out what to make of it," Hunsicker answered.

Kaylan looked at Zack, who went over to the comms station and began typing furiously.

"It doesn't look good from down here. There is talk of scrubbing the mission."

Jonah stepped forward. "With all due respect, Houston, that would be colossally stupid. There are a multitude of reasons for the video to cut off."

"I would have to agree with Jonah," Hunsicker said. "It would seem a bit premature to scrub at this moment. Why don't we take some time to analyze what we've got? And see if the surveyors send anything else. In the meantime we'll proceed as planned. We can always abort later on."

There was a few minutes of silence, during which Redford began pacing, muttering that they couldn't stop now.

"Houston, are you still there?" Hunsicker asked.

"Yeah, Michael, we're here. You're green for go to Titus Station. We'll work the analysis from down here and be in contact."

Hunsicker smiled, and Jonah sighed with relief. "Anyone want to venture a guess as to what happened to the rover?" Hunsicker asked.

"Like I said to Houston, there are a number of circumstances that could have resulted in what we saw," Jonah said.

"Fine. Let's list them," Hunsicker said.

"A gas pocket could have broken through the surface and knocked the rover on its side. The rover could have been damaged upon landing and just broke. A meteorite could have struck the rover," Jonah said.

"Or, something from the alien structure caused the rover to fail," Kaylan said.

Redford's mouth hung open and the group of them quietly thought about what Kaylan had just said.

"Uh, does the rover have a microphone?" Zack asked.

His question drew some strange looks from the others, and Kaylan answered. "No, it wouldn't. Why do you ask?"

"Hold on a second and take a look at this," Zack said. He stood up and restarted the video. "The rover pans the camera around. And here is when we first notice the light," Zack said, stopping the video. "If I slow the playback, you can see that the source appears to be coming from the structure itself. I'm wondering if there is some sort of optical effect. Something we can't see. The reason why I asked about a microphone is because I was wondering if there was some sort of challenge. Like "identify yourself" or something like that."

"He's got a point," Hunsicker said.

"Right," Jonah said. "Well done. Why don't Zack and I work on analyzing the video? Break it down frame by frame and see if there is evidence to support his theory."

"I'll make the images and video available for anyone to look at," Zack said.

Hunsicker nodded. "All right. We'll be getting underway in just a few moments."

The rest of the crew went back to their stations, but Zack stayed behind.

"Commander, will we need to strap in for this?" Zack asked.

"No, not for this. And good job," Hunsicker said.

Zack nodded and left the bridge.

Kaylan went to the front of the bridge and sat in the pilot's seat. She brought up the planned coordinates. "Commander, ready to go at your command."

Michael sat in the seat next to her and double-checked the readouts. "Let's go. Thirty-five percent capacity."

The plasma rockets had been on standby since they'd first come aboard. Kaylan entered the commands into the ship's computer. With a distant roar, the main engines surged to life as superheated plasma blasted out the rear thrusters. The Earth grew smaller in the window as they gained more speed, which was the only indication besides the telemetry readouts that they were going anywhere.

"Confirm, we're at thirty-five percent engine capacity. We should reach the station in two weeks, unless you would like to push the engines more?" Kaylan asked.

"That's fine. This will give the engines their first real workout. We'll save all that speed for Pluto," Hunsicker said. "Your friend really is quite clever."

"Zack has an uncanny knack for seeing things in the simplest terms," Kaylan said.

"Do you think he's right about what happened to the rover?"

"I'm not sure. He could be, but Jonah listed a few good reasons too. I keep thinking that if this structure were a secure facility on Earth, I wouldn't expect it to be unlocked. The same could be applied here. If that's the case, it's something we'll need to prepare for. At the same time, we could be reading too much into it," Kaylan said.

"Sometimes we get all these facts and theories, and then people make compelling arguments and what not. It all has its place, but sometimes we just need to trust our gut instinct. Right now I'm thinking Zack hit it pretty close to the mark. The farther away from home we go, the more we'll need to rely on ourselves," Hunsicker said.

Kaylan glanced at Michael for a second. They had worked together for the past few years on this mission. He was everyone's mentor. "When will we bring the rest of the crew in on the other thing Zack is working on?"

Hunsicker leaned back in his seat. "I think it would be best to wait until Zack has had more time to study what Dux Corp has kept hidden from the rest of us."

"I think the rest of the world should know about it—what my grandfather discovered and what they've done since then. All of it," Kaylan said. This thought had been weighing down on her since Ed Johnson had taken her to that hangar in Asheville, North Carolina. Things had moved so fast that she hadn't made up her mind about it until that moment.

"It's good to hear you say that. Ed assures me that Dux Corp will give a full disclosure about what they've done, but they won't do it until we're a bit farther away."

"Why?"

"They don't want the mission cancelled. As long as we're out here, all of the world's space agencies will be focused on this mission. The ISS being locked out of Athena's systems was a precautionary measure to prevent tampering," Hunsicker said.

"You can't believe anyone on the ISS would have done something to put the mission in jeopardy."

"No, but sometimes people do foolish things for the wrong reasons," Hunsicker said, and climbed out of his chair. "I'm heading down to see Efren and check on the reactor."

Kaylan was alone on the bridge. A week ago she had believed the Athena Mission would be purely a scientific journey. The recent measures taken to revise their mission had been a bit eye-opening. The things they could learn from the alien structure would hopefully be of benefit to the world. That was her hope for this mission. She brought up the images sent from Putin-1 and studied the aerial photographs, trying to glean any insight she could.

Chapter Ten

Kaylan woke up in her bunk. She could always sleep soundly wherever she was, and the tight quarters on the Athena were no different. She thought it helped a great deal that her room became pitch-black when she turned the lights off to sleep, but it hadn't helped when she'd awakened earlier than she was supposed to and couldn't see anything in her room. She'd decided to configure the wall screen to cycle through images of the stars taken by Athena's telescope. After that, when it came time for her to wake up, the image on the wall screen cycled through recorded sunrises from around the world. If they spent a year in space, she could wake up and see a different sunrise every day.

Showers on the Athena were the equivalent of a steam bath, but the steam wasn't scorching hot. Kaylan did come away feeling clean, but it wasn't the same as a full-on shower or a bath. After a few days of travel, they were settling into a routine. There was always something to be done. Kaylan checked her PDA, exhaled excitedly, and bounded to her feet. She would be shadowing Emma in the hydroponics lab this morning. Kaylan had done a semester abroad at Oxford at the same time Emma had attended, but the two had never met. Kaylan didn't meet the native Londoner until she joined the Athena program two years ago, and the two of them had become fast friends.

Near to the hydroponics lab was the med bay. Brenda Goodwin, the chief medical officer, stuck her head out and smiled when she saw Kaylan.

"I was going to come looking for you," Brenda said.

"I know I was supposed to stop in for a checkup. Sorry," Kaylan said.

"That's fine. I'm not worried about you. Zack has been avoiding me for the past two days. I can't believe he doesn't have any implants," Brenda said.

Kaylan followed her into the room and sat on the table. "He probably doesn't trust them."

"That's interesting, considering his specialty. Perhaps we should all have ours removed," Brenda quipped.

Brenda proceeded to give her a quick physical exam and recorded Kaylan's levels of bone density and muscle mass. She waved her handheld scanner in front of Kaylan's face and down to her stomach.

"You're the vision of health. If you wouldn't mind, could you ask Zack to come see me? It's important, especially since he's one of the last-minute members of the crew."

Kaylan promised her she would and headed over to the port observatory to check on Zack before meeting with Emma. She found him hunched over his tablet, frowning.

"Still running from doctors?" Kaylan asked.

"Yeah, she's been after me for a physical," Zack said. He leaned back and stretched his arms overhead.

The observatory had a breathtaking view of the stars. It was amazing to Zack how many could be seen out here.

"Nice view," Kaylan said.

Zack glanced out the window. "I like the quiet. Gives me some time to think, and Jonah hasn't found this hiding place yet. It's getting harder to keep him in the dark about what I'm working on. He knows a little bit about the alien data but not the complete picture."

"I agree with you. The rest of the crew needs to be informed. Michael told me that Dux Corp will inform all the space agencies after we reach Titus Station," Kaylan said.

Zack frowned. "They've been operating in the shadows for so long, I'm not sure if I believe they'll come clean about everything. What do you think?"

"I think they need to—otherwise someone else will put the pieces together and things will go worse for them. Have you learned anything from the data cache?"

"I've watched the surveyor video about a thousand times and still think there's something we're missing," Zack said.

"NASA has lost contact with Putin-1. They're not sure why it went dark. What else did you learn?"

"Well, I agree with Dux Corp's findings about the alien data. It's a warning about someone or something called the Xiiginn. It's almost as if it were added as an afterthought, like it wasn't part of the rest of the main dataset. I did a search for the word Xiiginn but couldn't find any other references. After the initial warning there is a reference to an element or a different set of compounds, some of which, I was surprised to learn, went into the construction of this ship. There's definitely a pattern to the data. It was smart of your grandfather to record everything. After the initial event, they took the raw recordings and transcribed them. Later on, the transcriptions were stored digitally. That made my job a lot easier. There is a mathematical pattern there. I just haven't solved it yet. I've also poked around the ship's systems," Zack said.

"You need to be careful," Kaylan warned.

"I'm not going to reconfigure the carbon dioxide scrubbers or anything. There are subroutines running in the ship's systems that I can't access along with this directory. BM1434OBC. I find pointers to it all over the place, but I can't figure out what it is."

Kaylan frowned and pursed her lips in thought. Zack's PDA vibrated in his pocket.

"You're buzzing," Kaylan teased.

"It's Jonah. I was supposed to meet with him a half hour ago," Zack said.

"Well, you better get to it," Kaylan said.

"Maybe I'll go see the doctor first."

Zack left her on the observation deck. She stood at the window, gazing at the stars and lightly pulling on a strand of her hair. Something about the directory name tugged at her. She had seen those numbers before. Kaylan closed her eyes, seeing the directory name in her mind. *BM1434OBC*. An idea ignited in the depths of her mind, burning its way to the forefront. She recognized the numbers as the address of her grandparents' house on the north shore of Long Island in the town of Oyster Bay Cove.

Kaylan stepped away from the window and opened the standard terminal that was available in every room on the ship. She logged in and navigated to the directory Zack had just shown her. It was semi-hidden, tucked in an obscure folder. She tried to open the directory, and the following appeared below the command prompt:

Aus! Sasha

A challenge phrase. Kaylan smiled. Her grandfather had been a dog lover for as long as she could remember, and Sasha had been one of his favorite dogs. A beautiful red Doberman Pinscher. Kaylan remembered the dog because as a little girl she would throw the ball and Sasha would bring it back. She would only drop it with the command in German. *Aus! Sasha.* Kaylan racked her brain for what her grandfather would say after the command. After a moment she had it.

Heir! Sasha.

It didn't matter what was happening, Sasha would drop everything and come at her grandfather's command. After she entered the response, a few lines of code flicked by, and then an old, grainy video opened.

The Psychic Warrior Initiative. These highly trained individuals lend vital support to the intelligence community with the ability to see events at a great distance. A select few have the ability to see into complex situations and influence favorable outcomes. Some even have the ability to focus their minds in a trance to receive messages from other warriors.

Kaylan didn't recognize the voice in the video. After a moment her grandfather appeared. He was mostly bald and his shoulders sagged with age, but it was the light in his eyes that Kaylan remembered best.

Hello, Kaylan. I've recorded this video because I'm not long for this earth, if you hadn't already guessed. But you're a teenager now and already in college. The introduction you just heard may seem foolish and in no way could apply to anyone with a highly analytical mind such as yours. I'm here to tell you that you're wrong. My work with Project Stargate earned more than few strange looks and laughs. This was entirely by my design. If the military had known what we could do, they would have taken over, and who knows what would have happened then. Doubtless, by now you're aware that we have in fact received a message from a being not of this Earth. You, alone, of all our grandchildren, showed any inclination of breaking with the family tradition. You went off on your own, and I have no doubts you will pursue a career in scientific research. Just as there are two sides to a coin, there are two sides to the human brain. We've been training you since you were a little girl. You've always shown a great amount of intuitive curiosity. Some would call it a sixth sense or keen observational sense. The members of the program weren't fortunetellers or able to kill a person with their minds. We put that rubbish out there to throw people off of what we were really doing. Even the term "Psychic Warrior" is incorrect. What you're able to do is exert a great amount of intuitive observation, which makes you more sensitive to energy that we can't begin to measure. The New Horizons discovery in 2015 all but confirmed it for us. Since you're seeing this, it means you were placed on the mission that will take you to Pluto. I wish I could be there to see it. We had our viewers try and glean insights into the structure on Pluto, but they weren't successful. We're not sure why. I'm going to go over how they prepared themselves for a viewer session. Perhaps you'll succeed where they failed.

The video went on to explain the basics of meditation and then focused on what she wanted to see. If Kaylan hadn't seen the sincerity in her grandfather's eyes on the video, she would have thought it was a joke. He kept saying she was trained. She didn't have any idea what that meant. They had always played games, such as scavenger hunt, but nothing that she would consider training, unless those summer afternoons on weekends had been more than what she thought they were. *It couldn't be that simple.* Kaylan shook her head and closed the terminal. She headed for the door and stopped on the threshold, her hand resting against the doorframe. Whenever she attacked a problem she would come at it from all directions. It was how she had succeeded in designing the next generation aircraft for Dux Corporation, how she excelled in advanced aeronautical study. Edward Johnson would say that all problems were three-dimensional, but most people only thought in two dimensions—how did it affect them and was the price worth the reward?

Kaylan backed away from the doorway and walked over to the window. She let her mind relax and closed her eyes. After counting to thirty, she built an image of the alien structure in her mind. She pulled in what she'd seen from both the rover video and the surveyor images, then placed herself on the ground in front of the building. The pearl-colored dome loomed in the background. The proportions were extremely large, as if whoever made the structure must be a larger species than humans. She moved that piece of insight off to the side of her mind and focused on the smaller building jutting out from the dome. The dark, smooth walls shimmered a deep, lustrous purple that coiled along the surface as if it followed a current. As she moved closer to it, there was a hum in the back of her mind—a subtle vibration that she could almost hear, but it was as if her head were submerged underwater. A panel rose up from the ground and fanned out into a disk. She tried to get closer, but it was as if something was holding her back. Her legs felt weighed down. The disk glistened along the edge, catching some unseen light source. Suddenly there was a flash of blinding light and she was kneeling on the floor of the observation deck. She blew out a giant puff of air and sucked in a mouthful more. One of her hands was pressed against the window. She had trouble focusing, but the spinning sensation gradually relented and she felt things shift back to normal.

Kaylan slowly got to her feet, wondering if what had just happened was the result of her imagination. It had felt so real, but it couldn't have been. Her breathing slowed down as she relaxed.

There was a general chime over the speaker by the door.

"Kaylan, please report to the bridge," Hunsicker's voice said.

Kaylan took a few steps over and opened the ship communicator. "I'm ... I'm on my way."

Chapter Eleven

Zack was celebrating the survival of his first two weeks in space by pulling comms duty. This was where he got to monitor the comms station for any contact from NASA. At least he wasn't alone on the bridge. Katie Garcia was in the pilot's seat with one leg propped up, working on some calculations. She had her headphones on, listening to who knew what kind of music. All Zack knew was that out of the corner of his eye he could occasionally see her curly black hair bobbing as she kept time to the music.

Comms duty was a relatively quiet affair, so he spent the time working on decoding the alien message. He had to be careful. Dr. Jonah Redford—also known as Hawkman because of his long nose and beady eyes—had been checking up on him. Zack had dealt with stuffy intellectual types while working on his own three-letter acronym that would grant him recognition in exalted university ranks. He didn't think having a Ph.D. was a bad thing, but he had stopped equating them with truly intelligent people a long time ago. Jonah, however, *was* extremely intelligent, but he was also wound really tight. Sometimes the man would let something slip that got Zack thinking the astrophysicist wasn't as ignorant about all the details of their mission as Zack had initially thought. And Kaylan and Commander Hunsicker wanted to wait until after their visit to Titus Station before telling the rest of the crew about the alien message.

Whenever Zack needed a break from making sense of the alien data, he would poke around the satellite network deployed in the inner solar system. It was amazing. Millions of dollars' worth of equipment sent into outer space and it was entirely unsecured. It was as if the engineers couldn't fathom that someone, like maybe himself, would dare tap in and update the satellite's telemetry to report that it had somehow teleported itself to the other side of the Milky Way. Zack left a little file entitled "Just Kidding" that he was sure the mission analyst on Earth would find. Sometimes he couldn't help himself, and it was immensely pleasing to poke a little fun at this stuff.

Just outside the bridge was a multipurpose room that was currently being used as a classroom. They used it for running simulations for various types of equipment. He'd seen Kaylan go in there a couple of hours ago, and he'd been watching for her to come out. He thought he would see if she wanted to do some catching up on the observation deck.

Zack heard Kaylan's laugh as the door opened. He also heard someone else with her, and he craned his neck to see who it was. It was Hicks. Zack's stomach clenched as if he had been punched. Hicks's laugh dripped of that southern drawl. Zack clamped his teeth down and blew a breath of air out his nose. Judging by the look in Kaylan's eyes, she was actually falling for that good old country-boy charm. It shouldn't bother him at all. It wasn't as if he and Kaylan were anything but friends. There were times at MIT that it had felt like it could have been more, but he'd missed his chance. Now it seemed he had missed his chance all over again, if he'd ever had one.

"Easy there, Casanova. You've got a message," Katie said, sneaking up on him.

Zack gave a slight start at Katie's surprise attack. She had a knack for catching him in awkward moments like this.

"The queue is clear …" Zack said as he glanced back at the screen.

Katie giggled and gave him a playful pat on the back.

Zack glanced at the message and snatched up the microphone for a ship-wide broadcast. "Commander Hunsicker, we've got a priority-one message from Titus Station. Broadcast is all text."

Hunsicker replied within moments, saying he would be right up. Kaylan and Hicks came down the corridor to the bridge.

Kaylan smiled as she came over to him and nodded to Katie. "What have you got?"

Before Zack could answer, Commander Hunsicker jogged in.

"It says there has been some type of malfunction on the station affecting the airlocks. Long-range communication is down. Power is being drained. Looks like it's a few hours old," Zack said.

Hunsicker read the short message himself. "Okay, forward

that message on to NASA and tell them we're going to investigate. Send a response to the station and see if you can establish contact."

Zack nodded and began relaying the message.

"How much time until we reach the station?" Hunsicker asked.

"ETA is twelve hours," Kaylan answered. "We can cut the time down to two hours, but we'll need to allow time to slow down. Otherwise we'll fly right past them."

Hunsicker nodded. "Do the calculations and double-check them."

Kaylan headed for the pilot's seat and got to work.

"Sir, I'm assuming we're going to try and help them out. Katie and I were trained to do salvage duties, so perhaps we can help," Hicks offered.

"Sounds good. Let's get the others up here so we can work out a plan," Hunsicker said.

"I've updated my calculations and have a course ready to execute," Kaylan said.

"Do it," Hunsicker replied.

Brenda, Jonah, and Efren joined them on the bridge. They gathered around, and it made Zack feel good that Kaylan moved to stand at his side.

"It appears that our visit to Titus Station just got more interesting," Hunsicker began. "Brenda, I want you to get the med bay ready for possible injuries. If they're having power issues, we could be dealing with severe burns. Does anyone know how many people are on that station?"

"Six people man that station," Kaylan answered.

Brenda looked up in alarm. "The med bay is only equipped to deal with four people at a time."

"You can use my room. It's right by there. I know how to help with severe burns," Zack said.

This drew a few surprised glances from the others, but Kaylan moved closer and put her hand on his shoulder. At least she understood why he would be so eager to help burn victims.

"Thank you for volunteering," Hunsicker said. "Efren, you're going to see an energy spike from the reactor. We're trying to reach the station in two hours instead of twelve at our current speed."

Efren pushed his rimless glasses up his nose and pressed his lips together. "It won't be a problem. The reactor can handle this easily." His jet-black hair and slight Moroccan accent made him seem as suave as he was cool. Zack guessed he must be cool to deal with a nuclear fusion reactor on a day-to-day basis. Zack purposefully chose not to explore that scientific bit of truly profound technology that was changing the world. He knew that if containment in the reactor failed, there would be a brief fiery brilliance as they were instantly killed by a plasma breach. That was all he needed to know.

Warbled static sounded from the comms station. Zack had left it open when he joined the others. He returned his attention to the comms station and aligned the signal as best he could. The reception cleared.

"Athena, this is Titus Station," said a man with a thick Russian accent.

Just then, the signal went out of whack again and Zack adjusted it. He made a mental note to write up an algorithm that would automatically adjust the signal without him manually having to do it every time.

"This is Vitomir Mikhailovich of Titus Station."

Hunsicker clicked the microphone. "We read you, Titus. This is Commander Hunsicker of the Athena. We got your message. What's your status?"

"Two are dead. There are four of us left. I'm trapped in the command center. Two crew members are somewhere in the station. One of us is outside in the LSS. He cannot dock. Half the station is dark," Vitomir said.

The crew of the Athena shared a solemn look.

"Copy that," Hunsicker said. "We're en route and should be there inside two hours. Are you or anyone else able to reach the life pods?"

"Ja, there is a pod here that is accessible, but I will not leave my crew behind," Vitomir replied.

"Understood. Can you tell us what happened?" Commander Hunsicker asked.

"Drones stopped working while bringing a large sample to the station. Some type of substance ate their … Uhh, what's the word? Skin? This substance came in contact with the station and began devouring components. It destroyed the power lines, causing overload. Tobias and Simmons attempted to fix a work-around. An explosion took their lives," Vitomir said, his voice growing thick with regret that could be heard over the connection.

"Copy that, Vitomir," Commander Hunsicker replied gently. "I need you to focus. Help is on the way. We're going to do everything we can to help you and your crew. Can you give us the names and last known location of the rest of the crew?"

Redford began to say something, but stopped himself and shook his head.

Static played through the speakers, and then Vitomir continued. "Yoshiko Jin was on E-Deck. Nikolai Vratowski was in the LSS, and Natalya…"

Vitomir's voice trailed off in a sea of static.

"Can you get him back?" Hunsicker asked.

"Working on it," Zack replied.

"Say again, Vitomir. Repeat the last, after Nikolai Vratowski," Hunsicker said.

"Natalya," Vitomir said, and stifled a sob. "Natalya Mikhailovich, my wife, was last on H-Deck."

"His wife!" Zack gasped.

Hunsicker took a breath, and his brows pushed forward in determination. "Copy, H-Deck. Vitomir, give us a few minutes while we come up with a plan."

The silence dragged while they waited for Vitomir to reply. "I copy. Will be standing by," Vitomir's garbled reply finally came through comms.

"Sir, he's barely holding it together," Hicks said.

"You think? He might have lost his wife and has already had two people die," Zack snapped.

"Let's focus," Hunsicker said. "We need to work the problem."

"Well, we can't risk docking the Athena with the station," Redford said.

"That's crazy. How are we going to help them then?" Zack asked.

"He's right," Hunsicker said. "If we bring the Athena in, then we risk exposing the ship to whatever substance affected the station."

Kaylan stepped forward and turned on the holodisplay. A small depiction of Titus Station appeared. "We use the shuttle, with both Hicks and Garcia running some reconnaissance with the Beagles. Hicks has been showing me how they work. They're a lot more maneuverable than the shuttle. They can fly in and assess the damage of the LSS and the station itself."

Hunsicker nodded, considering what she had said, then glanced at Hicks and Garcia. "What do you think?"

"We can do this. We can even exit the Beagle and assist in the rescue. If they have suits, then we could even bring them back to the shuttle," Hicks said.

"We'll bring some extra spacesuits in the shuttle," Hunsicker said.

Redford cleared his throat and ran his hand through the mop of charcoal-colored hair on his head. "I think we're forgetting something important."

"Why don't you tell us then?" Hunsicker said.

"There are four potential survivors on the station. We only have resources for two additional people if we're to make the trip to Pluto," Redford said.

"What are you suggesting? That we just leave them?" Hicks asked, barely keeping the contempt from his voice.

Zack had the impression that Redford would stray to the ruthless side of things, but this was something beyond simple ambition.

Redford glared at Hicks. "I deal in facts and data. While the cowboy may want to swoop in and save the day, the simple facts are that if we rescue all those people then we might put all of our lives at risk. Plus, we don't know what this substance is."

Hicks was about to reply, but Commander Hunsicker cleared his throat. "Jonah's right. If we take those people on board, we will have issues with resources. It's a fact, and it should be pointed out to us. However, we're not going to leave those people stranded to die."

Zack cleared his throat and raised his hand, drawing the attention of the others. "Wouldn't the station have food and medical supplies we could bring over to help offset the imbalance?"

Hunsicker smiled and nodded to himself. "Zack makes an excellent point. I was thinking along the same lines myself. So, we'll split into three teams. Hicks and Garcia will take the Beagles and assess the damage to the station. If they see an opportunity to assist a stranded crew member, they'll take it. Redford and I will pilot the shuttle and find the LSS that Nikolai Vratowski was piloting. Then we'll see about getting Vitomir."

Kaylan stiffened at this. "Sir, I can pilot the shuttle—"

"I know you can. I want you here on the Athena in case the rest of us get into trouble. Should the worst happen, you will still be able to get to Pluto," Hunsicker said.

Zack couldn't imagine how they could even think about going to Pluto at a time like this, but astronauts were of a different breed than him. Kaylan nodded. Zack knew she didn't like having to stay behind, but he was relieved that she wasn't going. Zack glanced at Redford, who looked as if he were about to spew fire, but he remained silent.

Commander Hunsicker called for their attention. "Ideally we'd want to restore power to the station. If we can get it stabilized, then they could hold out for the resupply ship. Our first priority is the lives of the people still alive on the station. Kaylan, I need you to send a message to NASA giving them an update and what we're planning on doing. They have rooms full of people who might come up with a better solution. Efren, can you speculate on the state of their reactor?"

Efren chewed on his bottom lip in thought. "It's powered by an older fission reactor. They simply dump the toxic waste from it on a nearby asteroid body. If they've lost power, there are some redundant systems that could be brought online, if they're not already, including a solar array. It's hard to say. The station started off as a purely autonomous robotic station. They've only been sending a team of humans there for the past six years. If their reactor is failing, the place is a ticking time bomb."

"How could we tell if the reactor is critical? We can always ask Vitomir, but I only want to do that if we have no other choice," Hunsicker said.

"If we could link up with their systems, then we could get a detailed damage report, but their long-range communications are down," Efren said.

"Russian systems are different than NASA's. We can't just link up," Redford said.

"Well, it's a good thing we have someone like Zack here," Commander Hunsicker said.

Zack grinned. "I've been playing with your satellites all day. Getting into a fifteen-year-old station network isn't going to pose too much of a problem. We just need to get close enough so we can connect."

"There you have it, Jonah. Let's make this happen," Hunsicker said.

The crew broke apart, each going to their assigned task. Commander Hunsicker came over to Zack.

"Playing with satellites?"

Zack smiled guiltily. "I just had their transponders report that they were on the other side of the galaxy."

"Zack, please," Hunsicker said, giving him that look like his father had when he'd been caught doing something he shouldn't have been.

"Okay, I'll change them back," Zack said. "Uh, Commander, quick question. Are you a father by any chance?"

"I'm a grandfather. Why do you ask?"

"You reminded me of my father just now with that look you gave me," Zack said.

"Oh, *that* look. You'll get it when you become a father," Hunsicker said.

Zack's face flushed, and he thought he heard Katie Garcia let out a small laugh.

"I've heard you've taken on evil giant corporations and brought no small amount of justice to those who deserve it, but you balk at the mere mention of becoming a father?" Hunsicker asked, clearly amused.

"Don't kid yourself, Commander. He's a regular Casanova," Katie said as she went by.

"I'll leave you to it. As soon as you're in the station's systems, we'll need to know the current status of that reactor. You may even find the tracker signals for the crew," Hunsicker said as he was leaving.

Zack went back to work. This was something he could help with, and he didn't want to let the crew down. He quickly scripted some automatic subroutines that would alert him when they were within range of the station's systems. They would be at the station within the hour, and to pass the time he updated the comms system so it would automatically keep the strongest signal. As he performed these tasks, he listened to Kaylan give an update to NASA and then speak to Vitomir, who was stuck alone in the command center of the failing space station.

Chapter Twelve

The bridge of the Athena had a conference table near the back so the crew had a place to meet. Kaylan had read that the original designers of the ship had argued furiously to have it added but were met with heavy resistance. They eventually won based on astronaut feedback citing that a lack of a place to collaborate interfered with scientific research and experimentation. The bridge of any ship, whether it sailed the sea or the stars, was the head, and perhaps the most important place next to the heart. In the case of the Athena, the heart was the reactor. This same design also applied to space stations. The Athena was rapidly approaching Titus Station, and Kaylan had already started the braking thrusters.

"I'm in their system," Zack announced from his seat at the comms station.

"I guess you weren't kidding about how easy it would be," Kaylan said, coming to his side.

"It makes sense. Why would they need to harden their systems? The only people out here are us," Zack said.

Kaylan and Zack joined the others gathered around the bridge conference table. The holodisplay flickered to life as the output from Titus Station's computer systems were piped in. They were in regular contact with Vitomir Mikhailovich, but this was their first real glimpse into how extensive the damage had been. Damage reports showed that the station had suffered several catastrophic failures.

"The containment fields around the reactor powering the station are failing. If they fail it could compromise the battery storage array," Efren said, and brought that report to the forefront of the feed.

Hunsicker frowned and engaged the comms channel to Titus Station. "Vitomir, can you confirm the readings from the reactor core?"

"They are correct, Commander," Vitomir replied.

Efren gasped. "The failsafes should have been engaged by now—"

Hunsicker closed the comms channel and held up his hand. Efren quieted down. "Take it easy. He's under a lot of pressure," Hunsicker said, and opened comms back up. "Vitomir, are you able to engage the failsafes and close off the reactor core?"

"Ja, I can do this, but not before I know the status of my crew. Switching to the emergency solar array can be even more dangerous," Vitomir said.

"Acknowledged. Give us a minute," Hunsicker said.

"Switching to the solar array is more dangerous than an exploding nuclear reactor?" Zack asked.

"The reactor wouldn't explode, but it can trigger an explosion from the battery storage array," Kaylan said. "Can you bring up a schematic of the station?"

"Sure," Zack replied.

Kaylan studied the schematic and brought up an interface so she could control the holodisplay. An overlay of blinking red circles appeared on various parts of the station. "The damage appears to be concentrated in the middle and on the far end away from the command center. And here are the deck IDs."

"Where is the reactor and the battery array?" Zack asked.

"The actual reactor is located beneath the surface of the asteroid along with the main battery array. There is a tunnel with a direct connection that runs through the middle of the station. Unfortunately, the main docking area the robotic drones use is also located in the middle," Kaylan said.

Hicks blew out a breath. "So whatever those drones brought back ate through some of the exterior and is gradually making its way to the heart of the station."

Hunsicker narrowed his gaze at the schematic. "H-Deck is near the entrance to the reactor core. If Vitomir activates the fail-safes and closes off the core, then his wife is dead."

Redford shook his head. "She could be dead already. If that core blows, it could kill us all."

"What do the failsafes do, exactly?" Zack asked.

"Efren, please correct me if I'm wrong," Kaylan began. "They pump a mixture of liquid nitrogen to help cool the reactor momentarily. Then they blow the tunnels between the reactor and the station. The rock and debris will protect the station's occupants for a period of time, allowing part of the station to detach itself and move to another asteroid."

Efren nodded.

"But with damage this extensive they can't use the station as a lifeboat," Hunsicker said.

"Yoshiko Jin was on E-Deck. He might be far enough away from the damaged sections to have survived. I say we stick with the current plan," Hicks said.

"We didn't come all this way to turn around and leave now," Hunsicker said. "Do the station's systems give the last known position of the LSS?"

Zack went to work. "According to the logs it was en route to dock when the explosion occurred."

Kaylan brought up a quick simulation and highlighted an area a short distance from the station. "You would have a search grid in this area for the LSS. If the explosion pushed the LSS away, its own thrusters should have stabilized it."

"Excellent work," Hunsicker said.

"Athena, I have a visual of you," Vitomir said, sounding relieved.

Hunsicker relayed their plan to Vitomir. "The last piece will be to collect you from the command center. In the meantime, can you gather supplies that can be easily transferred to the shuttle?"

"I can do this. I will gather medical supplies and provisions. Commander, please find my wife," Vitomir said.

"We'll do everything we can," Hunsicker replied, and closed the comms connection. He looked at Hicks and Garcia. "I want you to head to E-Deck first and try to get to Yoshiko Jin. He's the easiest of the two. Then proceed to H-Deck. We should be back with the shuttle to assist. If the area around H-Deck is too dangerous, then I don't want you going anywhere near it."

Hicks and Garcia nodded, but Kaylan could tell that neither

of them liked the thought of leaving someone behind. Dale Hicks was turning into something she hadn't quite expected. He'd made a real effort to get to know all of them and lend a hand where he could. She was finding that she didn't mind spending time with him, and she really liked his smile. She was even growing to like that southern good-old-boy charm he'd acquired growing up well south of the Mason-Dixon Line.

Hunsicker came over to her and waved Zack over.

"Listen up," Hunsicker said quietly. "Kaylan, I need you to keep the engines hot. I want you ready to execute a course that will take the ship to safety if things don't go as planned and we can't make it back. Zack, are you able to control Titus's systems from here?"

"I can try," Zack said.

"I didn't ask if you could try. I need to know if you can do it," Hunsicker said.

Zack glanced at Kaylan and then gave Hunsicker a determined look. "I can. I just need a little bit of time. Vitomir has the core systems locked out, but I can look for a way to bypass them."

Hunsicker nodded. "Understood. Once you're in, I may need you to force the failsafes to execute."

Zack's eyes widened. "But you just told him you'd try to save his wife."

"We will. I wasn't lying about that. But my first responsibility is for the safety of this crew and the ship. I'm not about to condemn us all to death for Vitomir or his wife. In this, Redford and I are in agreement," Hunsicker said.

Zack nodded. "I won't let you down."

Hunsicker smiled. "I know you won't," he said.

"Commander," Kaylan called as Hunsicker was leaving the bridge, "be careful."

Hunsicker waved and left Kaylan and Zack alone on the bridge.

"I didn't realize it was that serious," Zack said, and shook his head. "No, that didn't sound right, but you know what I mean. Every decision we have to make is weighed against the risk to the crew, the ship, and the mission."

"Michael will cover all his bases even if he doesn't like them. It's why he was selected for the Mars mission and why he's still alive today for this mission," Kaylan said.

They headed to the front of the bridge. Kaylan took the pilot's seat, and Zack sat next to her in the commander's seat.

Zack looked out of the window at the large asteroid that had been Titus Station's home for the last fifteen years. "How did they even build this?"

"They did it based on what they learned building the Luna Base on the moon. If you take some of your operations under- ground, then you have a safe haven from harmful cosmic radia- tion," Kaylan said.

"Any idea what could eat through the metal the station is made of?"

"It's not just one component. It's composites from materials mined from the asteroids out here."

"Is the Athena made of the same composites?" Zack asked.

"The Athena is stronger. The outer layer is a more advanced ceramic alloy that is highly resistant to things like heat and corrosion."

They continued to work in silence. Kaylan calculated a

course to take them away and uploaded it to the navigation system. She hoped they wouldn't need it.

"I'm still not used to seeing so many stars out. If it were colder in here, I bet I could almost hear the sounds of the Charles River when we used to go there with Gary, Tracey, and Pete," Zack said.

Kaylan laughed. "I can remember when you fell in. 'Don't worry, Kaylan, the ice can hold me,'" she said, mimicking his voice.

"It should have held me," Zack said, frowning. "Those were good times. I've thought about those times a lot."

Kaylan had a good idea which of those times he was thinking about. One night, walking home from their group's favorite coffee shop, one of them had brought out a small bottle of Irish whiskey and their normal coffees became Irish coffees. Kaylan remembered not feeling the frigid cold weather. Near an old-style lamp post, Zack took her by the hand, and, in a blur of whiskey-filled courage, kissed her while the Charles River flowed in the background. She remembered the tender feel of his lips pressed against hers, and, while she hadn't expected Zack to kiss her, she was glad he had at the time.

Kaylan turned toward him. He was older now, and he'd lost much of that schoolboy innocence. His dark eyes were infused with mysterious curiosity but inviting at the same time.

"I'm sorry for leaving the way I did. I should have come to you and said goodbye," Zack said.

"Why didn't you?"

Zack looked away from her. "Because I was afraid that if I saw you, I wouldn't have been able to leave."

Kaylan's heart twisted, and old, forgotten feelings surged forward.

"Athena," Hunsicker's voice sounded through the comms. "We're on the shuttle and are about to detach."

"Copy that," Kaylan answered.

Hicks and Garcia checked in, too, and Kaylan apprised Vitomir that the others were on their way. At some point, Zack went back to the comms station. Every now and then they caught each other's eye.

Oh boy, Kaylan thought. She brushed aside the ghosts of the past for the moment and focused on what had to be done right now.

Chapter Thirteen

Michael Hunsicker piloted the shuttle away from the Athena. Jonah Redford sat in the copilot's seat, and Brenda Goodwin sat behind them. She'd brought additional medical supplies. One thing Michael could guarantee about space travel was that the unexpected can and will happen. On Earth, space was mysterious and sometimes romantic. The reality was that working in space was among the most dangerous ventures to be taken on by humans. Lives could be lost in the blink of an eye, and it could take years to come to grips with the aftermath. After the Mars mission he had promised himself that he was done. He would stay on Earth and teach others how to survive in the most inhospitable of environments. Many people greeted him like he was some kind of hero. Truth be told, he just did what he had to do to survive, and that included a successful year-long mission on the surface of Mars. He had told Caroline to get used to having him around at home. She did.

They had a few years together before cancer took her from him. He had stayed around and enjoyed spoiling his grandchildren for a while, but the empty void left by Caroline had gotten to him. It was around that time that Edward Johnson had come to him with an offer to lead an ambitious undertaking—a manned mission to Titan, along with Saturn's other moons. Never in his wildest dreams had he ever thought he would be going to Pluto. The asteroid belt was supposed to be a flyby on their way to Titan, but the unexpected had happened, and here they were. Michael valued the entire crew. He was determined to bring them through this journey safely. At least he had managed to keep two of the mission's most important people out of harm's way. Kaylan Farrow was among the best he'd ever worked with. And he had voiced serious reservations about Zack Quick in the beginning, but he was glad to have been proven wrong in that case.

"I have a strong ping on the LSS," Jonah said.

A blip appeared on the shuttle's HUD, and Michael laid in a course to it.

"How did it get so far from the station?" Brenda asked.

"My guess is that the explosion sent it tumbling out here and the autopilot engaged to bring the craft to a stop, but it requires the pilot's command to bring it back to the station," Hunsicker said.

"We won't be able to tell if there is any damage until we get closer," Redford said.

"Or if Nikolai Vratowski is alive inside," Hunsicker added.

The Lenoy Salvage System was essentially a flying spider. It had six legs with clawed feet capable of grasping onto rough, uneven surfaces. The command module had enough room for two people, with a storage compartment accessible from the outside. The LSS had a drill attachment used for taking core samples of asteroids, which could penetrate up to fifty meters. Like most space vehicles, it could be remotely piloted, but whatever damage the LSS had sustained had knocked out its systems.

Michael slowed the shuttle down and turned on the overhead spotlight. Blackened swaths adorned the command module's white hull, but it looked intact.

"I'm going to circle around," Michael said.

As they moved around the LSS they didn't see anything leaking from the craft, so there were no indications of a hull breach. Whatever oxygen the LSS had originally had onboard could have already vented into space.

"Athena, other than a few scorch marks on the LSS, we're not seeing any traces of the substance Vitomir warned us about," Hunsicker said.

"Acknowledged," Kaylan said.

Hunsicker turned toward Brenda. "Are you able to pick up Nikolai's suit vitals yet?"

"Yeah, just now. His heart rate is low and steady. I'd say he's been knocked unconscious by the blast. Suit pressure is holding, though it doesn't have much oxygen left. He may have had minimal oxygen when he returned to the station," Brenda said.

"I can't access the ship's systems," Redford said.

"All right, the module looks intact. I'm going out there to see if I can bring up the ship's systems from the inside," Hunsicker said.

He swung the shuttle around so the rear of the craft was

nearest to the command module of the LSS. He climbed out of the pilot's seat and closed his helmet, pulling on his gloves and pressurizing his suit. The others followed his example.

"Depressurizing," Redford said, once everyone had given him the okay.

"Don't go anywhere without me," Hunsicker said.

"I won't let him," Brenda replied.

Redford gave a half smile. "Good luck, Commander. We'll be right here."

Hunsicker nodded and headed for the airlock. He closed off the passenger compartment, and once he was sealed in, the indicator light went from red to green. Hunsicker opened the outer airlock. The LSS command module was about five meters away. Hunsicker took a moment to comprehend the vastness of space beyond. Astronauts of every caliber were often taken aback when they performed their first spacewalk. The sheer overwhelming reality that came when an astronaut left the safety of their ship could be awe inspiring. He'd always found it truly amazing, and it left him with a heartfelt respect that they were even alive at all. That the conditions conducive to life had aligned to thrive on planet Earth was a miracle.

Hunsicker brought his gaze back down. "Heading to the LSS."

His suit thrusters gave him a gentle nudge toward the LSS. As he closed in, he engaged his thrusters for a few seconds to slow his approach. He grasped at the handles along the hatch and came to a stop. He could only see the vague outline of Nikolai Vratowski. Hunsicker opened the hatch and went inside.

"It looks like he's just knocked out. He has a gash on his

forehead, but his helmet is intact. I'm going to try and bring up the computer," Hunsicker said.

The instrument panel on the power core monitor indicated an overload, which had probably occurred when the explosion from Titus Station impacted the LSS. Since the ship was designed to withstand impacts, the explosion must have been bigger than they'd originally thought. He closed the breakers and pressed the power button. The internal lights flickered on, and Hunsicker moved into the seat next to Nikolai.

"The engines are offline. The damage report shows an issue with the couplings. Main life support is depleted. Nikolai is lucky he was wearing his suit. There is no way I can fly this back to the Athena," Hunsicker said.

"Perhaps we get the LSS to grab onto the shuttle. Can you control any of the grasping legs?" Jonah asked.

"Won't that damage the shuttle?" Brenda asked.

"Not if we don't overdo it. The LSS is designed to latch itself onto any object with as much or as little force as required," Jonah said.

"The legs are online, so that could work, but I don't know how to operate them. First, we need to get Nikolai into the shuttle. Athena, can you patch in Vitomir?" Hunsicker said.

Kaylan patched in Vitomir, and Hunsicker relayed the plan. Vitomir said he could walk someone through the controls of the LSS.

"Commander, have your people been able to locate Natalya or Yoshiko?" Vitomir asked.

"Not yet. I have Hicks and Garcia assessing the damage to the station and looking for them," Hunsicker answered.

"I will wait," Vitomir said.

"Jonah, I need you to head to the airlock and bring a tether," Hunsicker said.

He unstrapped Nikolai from the chair and pulled his body up, which was easy in zero gravity. There was no way for him to know if Nikolai had broken any bones, so Hunsicker carefully guided him to the back of the module. He opened the hatch and saw Brenda and Jonah waiting at the shuttle's airlock. Hunsicker waved for them to send the tether over. The bright orange tether shot forth, and Hunsicker grabbed it, securing the tether to Nikolai's spacesuit.

"Okay, retract it," Hunsicker said.

The unconscious form of Nikolai crossed the distance, and Jonah and Brenda caught him. Hunsicker left the hatch open on the LSS and crossed back over to the shuttle. Jonah waited in the airlock after Brenda brought Nikolai inside.

"Once you're on the LSS, I'll position the shuttle underneath. Are you sure you're up for this?" Hunsicker asked.

"I'll be fine," Jonah said, and headed to the LSS.

Hunsicker went through the airlock and checked with Brenda.

"He's stable for now. I won't know if he has internal injuries or broken bones until we get him to Athena's med bay."

Hunsicker nodded and went to the pilot seat. "Jonah, what's your status?"

"Ready when you are. Vitomir says there are smaller arms that can extend from the legs that we can use to latch onto the shuttle. They only have a one-meter range," Jonah said.

With the LSS engines offline, they didn't have a choice. "Not a problem. I'll let you know when we're in position," Hunsicker said.

He checked to see that Brenda was secure and circled around the LSS. Redford had retracted all but two of the legs that extended out away from the ship, and Hunsicker eased the thirty-foot shuttle underneath the LSS. With the lightest touch, he moved the shuttle up into position. The sensors reported that the LSS was two feet directly above.

"We're in position. Take your time, and don't tear any holes," Hunsicker said.

"Acknowledged. Extending the arms now," Jonah replied.

Hunsicker closed his eyes and listened. There were guide rails for astronauts to use that ran along the shuttle. NASA had joined them to the actual frame of the shuttle, so if Jonah could get four of the legs connected, then it should bear the distributed weight of the LSS once they began moving.

A loud clang from above announced Jonah's first attempt.

"Jonah, you need to ease up just a little bit," Hunsicker warned.

The other legs connected with much less force.

"Attached, and the legs are locked, Commander," Jonah said.

"Acknowledged."

He laid in a course for the Athena, and the shuttle began to move. The LSS stayed in place, and none of the shuttle's sensors reported any stress overload. During the trip back to the Athena, Jonah was able to get the maneuvering thrusters online with Vitomir's help.

Hunsicker lined the LSS up with the docking clamps on the Athena. The docking clamps would hold the LSS in place, but the only way to access it would be from the outside. It was like hauling something on the roof rack of a car. The idea for using the LSS on Pluto was last minute, so it hadn't been built into the design of the ship.

After the LSS was secure, Hunsicker docked the shuttle. Brenda took Nicolai to the med bay and Jonah came back on board the shuttle. It had taken them just under an hour to retrieve the LSS. Now they would head to Titus Station and get the others out.

Chapter Fourteen

The Beagle 4S was a small, one-man spacecraft developed for satellite salvage and repair. It had been intended for service on the second-generation International Space Station, but as it proved more useful, its operational and application ranges were increased. Private corporations paid a lot of money to maintain a small fleet of these spacecraft at the ISS. The United States Air Force used them in a joint venture with NASA to train astronaut candidates from the military in salvage and repair. The Beagles were sixteen feet in length with stub wings. They weren't meant for atmospheric flight. The pilot sat close to the nose of the spacecraft. They were highly maneuverable and quick, which made them ideal for navigating the debris field that stretched out from Titus Station.

Hicks and Garcia approached the station slowly.

"The debris field seems mostly made up of pieces from the

station. I'm not detecting any asteroid fragments at all," Garcia said.

"I keep wondering about the substance that caused all this," Hicks said.

"Whatever happened here, it wasn't quick. Perhaps there was a buildup on the outside of the station that eventually led to corrosion and the explosion."

"Would you look at that," Hicks said.

They closed in on the station. The middle of it was a mass of twisted black metal. Titus Station was home to a small army of robotic drones whose sole purpose was to catalog asteroids. The asteroids rich in metals and mineral deposits were tagged with a beacon, then eventually collected and inserted into Earth's orbit. And with the advent of quicker space propulsion, a human presence could be maintained in the asteroid belt.

"There's a lot of damage to H-Deck. The commander was right. Let's head to E-Deck first," Hicks said, and sent an update back to the Athena.

"What are you doing?" Garcia asked.

Hicks frowned, his eyes darting around him. "What do you mean? Did I miss something?"

Garcia sighed. "With Farrow."

"You're bringing this up now?" Hicks asked.

"Well, it's just you and me up here. No one else can hear, unlike on the ship," Garcia replied.

Hicks and Garcia had been paired together for almost four years—enough time for both of them to go in and out of relationships. They'd always been friends. She was like a sister to him and, like a sister, she could be overly blunt.

"We need to focus," Hicks said.

"Now you're dodging the question, cowboy. Can't you do two things at once?" Garcia challenged.

People had been calling him cowboy since officer candidate school. He guessed since he was from Texas, people expected the cowboy thing to go hand in hand. The funny thing was that he had never even ridden a horse.

"Nothing is going on between us," Hicks said.

"Sure."

"We're supposed to watch out for Kaylan and Zack. I've been getting to know both of them," Hicks replied.

"Well, you're not flirting with Zack," Garcia said.

Their deployment schedule hadn't allowed them much in the way of personal relationships beyond a fling. Ever since their aerial stunt show over the Appalachian mountains, Kaylan had been in his thoughts more often than not. He was attracted to Kaylan—from the way her dark hair met the contours of her neckline to the color of her eyes like glistening drops of honey in the early morning sun.

"Fine, I might have flirted a little bit," Hicks admitted.

"Well, I'm not the only one who's noticed," Garcia said.

Hicks was about to reply when he realized they were closing in on E-Deck. The pockmarked surface of the station stretched back the way they had come.

"I can't detect any suit signals from this far out," Hicks said, and glanced at the multiple hull breaches venting into space. "It looks pretty unstable, but I want to go in for a closer look and see if I can detect Yoshiko's suit signal from inside. You stay out here and monitor the station. This place could blow at any moment."

"Will do, and be careful. I don't want to explain to your

mother and sisters that you got yourself blown to pieces trying to be a hero," Garcia said.

Hicks chuckled. His family adored Katie, and his mother hinted that he and Katie should get together. They'd glanced at each other and laughed it off. Their lack of physical attraction to each other was mutual. Hicks eased his craft closer to the station until he was two meters away from its surface. Katie maintained her distance so she could observe his approach. Yoshiko's suit signal appeared on the HUD.

"I've got a signal. He's alive. His pulse is elevated. He could be trapped in there," Hicks said, and tried to contact him, but there was no reply. "I'm going inside for a look."

"I'm detecting vibrations coming from the surrounding area," Garcia said.

"I'll go as quick as I can."

Hicks opened the canopy and climbed out of the Beagle, using his thrusters to cross the distance to the hole. It would be a tight fit, but he was certain he could make it through. Emergency lighting shined through the dimly lit corridor. E-Deck was part of an older section of the station, so it was designed for zero gravity. Hicks pulled himself along the corridor and tried raising Yoshiko Jin on comms but didn't get a reply. There was some blockage ahead, and he heard the groaning protest of the station's supports. The emergency lighting went out, and the only illumination cutting through the darkness came from Hicks's helmet. A short distance away from him the corridor was entirely blocked off, but it looked like there was a turn before the blockage that could take him further into the station's interior. He pulled himself along, and his comms system picked up a staticky message.

"Katie, are you receiving this?" Hicks asked.

"I just heard static," Garcia replied.

"The way forward is blocked, but there is another corridor heading to the interior that's clear. Yoshiko's comms system could be damaged," Hicks said.

Shafts of light coming from his helmet penetrated the darkness, and Hicks floated down it, moving faster. He closed in on the end of the gray metal corridor, and there was a dim orange glow beyond. Hicks rounded the corner and heard the last vestiges of twisting metal snap as the entire corridor shifted into him. It took him a few seconds to stop bouncing between the walls and gain his bearings.

"What's going on, Katie?"

"Sections away from your position are popping. Each pop depressurizes a small section, but it's straining against the structure as a whole. Where are you?"

Hicks pulled himself around a pile of twisted metal and saw a man in a gray and orange spacesuit pinned against the wall. He waved both his hands at Hicks when he saw him.

"I've found him," Hicks said.

Hicks pulled himself toward Yoshiko, and the man waved his arms furiously, gesturing up above him. A greenish vapor coiled along the piping on the ceiling.

"Katie, can you patch in Athena?"

"Done, you're go for Athena," Garcia said.

"Kaylan, I've found Yoshiko. He's pinned against the wall. There's some type of greenish vapor coming through the piping overhead. Do the schematics tell what that is?" Hicks asked.

"The piping above you is used to fuel the drones. You've got to get him and yourself out of there now," Kaylan said.

Hicks turned off comms and swore.

"Hicks, did you copy? The area you're in could explode any minute," Garcia said.

"I'm going to see if I can get him free," Hicks replied.

He closed in on Yoshiko, who was shaking his head. Yoshiko raised his arm so Hicks could see the suit readout.

Hicks nodded. "He's almost out of oxygen. I'm going to try and get him free."

He heard Kaylan start to protest, but Garcia cut off comms back to Athena, and Hicks thanked her. He needed to concentrate.

Yoshiko was pinned against the wall by a large metal shaft from the opposite wall.

"I'm gonna try and pull this out enough for you to get out," Hicks said, getting close enough so that Yoshiko could hear him.

Yoshiko nodded. He looked to be in his late forties, and Hicks figured this was his last mission. Hicks twisted his position so his feet were near Yoshiko's head. He squatted down and grabbed the metal cross section that had kept Yoshiko's suit from being ruptured. He counted down from three and pushed with his legs. Nothing moved. Hicks shifted his position and tried again, straining to move the debris, but it was no use. Yoshiko was wedged in. He let out a low growl and pushed as hard as he could. He heard Yoshiko doing the same.

"It's the damn hard spacesuit he's wearing," Hicks said, finally answering Garcia's call for status. "If I had a pressure-jack, then I bet I could get him loose."

Hicks glanced at Yoshiko. The Chinese astronaut returned his gaze calmly and gave Hicks a single solemn nod. Hicks kept looking around for anything he could use to pry Yoshiko loose.

Yoshiko waved him over, and Hicks leaned in so he could hear him.

"Leave."

"No!" Hicks cried, grabbing onto the shaft and pulling, screaming for all he was worth.

It was no use. The shaft wouldn't budge. The greenish gas was getting thicker. Yoshiko patted his arm and shook his head, then pointed at Hicks and down the corridor.

"I won't leave you," Hicks said.

Be it military bravado or heroic foolishness, Hicks couldn't leave the man behind. Yoshiko mouthed the words, "Thank you," and raised his hands to his helmet. Before Hicks could react, Yoshiko pulled the release mechanism, exposing his head to the frigid vacuum of space. Hicks cried out, but Yoshiko was already dead.

"Hicks, what happened? Are you all right?" Garcia asked.

His breaths came in gasps, and he clutched the dead astronaut's spacesuit.

"You need to get out of there now. Move it, soldier," Garcia said with a steely tone.

Hicks looked back at the dead astronaut. Tiny icicles wreathed his head, collecting along his thinning hair. Yoshiko's frozen visage was burned into Hicks's brain. Grim-faced, Hicks pushed away from the dead astronaut. He rounded the corner and used the jets on his spacesuit to propel him faster, closing the distance to the breach where his ship was in no time.

"Hicks, were you able to get Yoshiko out?" Commander Hunsicker asked.

Hicks pulled himself back into the Beagle. "Sir, I couldn't get him free. Yoshiko … took his own life."

There was a short span of silence before Hunsicker answered. "Understood. You did everything you could. We've retrieved the LSS and are heading to the Command Center."

"Garcia and I are heading to H-Deck to look for Natalya."

Hunsicker acknowledged, and Hicks rejoined Garcia. He didn't want to talk. He just wanted to continue on to see if they could at least rescue Natalya. Whenever he closed his eyes, he saw Yoshiko's face turn gray as it instantly froze.

Titus Station's exterior lights were out further along the center of the station. Hicks saw the occasional ghostly flicker through smaller hull breaches. There weren't any windows, so he couldn't see inside. The station was home to more robots than people. The Command Center had been added after the station had been built.

A blip appeared on the Beagle's HUD.

"I have contact," Garcia said.

"I see it," Hicks answered.

There wasn't as much wreckage floating near the station, but the occasional ding on the Beagle's hull made his stomach clench. The signal grew stronger as they closed in on the western-most point of the wreckage. Above them, the explosion had left a gaping hole, but below was a mass of former decks that were scrunched together. Flashes of electricity in the form of blurred arcs rippled through the interior.

Hicks called out to Natalya, but there was no response. The Athena comms channel pinged them, and Hicks opened it.

"Hicks, try scanning for low-level suit frequencies. The damage might be too thick for anything else to make it through," Kaylan said.

Hicks expanded the frequency level, and there was a faint response. "Got it. Thanks."

He moved his ship lower, and the signal got stronger.

"This is Natalya Mikhailovich, Titus Station."

"Hello, Natalya, I'm Major Dale Hicks of the spacecraft Athena. We're here to get you out of there."

"Reactor core unstable—" Natalya's reply broke up. "Unable to leave."

Hicks looked for a way they could get inside but didn't see anything.

"Several decks down looks intact," Garcia said.

She was right. They could use the plasma cutter to clear a path inside. He started calculating how much time it would take and couldn't come up with more than a vague estimate. He needed Natalya's exact location.

"Hicks," Kaylan said through comms. "You can't reach her. Natalya was heading to shut down the reactor core. The interference with comms traffic isn't entirely from the wreckage. It's because she's near the core."

"How do you know that?"

"Trust me. If you try cutting your way inside, both you and Garcia will die," Kaylan said.

"She could be right," Garcia said. "The station wasn't built with safety measures for people in mind."

Hicks saw Garcia's solemn expression through the canopy in the Beagle next to him. He clamped his teeth down, trying to think of something he could do.

"Natalya, are you able to get yourself to another part of the station, away from the core?" Hicks asked.

"I'm trapped, Major. Please, can I ask if you've had word of my husband, Vitomir? He was in the Command Center."

Hicks closed his eyes. "Your husband is safe. Are you sure there is no other way—"

"Please, Major, I would like to speak to my husband. Can you make this happen?" Natalya said. Her voice sounded like she was weakening. He wanted to ask her if she was hurt. Hicks looked at Garcia helplessly, and she gave him a grim nod. He wracked his brain, looking for some alternative, but couldn't think of anything. The rules were different here in space. On Earth if things went south there was at least the option of bugging out, but here a person's life hung by a thread, precariously tied to their location when disaster struck.

"I can do this for you," Hicks said.

Chapter Fifteen

Titus Station had been built on a large asteroid about twenty kilometers in diameter. What had started off as a mining experiment had turned into a first-of-its-kind deep-space operation. The station had been built from the materials found on the asteroid, and now it was a breath away from being destroyed.

Hunsicker got his first real look at the station on their approach in the shuttle. The station had three main sections. The larger sections were for space-probe maintenance and refueling. Long gray shafts connected the different areas. The Command Center's white outer hull was similar in design to the International Space Station. Emergency living quarters were part of the Command Center, but the main living quarters were below the asteroid's surface, which protected the astronauts from harmful radiation.

"Commander, this is Athena," Kaylan said over comms.

"Go, Athena," Hunsicker said.

"Hicks reported a substance venting inside the station. Vitomir believes it's the fuel for the space vehicles being used," Kaylan said.

"Acknowledged," Hunsicker replied.

Redford blew out a frustrated breath and was about to speak when Kaylan continued.

"Commander, that station could blow at any moment. All it would take is a spark to start a chain reaction," Kaylan said.

"Understood, shuttle out."

"This is getting too dangerous," Redford said. "We should leave now. You should pull Hicks and Garcia out."

The gray mass of Titus Station loomed before the shuttle. It was lopsided, and there was a gaping hole several decks wide near the center. Hunsicker ignored Jonah and flew the shuttle toward the Command Center.

"You're putting the entire mission at risk to rescue two people," Redford pressed.

"You know, you can see a person's true colors in a crisis. In an instant you know who's only concerned with saving their own skin and who the brave ones are," Hunsicker said.

Redford sucked in a breath. "There is a difference between being brave and being smart."

"And there is a difference between cowards and those with courage. This isn't a classroom, professor. Those are real people out there. Do you want their blood on your hands? I certainly don't. I won't abandon Vitomir or his wife while there is still a chance that we can get them out," Hunsicker said, then hit the comms button. "Hicks, have you found Natalya yet?"

"Commander, we've got the telemetry from her suit. It should appear on your HUD in a moment. She's alive, but her location is under several decks' worth of wreckage from the initial explosion. We think she's near the reactor core. She was heading to the reactor to engage the fail-safes, but she was locked out," Hicks said.

"Commander, this is Athena," Kaylan said. "A lockout can only be authorized by the station commander."

"Acknowledged, Athena. Hicks, can you patch her signal through comms? I'm going to patch Vitomir in now," Hunsicker said.

He navigated through the interface and quickly merged the comms signals.

"Vitomir, we've found Natalya. She's on the line now," Hunsicker said.

"Natalya, are you there?" Vitomir asked.

"I'm here. Are you safe?" Natalya asked.

"I'm in the Command Center. The way is blocked to the station's interior."

"Vitomir, the reactor fail-safes must be engaged."

"I cannot. You'll die down there."

There was a long pause. "*Vitomir*," Natalya said gently. "You need to get out. I will not be leaving Titus Station."

Vitomir let out a mournful howl. "I cannot leave you. I won't leave you."

"Yes, you will. Dominika will need one of her parents to return home."

"Please," Vitomir pleaded. "Please don't make me do this. Please don't go," he whispered.

"I won't be far as long as you live. You will find me in our daughter's smile and in the echoes of her laugh. There you will find—"

The connection cut off. Vitomir screamed his wife's name, but there was no response. The vitals from Natalya's suit all flatlined.

"I'm sorry," Hunsicker said, his throat growing thick. "She's gone." Hunsicker waited a moment before continuing. "You're all that's left, Commander. We're right outside. All you have to do is come through the airlock."

They waited there in silence. The HUD showed that Hicks and Garcia were approaching.

Hunsicker opened a secure comms channel back to Athena. "Zack, are you able to engage the fail-safes?"

"I'm in command, but if the station explodes, will the fail-safes make a difference?" Zack asked.

"Yes, it will prevent a much bigger explosion. Engage the fail-safes now."

"Executed," Zack confirmed.

Proximity alarms blared. Flashes of orange were spewing out the center of the station, expanding in both directions. Hunsicker turned back toward the airlock, which hissed open. Vitomir stood in his red and orange spacesuit. He carried a metal container.

"Hicks, Garcia, head back to the Athena. Double time," Hunsicker ordered.

The Beagle 4S's swung around and sped away.

Redford raced to the back of the shuttle and opened the airlock. Vitomir used his suit jets to navigate to the opening. As soon as the airlock closed, Hunsicker punched it. The proximity alarm blared again, and the HUD lit up. An orange glow blazed behind them from where the Command Center had been. There were several large clangs from small objects striking the shuttle. Hunsicker was on the maneuvering thrusters, trying to stay on course. More debris from the station rained on the shuttle as it sped away, but nothing punched through. The pieces hitting the shuttle became less frequent, but Hunsicker altered course to be on the safe side.

The shuttle arrived at the Athena within minutes of Hicks and Garcia. Hunsicker docked the shuttle and ordered Kaylan to move the Athena away from the station. They would need to do a damage assessment of the shuttle later on.

Brenda met them as they came onboard and took Vitomir to the med bay. The cosmonaut hadn't said a word since coming on the shuttle. He just stared off into space.

"I'm not sure bringing him on board was such a good idea," Redford said.

"He's in shock," Hunsicker replied.

Redford grunted.

Having all he could stand of the astrophysicist, Hunsicker quickened his step to the bridge before he did something he would regret.

Kaylan and Zack were on the bridge. Kaylan had the holodisplay up, and she was shaking her head.

"That bad?" Hunsicker asked.

Kaylan nodded. "The explosion altered the asteroid's orbit. If my projections are correct, it might make it to Earth's orbit."

"Are you saying the explosion is going to send that asteroid into Earth?" Zack asked.

"I said 'might,'" Kaylan said.

"We need to alert NASA. Given the amount of lead time,

they should be able to run their own numbers and come up with a way to deal with it," Hunsicker said.

"Shouldn't we stick around in case they need us to assist?" Kaylan asked.

Hunsicker shook his head. "No, this ship isn't equipped to deal with that." He noted Zack's unconvinced expression. "They have rooms full of people who can work this problem with the attention it deserves. Kaylan is right. This is just preliminary. Just because an asteroid might pass through Earth's orbit doesn't mean our planet will be anywhere near there when it does. Also, we've guided asteroids into Earth's orbit before, so they're prepared for this."

Zack nodded.

"Engaging the station's fail-safes allowed us to escape. Good work, you two," Hunsicker said, and meant it.

If the day's events were any indication of what was to come, then they needed to be able to work together. He also needed to keep a closer eye on a certain astrophysicist who might be the problem Edward Johnson had warned him about.

Chapter Sixteen

A few hours after the destruction of Titus Station, Kaylan was still on the bridge. Zack had stayed and was quietly working at the comms station. They hadn't said anything since the others returned. Sometimes she heard him talking to himself as he worked on some type of problem.

She was calculating the best course for Pluto, and each time it came to the return trip back to Earth, the computer warned of a lack of resources. In addition to retrieving the LSS, or the creepy robotic spider as Zack liked to call it, they had been supposed to resupply at Titus both on the outbound and inbound treks through the solar system. With Titus Station gone, they needed to find another option.

Commander Hunsicker walked onto the bridge and joined her at the planning table.

"What have you got?" Hunsicker asked.

Kaylan looked at him and noted the bags under his eyes.

"NASA is working to get the families informed of the deceased astronauts. They requested a video message from Vitomir and Nikolai to send to their families. News of Titus Station's destruction will be reported soon."

Hunsicker nodded. "Right now they're both sleeping in med bay. Brenda will let us know when they're able to send the message."

"We lost our supply channel. We can make it to Pluto, but we don't have enough supplies to make it back to Earth," Kaylan said.

Zack turned around and got out of his chair. "When you say supplies, I think of things like food, water, and oxygen. Is that what you're talking about?"

"Partially, but in this case I mean fuel. Athena runs with a fusion reactor core. It's highly efficient and powerful, but eventually we'll need to replenish the fuel supplies," Kaylan said.

Hunsicker rubbed his chin, and his eyes narrowed in thought.

"Where can we get what we need?" Zack asked.

"We could collect what we need as we go, but that could take a while," Hunsicker said. "How far back does the return trip get us?"

"Depends on how long we stay on Pluto. Most of my projections show us intercepting the orbit of Neptune," Kaylan said.

"That's no good," Hunsicker said.

Zack frowned. "I'm not following. What's so bad about Neptune?"

"The upper atmosphere of the gas giant has what we need to fuel the reactor, but studies of Neptune show that it has super hurricane-force winds. It would tear us apart if we tried to go there," Kaylan said.

"Well, Jupiter is the biggest gas giant in the solar system. Can't we just swing by there on the way out to Pluto?" Zack asked.

Kaylan frowned. "No, not Jupiter, but ..." She stopped speaking and started entering commands into the holo-interface. The display cycled through images with possible Athena routes.

Zack leaned over to Hunsicker. "Why not Jupiter?"

"Because it would take us in the opposite direction, and because its gravitational pull is too great," Hunsicker said.

Kaylan's eyes widened, and she smiled. "Uranus is perfect for our needs."

Zack burst out laughing. He tried to apologize, but small laughs kept getting out. Hunsicker rolled his eyes.

"You really are a child sometimes," Kaylan said.

"I'm sorry. I really am," Zack said, catching his breath. "What makes the most poorly named planet in our solar system the ultimate place for a pit stop?"

"Because its gravitational pull is the least of all the gas giants. It's actually less than the gravitational field of the Earth. That alone would make it a good choice. What makes it even better is that there is a surveyor probe already there, collecting the resources we need. We just need to go there and get it," Kaylan said, smiling.

Hunsicker nodded and brought up the probe's information. "The Ulysses probe, put out there by SpaceX, was sent to help them calculate how much heavy hydrogen, helium 3, and other elements there were to see if it was worth setting up a mining operation there in the next fifty years or so."

"I'll run some numbers and send our proposal to NASA," Kaylan said.

"Why wouldn't we just go? Do we have to clear everything with them?" Zack asked.

"It's standard protocol. They also need to get us clearance to utilize Ulysses to refuel the ship," Kaylan said.

Zack pressed his lips together and eyed her and Hunsicker, considering. "Standard protocol. For a public organization, NASA has a lot of subroutines running in the ship's systems."

Kaylan exchanged a glance with Hunsicker. "Well, they're needed. They could remote-control the ship if they needed to."

"That's the part that scares me. I recognize the need for NASA to be in the loop in case of a catastrophe, but at the same time it leaves us extremely exposed. Given the sensitivity of our mission to Pluto, what's to stop any one country from taking over this ship remotely? They could engineer a disaster and tell the world anything they wanted. Regardless, we would all be dead."

"Are you really this paranoid?" Kaylan asked.

"Are you really this naive?" Zack replied.

Kaylan felt heat rise in her face.

"Zack raises a good point," Hunsicker said. "I don't like it. Not one bit. The idealist in me wants to believe the scenario Zack just described could never happen, but the realist ..."

"I'm sorry, but I don't agree," Kaylan said. "We can't go through this mission constantly looking over our shoulder and wondering if the people back on Earth, who are supposed to be there supporting us in this mission, will turn around and stab us in the back."

"I don't intend to give them the chance, or anyone else for that matter," Zack said.

"What have you done?" Kaylan asked.

"I took away their ability to seize control of the Athena," Zack said.

Kaylan's mouth dropped, and she glanced at Hunsicker. He was just as shocked as she was. "Are you insane? How … You … Whatever you've done, change it back to what it should be."

Zack drew himself up stubbornly.

"Commander, he needs to change back whatever he's done. People on this ship's lives are at stake," Kaylan said.

"It's for the people on this ship that I made those changes," Zack replied.

Hunsicker held up his hands and turned toward Zack. "I'd like to better understand what you've done."

Zack nodded. "First off, I didn't change any of the processes that are running on the Athena. Safety protocols, sensors, life-support are all functioning the way they should be," Zack said, and glared at Kaylan. "I'm not an idiot. I wouldn't do this on a whim."

"Zack, focus," Hunsicker said.

"I isolated the accounts that NASA would use to remote-pilot the ship and control the systems. I then revoked their privileges. They can still access the systems, but they can't control them without permission. In the event of catastrophic failure and we all die, then the privileges would be restored," Zack said.

"Whose permission?" Hunsicker asked.

"Well, yours, Kaylan's, mine. And in the event that we aren't here, a confirmation prompt will present to whoever *is* here. I didn't do this without giving it a lot of thought. I just want us as a crew to be in control of our own destiny," Zack said.

Hunsicker gave a small nod while he considered what Zack had said.

Kaylan felt a flush creep across her cheeks. "I'm sorry."

The anger melted away from Zack's gaze instantly. "It's okay."

"I understand why you did what you did. I even agree with it to a certain extent. Next time, give me a heads-up," Hunsicker said.

Zack nodded.

"Now that we've worked that out, have you made any progress with the alien message?" Hunsicker asked.

"I've confirmed the conclusions that were drawn before. Most of them were fine. I keep finding a coded reference within data sets that have been decoded and the same reference in things we haven't gotten to. I'm not sure what it is. To be honest, I need some help," Zack said.

"What do you need?" Hunsicker asked.

"Well," Kaylan said. "The rest of the crew, to be honest. We need to tell them what we know."

Zack nodded. "I need—and I can't believe I'm saying this—but I need Jonah's help. I suspect that some of the references I'm finding are for things in our solar system, but I can't be sure. Decoding this data is meant to be a collaborative effort."

"I agree we need to tell them. We're all in this together. They all know bits and pieces, but this will be the first time they learn about the rest," Hunsicker said. He activated the broadcast comms. "This is Hunsicker. I'd like everyone to come to the bridge please."

After a few minutes the crew of the Athena made their way

to the bridge, with the only exceptions being Vitomir and Nikolai, who were both resting in the med bay. Hicks and Garcia stood next to each other and were soon joined by Efren Burdock. Brenda and Emma joined them at the table. Jonah Redford came in last. He was rubbing the back of his neck and pressed his lips together when he caught sight of them.

"Thank you for coming," Hunsicker said. "There are a couple of things I need to go over with you all. First, we're heading to Uranus to leverage the proof-of-concept surveyor probe, Ulysses, to refuel the ship. Efren, we'll be looking to you to confirm Kaylan's fuel estimates. The reason we're not heading directly to Pluto is because we won't have the fuel to make it back after we're done there."

Jonah raised his hand. "How will we know when we're done there? There is no precedent set for what we're doing."

"We'll be done either when we've learned all we can about the alien structure or we run out of resources for the return trip. Resources like food," Hunsicker answered. "Any other questions?"

Emma raised her hand. "I'm getting excellent results in the hydroponics lab. I'm sure I could increase the yield to extend our food supplies."

Efren groaned. He hated raw vegetables.

Emma smiled sweetly at him. She had taken it upon herself to get Efren to eat more vegetables. "Don't worry. You can just add a few protein cubes, and you'll be good to go," Emma said.

"Could you perhaps make a few bottles of wine in that lab?" Efren asked.

"Sorry, only the essentials," Emma replied.

"I brought a bottle of scotch and some wine that I was going to bring to dinner tonight," Hunsicker said, and Efren rubbed his hands together. "Brenda, I meant to ask, how are Vitomir and Nikolai?"

"Vitomir is asleep. I gave him a mild sedative to help him rest. Nikolai hasn't woken up, but he has a concussion, so rest is the best medicine. I've hooked up an IV so he'll be hydrated. I'm afraid we'll have to wait and see. Blows to the head can be a tricky thing," Brenda said.

Hunsicker nodded. "Now for the second reason I've asked you to come. There's something you all need to know. Some of you know bits and pieces about the history related to the alien structure, but not all of you. It's time we're all on the same page. To be honest, what Kaylan, Zack, and I are about to tell you may seem quite shocking. Zack, why don't you start? By and large you're one of the main reasons we're all here."

Zack glanced guiltily at the others. "As most of you know, about a month ago I hacked into a data storage facility that was owned and operated by a subsidiary of Dux Corporation. It was there that I found older data files and the images of the alien structure. I released them to the world. Along with the images, I found raw data caches that I began decoding. I didn't know what I had stumbled onto at first. When I found the images of the alien structure from 2015, I tried to run." Zack stopped and nodded to Hicks. "Needless to say, I didn't get far. One of the reasons I'm here is to decode the remainder of the alien data, but the more I work with it the more I realize I can't do it alone. I can get to a point where I need someone who is much more familiar with a specific subject than I am. I'm able to decipher the patterns, but for some of these references I'm at a loss because I didn't study astrophysics in college, or xenobiology and nuclear physics, for example. That's why I believe this data is meant to be worked on in a collaborative way."

The crew exchanged glances, appearing unsure of what they needed to do.

"Zack, why don't you show us an actual example of what you mean?" Hunsicker suggested.

Zack nodded. He entered a few commands, and the holodisplay changed to show a grouping of windows with streaming characters. The data stream stopped and a group of numbers was highlighted across a few windows. "Here is one I see reference to a lot. On the simplest level, they appear to be coordinates, but I couldn't say where. For something like this, there isn't anything left for me to decode. I either understand the meaning or I don't. I've seen other references to it, particularly with this mathematical formula. Does this look familiar to you, Jonah?"

Redford scanned the formula. "It's the basis for laser communications we use in space."

Zack nodded. "In many ways, working with the alien data is like translating an unknown language, except it's through mathematics. This begs a number of questions—from the basic 'what does this mean?' to the more complex 'why is this data here in this particular place?' What are they trying to tell us?" Zack said.

Redford pressed his lips together thoughtfully and glanced at Hunsicker. "I think he's on to something."

Hunsicker nodded. "I want you all to work with Zack on this. Perhaps the information we learn will help us with what we'll face on Pluto."

"Where did all this data come from?" Efren asked.

Kaylan cleared her throat. "I'll take this one. During the 1980s my grandfather, Bruce Matherson, was a military contractor with Dux Corporation. He was directly involved in an obscure program called Project Stargate. It was run out of Maryland for the U.S. Army. The purpose of the project was to investigate the potential for psychic phenomena in military and domestic applications. They tested people to see if they were receptive to being trained in remote viewing."

A few chuckles trickled through the crew, and Kaylan smiled. "Sounds crazy. The project was canceled after several reviews by the CIA revealed that it wasn't yielding any results. It was then swept aside and forgotten. Two years prior to the cancellation of the program, an event occurred that affected the viewers who were on duty at the time. Viewers are the men and women who participated in the program. They were constantly monitored during a series of sessions. On the night of the event, my grandfather's team recorded everything—from what the viewers said to body movements and viewer testimonies afterwards. The event was never reported to the army. My grandfather collected the data and had a team analyzing it in secret for the past sixty years. As his team made discoveries, they would farm out the research to different universities throughout the world. This is one of the main reasons Dux Corporation has such global influence."

"You can't seriously believe any of this," Redford said.

"Not at first. The idea of a true psychic phenomenon was the fuel and lifeblood of conmen. As a scientist, if I can see it and study it, then it's real. The alien structure on Pluto is real. We've confirmed it. So if that's real, why wouldn't the event that occurred in the '80s not also be real?" Kaylan said.

"The two could be unrelated," Redford replied.

"Perhaps. Hold that thought for a minute. Over the years,

Dux Corp was able to make sense of some of the data collected. Like Zack said, it's not meant to be decoded by any one individual or even all at once. It's like the pieces of a puzzle, with one piece leading to the next to create a much larger picture. What they learned led to technological advancements that we're using today. The alien data didn't send a schematic on the atomic matrix of the components for the advanced ceramics that was used to build the Athena. According to Edward Johnson, they decoded references to different chemical compounds. People did the actual research and learned their properties. The knowledge gained was earned by us. The alien data was a nudge in the right direction. We would have gotten ourselves there eventually," Kaylan said.

"I'm sorry, but I'm having a hard time believing any of this," Redford said. "The concepts used for this ship, like the fusion reactor, were well-established ideas since the Manhattan Project, well before this event that occurred in the '80s."

Kaylan nodded. "That's right. They didn't give us anything we wouldn't already be doing. Like I said, it was a nudge in the right direction."

"We just don't understand why they did what they did," Hicks said. "I may be a bit biased, but if I accept everything about this whole thing at face value, then I need to ask what's in this for them. Why send us this information at all? Why nudge us in the first place?"

"That's one of the reasons we're going to Pluto. One of the clearest parts of the message was a warning," Commander Hunsicker said, and nodded toward Zack.

Zack brought up another window that showed a grainy video. A man in a gray jumpsuit sat in a chair. He had electrodes connected to his head and chest. Old-style tube monitors were behind him.

"... *So much space. The void is empty. The cold burns. The nine is the key ... they must get to the nine ...*"

A taller man in a shirt and tie leaned over the man who reclined in the chair. Someone off camera asked what they were saying. The man turned toward the camera, and Kaylan sucked in a breath. It was her grandfather.

"*They are coming. They are coming. Must go,*" the voice of Bruce Matherson said.

Zack stopped the video.

Redford sighed. "It makes for interesting conversation, to be sure. If these viewers were so instrumental in this work, where are they now? Why aren't they used anymore? Why were people kept in the dark about all this?"

"It was believed by those in charge of Dux Corp that this was beyond any one nation on Earth. No single nation could have gotten us where we are today. Space exploration is a joint effort among scientists around the globe," Kaylan said.

Redford looked at Hunsicker. "Too bad we don't have any of these viewers on the ship. They might have saved us the trip."

Jerk, Kaylan thought, and resisted the urge to kick Redford in the balls. He might be a brilliant scientist, but he was obnoxious. His comment reaffirmed her decision to keep the vision she'd had of Pluto to herself. She still didn't know what to make of it.

Hunsicker ignored Redford and nodded to Zack.

"I've organized the material in groups that I think are appropriate. You all have access to it, but I'll be coming around to take you through it," Zack said.

"What about the probe we sent to Pluto?" Redford said. "Do you still think it's a challenge of some kind?"

"Yes," Zack said.

"Does any of the data you've reviewed so far mention the planetary body known as Pluto and an alien structure there?" Redford asked.

Zack shook his head. "Not yet. But judging from how the message was handled and the fact that they built a structure so far from Earth, I believe we're meant to go there in person and find out," Zack said.

"I agree with him," Kaylan said. "Before you ask, I'll tell you why. In the simplest of terms, if I were testing the waters to see if I wanted to be friends with a new alien species but they just weren't developed enough technologically, I might put a few things in their path to help move them along. If they were smart enough to figure it out and get there, then they'd have proven themselves worthy."

Redford grunted. "A club that you have to earn your way in. I can see your point, but on the flip side the two events could be entirely unrelated."

"Who was coming?" Hicks asked suddenly. "Is there any other mention of it?"

"There is only one reference in the beginning. It says, beware of the Xiiginn. That's it, and there is no other reference to who or what the Xiiginn actually are. It's almost like it was added after the fact," Zack said.

Hicks nodded and looked back at the holodisplay.

"There is also another thing," Hunsicker said. "There will be an away team that will go down to Pluto's surface. Zack, you need to be on that first team."

Zack's eyes darted to Kaylan. "Um, are you sure about that? I'm not even a real astronaut. What help could I be down there? Not to mention that I have this aversion to dying."

"We'll start training you to do EVAs. You can start by helping with the shuttle repairs. You'll observe, but it will give you the experience you'll need. The reason is that I will need someone on the ground with me who understands the alien system down there," Hunsicker said.

"That's just it. I don't understand the alien system. That's why I'm asking for help from the others," Zack replied.

"You understand it far better than any of us," Hunsicker said.

Katie Garcia gave Zack a wide smile and winked at him. "Don't worry, Romeo, I'll take good care of you."

Zack's shoulders slumped for a moment, and then he straightened himself. "Bring it," he said.

Katie laughed and gave Zack a pat on the shoulder. "That's the spirit. We can start physical conditioning tomorrow."

The smile drained from Zack's face, and he knew he was going to regret that last comment.

"We all know what's coming. We'll head to Uranus first, and from there we go to Pluto," Hunsicker said.

"ETA to Uranus is three weeks," Kaylan said.

Hunsicker dismissed them, and everyone filed out to get some rest.

Chapter Seventeen

When Zack was a kid, he used to hand his father tools while he worked on an old 1968 Dodge Charger. The massive black hood opened to a chrome-covered engine that dripped raw power, befitting the classic automobile. He used to imagine that there were teeth on the inside and if he weren't careful, he would get fed to the beast. They'd needed a special historical license to drive a car that was eighty years old and ran on gasoline. Zack did like the sleek black look and the curvy body with the gleaming chrome lines. His father used to say the car was timeless. The new cars were way more efficient, but there was just something different about the beast. Mostly he liked his father's enthusiasm for the car.

"Zack, are you paying attention?" Hicks asked.

Zack blinked his eyes and tried to ignore the millions of miles of expansive space stretching out in all directions. Hicks had told him to think about something else to help calm himself down.

"Just focus on the ship," Hicks said.

Zack pulled his eyes back to the white outer hull of the Athena and gave the tether strap attached to his spacesuit a quick tug to reassure himself that he was still connected to the ship.

"Thanks," Zack said. "I was thinking about something else."

In the past few weeks he must have done about twenty EVAs with Hicks, Hunsicker, or Katie Garcia. All of them offered a different perspective on working in space. Since Commander Hunsicker had insisted he be on the ground crew when they finally got to Pluto, they put him on a training regimen that included spacewalks and physical conditioning. It was as much for their protection as his.

"What were you thinking about?" Hicks asked.

"Are you sure it won't distract you?"

"It won't," Hicks answered.

A small part of him envied the mountain of confidence that Hicks put forth in any endeavor of which he was a part. The only time Zack had seen him shaken up was after the destruction of Titus Station. Even that only consisted of a quiet withdrawal from the rest of them. Zack knew he would have freaked out if someone had died in front of him. Hicks bore it as a personal responsibility, but it seemed to Zack that Hicks had done everything he could, and perhaps more than he should have.

"I was thinking of my father and a car we used to work on together. Maybe on one of these trips you'll actually let me do something useful," Zack said.

Hicks grunted. "I thought you only worked with comput-

ers," he said, while screwing in a panel to the exterior of the shuttle. "Besides, this is useful. We're repairing the shuttle."

"No, you're repairing the shuttle. I'm just holding various
pieces and trying to control my fear of being sucked away into
space," Zack replied.

"Fine, next time I'll let you screw the panel in, and as long as
you're tethered to the ship, you're not going anywhere," Hicks
replied. He brought his feet under him and stood up on the
shuttle wing.

Zack executed a similar maneuver and stood next to Hicks.

"You've got to admit being out here is pretty cool,"
Hicks said.

"Isn't it time to head back?"

"What's the rush?"

"Not rushing. It's just that after this, Katie gets to make me
wish I'd never been born. The only exercise I got back home was
the occasional run. This whole strength-training routine she's
putting me through is a whole other ball game," Zack said.

The magnets in their boots helped them walk along the wing
as they headed back to where the shuttle was attached to the
Athena. The airlock wasn't far from there, but they would have to
pull themselves along.

"She's tough," Hicks said.

"And relentless. Sometimes I think I've offended her somehow, and she's making me pay for it."

Hicks laughed. "She just wants you to be in the best shape
for Pluto, and besides, most people don't mind spending time
with her," Hicks said.

"I could say the same thing about Kaylan, but you already

knew that," Zack said, and immediately wondered if he had said too much.

Hicks turned toward him. "Does me spending time with Kaylan bother you?"

"No. Yes. I don't know," Zack stammered and sighed. "I'm sorry. Kaylan and I knew each other in college. It's nothing."

Their suit-comms chimed. "Are you guys almost done with your little spacewalk? I've only got an hour to whip that rookie into shape," Katie said.

"Almost there," Hicks replied, and smiled at Zack mischievously. "Oh, and Katie, Zack said you've been taking it too easy on him and wants you to step it up a notch. He said your workouts are nothing compared to mine."

Zack looked at Hicks, his mouth opening but no words coming out.

"You're mine now, rookie." Katie laughed wolfishly.

"I hate you," Zack said to Hicks as they got in the airlock.

Hicks kept grinning but didn't say anything else. Zack got along well with Hicks. His easygoing manner stood in stark contrast to the dry personality of one Jonah Redford. Given the choice, he'd almost prefer these EVAs to being around Redford, but the work he was doing with the astrophysicist was important.

Kaylan and Hunsicker met them in the airlock already suited up.

"I didn't think anyone else was scheduled to go out," Hicks said.

"We're just doing some safety checks before our final approach to the planet," Hunsicker said.

"Mind if I tag along?" Hicks offered.

"Not a problem," Hunsicker said.

Kaylan smiled at him as she passed. The three of them closed the airlock and headed back outside. Zack shook his head and bit back a small bit of jealousy. He did have feelings for Kaylan, but as time went on they seemed less than what they had been before. He removed his spacesuit and stored it in his locker. He had seen the videos of the bulky spacesuits the astronauts used to wear and was thankful for the much more functional version they had now. The suit was a tad heavy in artificial gravity, but once they were in zero G it was fine, and suits weren't so bad now that he was getting stronger. He had always been wiry and lean, but the conditioning program Hicks and Katie had him doing made him feel a lot better, even if he begged for mercy during the actual training session.

"Ready to go, Romeo?" Katie asked from the doorway. She wore gray sweatpants and a white tank top that revealed a slice of her taut abs. Simple enough garment, but the way it clung to her shapely form was enough to distract him from his thoughts. She enjoyed his reaction at seeing her, and her full lips curved into a small smile. "The gym awaits, rookie," she said, then turned around and left.

Zack followed, and his eyes slid down to admire her backside. It was like he was flying on autopilot and couldn't help himself. Zack knew his strengths, and women weren't one of them. It seemed that Katie excelled at making him squirm.

The gym had padded mats, an exercise bike, and a rowing machine, along with cables to enhance bodyweight exercises. Weighted Swiss medicine balls were secured on a rack to the side. Those hellish balls made the muscles in his arms and shoulders scream for mercy.

Katie turned around, all the suggestive flirtation leaving her dark eyes. It was amazing how she did it—going from a dark-haired beauty into the queen of drill instructors in under a second. It was scary.

Thirty minutes later, sweat was pouring off of him and he lay gasping on the floor. Katie was only slightly winded, but she did have a sheen of sweat adorning her tanned skin, which Zack counted as a small victory. She threw a towel at him, and he started wiping himself off. When he stood up, he found that he didn't have to gasp for breath for as long as he used to.

"Time for some light sparring," Katie said.

Zack bit back a groan. "We're not going to be fighting anyone on Pluto."

Katie laughed. "It's good exercise, and everyone should know the basics."

They had started this about a week ago, and it was humbling how easy it was for Katie to take him down. At first he'd been afraid to hurt her, but she'd just laughed and told him not to hold back. He'd been an idiot. He couldn't have physically hurt her if he'd tried. Hicks later told him that Katie was top of her class.

They went over some basic takedowns and she let him practice the techniques on her. The moves were becoming much smoother than his clumsy display had been on the first day.

"Head still stuck in the past?" Katie asked.

The question took him off guard, and in a second he was staring up at her from the matted floor.

"What do you mean?" Zack asked, rising to his feet.

He went to grab her, but she countered and he was on the floor again. "This whole Kaylan thing you've got going on," Katie said.

"Well, we could talk about you, but you might have to take a break from all the nicknames you give me," Zack said.

Katie helped him up and held him in her gaze. "You sure you want to open up that can of worms?" she asked, pursing her lips temptingly.

Zack had the strangest feeling that he had unwittingly wandered onto thin ice, and he was seconds from falling through. He brought his hands up, but Katie weaved through his pitiful defense and he was on the floor again. This time Katie came down to the mat on top of him, her face inches from his. She leaned in and kissed him, slowly at first, then with more intensity. Zack's mind was reeling as he was swept into desire. *We're kissing! Oh my god, I'm kissing Katie,* came the thought somewhere in his muddled mind.

Katie pulled back, but remained a finger's width from his face. He felt her full breasts pressed firmly up against him. "You've been so concerned about the past that you never stopped to consider what was right in front of you."

Zack's mouth hung open, the breath rushing in. "Katie … I … you—"

She silenced him with another kiss, in which he gleefully lost himself, feeling like he was flying so fast that his thoughts didn't have a prayer of catching up. He rested his hands on her hips and surrendered.

The ship's communicator chimed from the door.

"All hands, this is Hunsicker. We're on approach to Uranus. Ready your stations. ETA is one hour."

Katie pulled away from him and helped him to his feet.

"I had no idea, you're … well, it's you. And you're so … You could have anyone you want. I didn't even think—" Zack said.

"I know you didn't. This isn't over. We'll finish this later," Katie said, and left. Zack watched her walk away.

Zack left the gym, heading to his quarters. Katie had gone a different way. The questions kept tumbling through his mind, going from Kaylan and their past to Katie and *that* kiss. It had been amazing, and it stayed in the forefront of his mind while he changed clothes. *God, that was one hell of a kiss.* He would have liked to have taken a cold shower, but that would have to wait. He needed to meet Jonah in the observatory.

As Zack climbed up to the top deck where the observatory was, his mind kept going back to the gym and the feel of Katie's lips pressed against his. It had been a long time since he had kissed anyone, and he was pretty sure none of those kisses had been as good as that one. His lone crusade against corrupt corporations and those who ostensibly led them had taken up much of his time. He had grown somewhat bitter in his self-imposed isolation. Life on the Athena had reawakened what had been missing in his life. The people he was traveling with were all good people, and he liked being around them.

Zack entered the observatory, and Jonah was at his console. He had on a thin blue sweater and sported about a week's worth of beard growth on his angular face. Redford preferred to stand while working, which had taken Zack some getting used to. When Zack had first met Jonah in Houston, he had labeled him as the human version of a hawk. His thin, shoulder-length hair and pronounced nose gave his face an almost aerodynamic shape. He'd commented as much to Kaylan, who'd had to stifle a laugh and urged him never to say that to Jonah's face.

Zack had to admit that the sessions with the exceedingly dry personality of Jonah Redford had been productive, but Zack couldn't imagine spending any sort of time with the man that didn't involve work. At least Jonah treated him as a peer, which put him slightly above some others of the crew who, in his opinion, Jonah thought of as merely necessary.

"Excellent," Jonah said, waving Zack over as he walked in. "I've had some thoughts on those coordinates you decoded from the alien message. Here, take a look at this formula and tell me what you think."

Redford minimized some of the windows in the holodisplay and brought another one to prominence. Zack narrowed his gaze and worked through the calculations in Redford's new formula.

"Are you using the sun as a point of origin?" Zack asked.

Redford's lips curved slightly in the manner of a teacher pleased with his student. "Very good. That's exactly what I did. When we tried using Earth as the point of origin, it didn't work. I tried all the other planets in the solar system, but none balances the equations as well as using the sun. And it makes sense if you think about it. The single most defining characteristic in our solar system is the sun. Earth just happens to be lucky enough in its creation and position for life to flourish."

Zack entered a few commands from his interface and traced where the new calculations took them. "It's well beyond the solar system."

"The solar system is actually quite large, much larger than people think. A significant portion goes beyond Pluto's orbit, like the Kuiper belt, but these coordinates put whatever they referenced firmly within the area known as the Oort cloud," Jonah said.

"What's the Oort cloud? How far away are we talking here?" Zack asked.

"It's a theoretical sphere that surrounds our solar system. It's believed that the cloud extends almost halfway to the nearest star. Whatever these coordinates point to could be anything, but there are so many coordinates that they must have been put there by design," Jonah said.

Zack nodded, considering. "If whatever is there is mechanical, simply pointing the Athena's telescope at it wouldn't be able to pick anything up, would it?"

"That's right, and I doubt either of the Voyager spacecraft happened to fly by one. Regardless, let's say it's some type of machine related to the structure on Pluto. In that case, chances are we wouldn't be able to see anything. I tried anyway, and it will take a while to render the images if anything was detected," Jonah said.

"What if we sent a signal from the ship to some of these coordinates to see if we get a reply?" Zack asked.

Redford's eyes widened. "That's a great idea."

Zack frowned. "There's just one problem. If we send a signal and actually get a reply, the reply will be returned to where we were."

"Not if we tell it where we will be," Jonah said.

"I can put the data in a format that was used in the original message, but … I'm not sure if whatever is there will even reply. Look, they're spread around the entire solar system like a large net," Zack said.

"Still worth a try, I think," Jonah said.

"There's still the issue of encoding. We might be able to put the coordinates to reach us in there, but there's no guarantee the machine will even allow us to communicate. I keep thinking about the surveyor probe we lost contact with on Pluto's surface.

I still say it was challenged, which means we need a password or something that says we can communicate with it," Zack said. He took a closer look at all the pinpoints residing in the Oort cloud.

"What is it?" Jonah asked.

"If I forget the fact that this is outside of our solar system and assume it's around a planet, then I would say this is some type of satellite network. They seem to be within a certain proximity to each other. This can't be by accident," Zack said.

Jonah narrowed his eyes thoughtfully. "No, none of this is by accident."

"I have an idea," Zack said. "The alien data is broken up into sections. Each section has some type of header. I think if we input that header into our own crafted message and send it out there, we would increase the chance of a reply."

Jonah nodded. "Brilliant, Zack. We have a way forward. Now let's see about putting that message together."

Zack arched his brows.

"What?" Jonah asked.

"I've just never heard you compliment anyone before," Zack said.

Redford rolled his eyes.

Chapter Eighteen

Kaylan gazed out the window from the pilot's seat. The seventh planet in the solar system dominated her view. She knew the facts—how Uranus was sixty-three times larger than Earth—but words in a textbook and seeing the reality of it were two different things. The sight of the turquoise-colored gas giant was enough to silence all who were on the bridge. The crew of the Athena was the first to ever see the planet in person. The moons looked like pinpricks orbiting the massive celestial body. The sunlight reflecting off the planet cast a soft bluish glow that shined through the windows of the ship.

"It's amazing," Zack said, coming over from the comms station to stand behind them.

"It's quite a sight," Hunsicker said from the chair next to her.

"I didn't know there were rings around Uranus," Zack said.

Kaylan glanced back to see if Zack was making a joke. He wasn't.

"They're not as prominent as Saturn's rings, but they're still there. I wish we could spend time here and study this place," Kaylan said.

"I feel like a little kid asking this, but why is it that blue-green color? And why did the rings form over the top of the planet instead of along the equator like with Saturn?" Zack asked.

"First, the atmosphere is mostly made up of hydrogen, but it's the methane that gives it that color. Second, the rings do run along the equator of the planet. It's the axis that's different. We're actually looking at the south pole, which constantly faces the sun. For as big as the planet is, it has less of a gravitational pull than Earth. You might actually be able to dunk a basketball here," Kaylan said.

Zack smiled. "Probably not. I haven't played in a long time."

The others joined them on the bridge, except Redford, who was working from the observatory, and Nikolai Vitowski. Nikolai was still resting in the med bay. He had awakened from his head injury, but Brenda had prescribed bed rest since he was still weak. Nikolai could barely remember the explosion on Titus Station. Vitomir had stayed near Nikolai's bedside almost the whole time since they'd come on board and only left to send a video home to his daughter.

The others crowded the windows around the bridge, taking in the beautiful sight. Hicks leaned near Kaylan, looking out of the window, eyes wide. She could smell traces of the soap he used in the shower. She noticed Zack watching her and saw a slight resignation in his eyes. A small pang seized her chest for what might have been all those years ago. She wasn't sure if the idea of her and Zack was better left in the past or was something to be opened up in the present. In many ways he was the old Zack she remembered from college, with quick intelligence and charming on occasion, but shy at times. But she was no longer that girl anymore. There had been other men in her life, but mostly she buried herself in her work. Thoughts of a husband or starting a family didn't appeal to her, at least not anytime soon. There were times she was with Zack that got her thinking about what might have been, but she just didn't know. Hicks, on the other hand, knew what he wanted, but he was ever the gentleman. She found it charming that he was more traditional in his interest in her. Sometimes that southern charm did have a way of making her smile. Most of the time she brushed those thoughts aside so she could focus on the mission, but after the catastrophe at Titus Station she wondered if burying herself in her work was how she should live her life.

Katie leaned toward the window next to Hunsicker's seat. Katie was blessed with womanly curves in all the right places and was the type of person she would have expected one Dale Hicks to be attracted to. Kaylan was more on the slender side—not to say she was a rail, not even close—but she noticed that Katie garnered the attention of more than one man when she walked in the room.

Katie noticed her gaze and nodded in greeting, then moved back to join the others at the table. Kaylan ran a final check on their approach to the planet. They had been steadily slowing down and would insert into orbit near the south pole.

Kaylan rose from the pilot's seat and joined the others. "On schedule for orbit insertion around the planet."

Commander Hunsicker nodded. "Take in the sight while you can. We're only going to be here for a short while. I'd like to go over the plan for retrieving the payload from the Ulysses probe."

Kaylan took control of the holodisplay and showed a mockup of the probe flying in the upper atmosphere of the planet. "The Ulysses probe has been steadily increasing its altitude to reach the upper atmosphere. When we arrive, it will be as high as it can go. I've set Athena's orbit to follow the Ulysses's position, but we will be well above the planet's atmosphere."

Hicks stepped up and started the next part of the presentation. "Katie and I will fly in, and using the salvage arms, we'll retrieve the payload from the probe."

"Why does it take both of you?" Zack asked.

"Well, for backup for one thing. One of us—me—will be observing the approach, while Katie will get close enough to actually retrieve the payload. The container is about two meters in length. Once we have it, we'll come back to the ship," Hicks said.

Efren Burdock rubbed the stubble on his chin. "The helium-3 we need for fuel will be in the payload. This is truly amazing."

Commander Hunsicker nodded. "NASA told me there are plans to put a robotic mining facility here within the next hundred years. Uranus will become a major fueling station."

"What happens if something goes wrong with the retrieval?" Zack asked.

"Like what?" Hicks replied.

Zack shrugged, looking worried. "I don't know. Anything. Commander, didn't you say that the one thing we can count on being in space is that something will eventually go wrong?"

"They won't be alone," Kaylan said. "I'll be piloting the shuttle, monitoring both Katie and Dale. So if something does happen, help will be close by."

Zack's eyes widened, and he clamped his jaw shut.

"Don't worry, rookie. We'll be just fine," Katie said.

A small smile lit up Zack's face, much to Kaylan's surprise, but she could tell he was still worried.

Hunsicker cleared his throat. "Everything we do up here involves a certain degree of risk. It's why you all were picked for this mission. You are all the best at what you do. We work together as a team, and we'll all pull through this. The Ulysses probe was designed to have its payload retrieved. Granted, it was by a different type of ship that is not due to arrive for another year, but it's not beyond the capabilities of the Beagle spacecraft."

Zack took a deep breath and nodded. "Can I go on the shuttle?"

Kaylan glanced at Hunsicker, who looked at Hicks. "What do you think?"

"Zack and I have been on daily EVAs, and he's come a long way. He should be fine," Hicks said.

"Thank you," Zack said. "I won't be any trouble."

Kaylan nodded and smiled at Zack.

A few hours later the Athena inserted into Uranus's orbit, perfectly aligned with the Ulysses trajectory. Kaylan sat in the shuttle pilot's seat with Brenda Goodwin next to her. Kaylan had pointed out to Hunsicker that it wasn't right that the commander of the mission got to have all the fun. It was her turn. He had grudgingly agreed and told her it had nothing to do with her abilities as a pilot or as his second in command. He just had to be reminded or kicked if he did it again. Kaylan knew that, as commander, it was Hunsicker's job to look after the crew, but as time had gone on she'd noticed that both she and Zack had been more or less restricted to the ship. In Zack's case, she could understand. He didn't have years of astronaut training to fall back on and was getting the ultimate on-the-job training. At some point she and Hunsicker would need to sit down and talk about this.

The shuttle detached from the Athena, and Kaylan could hardly keep from smiling. Brenda, who was ten years Kaylan's senior, didn't look nearly as excited as Kaylan was. The two Beagles detached from the Athena and darted ahead. Kaylan had trained in the simulator for the Beagle spacecraft, but she just didn't have the experience that Katie and Dale had. Brenda was the Athena's medical officer, so she was there if someone needed medical attention. Kaylan hoped they didn't run into any problems.

Zack sat behind them, and though he put on a brave face, Kaylan could tell he also had a healthy amount of fear. He kept checking to see if his helmet was securely on.

"All set," Zack said, giving her the thumbs-up.

The Beagles were single-passenger spacecraft. They had small wings that allowed them to have some lateral control for upper atmosphere objectives, but they were designed to operate primarily in space. Their white hulls had a thick line of yellow that ran along the length of the craft. Kaylan maintained a visual of the two ships, and the HUD told her the actual distance from them, along with the status of the pilots inside.

Athena's shuttle could land on low-gravity moons and dwarf planets, like Pluto, and still be able to escape their gravitational pull. Landing on Uranus wasn't an option.

"So what they're heading to is only part of the Ulysses probe?" Zack asked.

"That's right. The actual craft that collects what we need operates in the atmosphere. The project that manages it is actually quite supportive of our objective to make use of it," Kaylan said.

"Not that I would want to look a gift horse in the mouth, but why are they so helpful?"

"This proof of concept was funded by venture capitalists, as well as state agencies. When we retrieve the container and validate that we can use the contents, it will open the doors for more funding. Hunsicker was right—there will be a mining operation here, but instead of in the next hundred years it could be a lot sooner based on our success," Kaylan said.

Zack glanced at the HUD. "I can barely see them. If it weren't for the HUD, I wouldn't be able to see them at all."

Kaylan had the HUD zoom in, and the two spacecraft became easier to see. "Hicks, Garcia, your approach looks good from here."

"Acknowledged," Hicks said.

"We'll be coming really close to the atmosphere," Katie said.

"Should we abort?" Kaylan asked. She knew Hunsicker was monitoring from the Athena, but she was on point for this mission.

"Negative," Katie said. "I can reach it."

Kaylan acknowledged. If they didn't get the payload, they wouldn't have enough fuel to return to Earth from Pluto. The HUD showed the Beagle marked Garcia moving ahead, gaining on the probe.

"How many containers does she need to get?" Zack asked.

"There are two available, but we really only need one of them. The containers are locked together, and NASA wants us to retrieve both to be on the safe side," Kaylan replied.

The Beagle was an elongated tube that came to a point, with its primary engines in the rear and maneuvering thrusters at different points on the nose and under the belly, which made it quite agile. Katie swung the Beagle so the nose of the spacecraft was perpendicular to the Ulysses probe. Three robotic arms extended from underneath the pilot's seat. The arms could extend three and a half meters each. The probe was designed to dock with another ship so the payload could be retrieved, but the design wasn't compatible with the Athena or the shuttle. The Beagle pilot would need to open up the probe and retrieve the contents manually.

"Sending the signal to open now," Katie said.

Kaylan and the others watched the HUD with rigid intensity. Two top panel doors opened on the black probe. The Beagle eased forward and one of its robotic arms latched on. The remaining two arms reached inside the probe.

"I'm feeling some vibrations," Katie reported. "I've got one of the holding clamps free. Moving to do the other two."

The only thing they could see was the arms reaching inside the probe. Kaylan sucked in her bottom lip for a second and moved the shuttle closer.

Brenda gave her a questioning look.

"I'm just moving in a little bit closer," Kaylan said.

"I can see the second clamp is removed," Hicks said. "Looks good from here, but what's the status of the vibrations?"

"They're increasing," Katie said.

Zack leaned forward. "This isn't right. There's not supposed to be any vibrations."

Kaylan nodded. "Hicks, is it possible for the Beagle to pull the probe into a higher orbit?"

"No, that would tear the arms off. If it was zero gravity, then I would say yes, but it's too risky here. She's almost got it," Hicks said.

They watched the HUD in silence.

"Got the last clamp. The little sucker was stuck," Katie said.

"Time check," Hicks said. "We've got ten minutes before the Ulysses probe auto inserts itself back into the atmosphere."

"Acknowledged," Katie replied. "I'm pulling the container out—"

Katie's transmission cut off and the probe jerked to the side, swinging the attached spacecraft into a spin. Maneuvering thrusters fired from the Beagle, attempting to correct the spin, but it wasn't enough. The container flew out away from the probe and spun away. One of the Beagle's arms remained attached to the probe, but it was spinning so fast that no one on the shuttle could see what was happening.

"Katie, can you release the arm?" Hicks asked.

"Negative, I think it's twisted," Katie answered, her breath coming in gasps over comms.

"She's getting pulled into the atmosphere," Zack said to Kaylan.

Kaylan thrust the shuttle forward to get a better look.

"Hicks, I can't stop the spin," Katie said, grunting with effort.

There were no inertia dampeners on the Beagles, so Katie was feeling the crushing effects of the spin. She could pass out at any moment.

"We need to do something!" Zack said. "Can't she eject or something?"

At the same time, Hicks began calling for Katie to eject. They looked on helplessly as the two spacecraft spun toward the atmosphere. A reddish glow started to envelope them. All the while they heard Katie Garcia's helpless cries as she tried to bring some semblance of control to her ship.

Hicks's Beagle drew in dangerously close, as if he waited for a chance to try and help.

"You can't help her, Major Hicks. You'll only die trying," Jonah Redford said over comms. "If she can't get herself out of this, then she's dead."

Zack grabbed the comms link on the shuttle. "Fuck you, Jonah. If you can't help, then just shut the hell up."

There was muffled arguing over the comms from the Athena; then Commander Hunsicker informed them that they wouldn't be hearing from Redford until he woke up. "Katie, can you hear me?" Hunsicker asked.

There was no reply.

"Sir, I have an idea," Kaylan said. "Katie, if you can hear me, the further you get into the atmosphere there is a chance that it will slow down the spin. You might be able to break away or stabilize enough to eject. Acknowledge."

Kaylan repeated herself, but there was no reply.

"She'll burn up before she has a chance to escape," Hicks said.

Kaylan's mouth clamped shut and she tried to think of something she could do. Zack stood up and started pacing.

"Hicks, retrieve the payload and head back to Athena," Hunsicker said. "Acknowledge, Major."

There was a long moment of silence. The spinning Beagle and Ulysses probe were almost completely engulfed.

"Sir, I can't leave her," Hicks's choked reply finally came through comms.

"You can't save her," Hunsicker said softly.

Zack looked at Kaylan. "How can he just tell him to leave her?"

"He's doing it so Hicks doesn't do something stupid. Like what we're about to do. Hold on," Kaylan said. She thrust the shuttle forward. "I'm going in there. Hicks, the commander is right. You can't help her, but maybe we can."

Commander Hunsicker and Hicks's replies came at the same time, but Kaylan ignored them. "Zack, I need you to strap yourself in by the airlock in the back."

Zack bolted toward the back of the shuttle and yelled that he was ready.

Come on, Katie, give me a sign, Kaylan thought.

A warning flashed on the HUD that they were coming dangerously close to entering Uranus's atmosphere and advised them to course correct. Pieces of debris were breaking off the two spinning craft. Kaylan focused all her attention on them, waiting.

"What are we waiting for?" Zack asked.

Kaylan barely blinked her eyes, afraid she would miss what she was looking for. Something broke away from the two ships barreling away from them. The cockpit of the Beagle shot forward, its emergency thrusters pushing it away from the planet.

"She's out, Zack. Get ready. Tether yourself to the airlock. You've only got one shot at this," Kaylan said.

Zack got out of the seat and hooked himself inside the airlock. "Okay, now what do you need me to do?"

"Open the airlock when I say. Then you'll use your suit-thrusters to get Katie," Kaylan said.

Zack gulped, silently urging himself not to screw this up.

"She's free of the cockpit and using her suit-thrusters to close the distance to us," Kaylan said.

"Will she have enough to reach us?" Zack asked. He placed his hand on the airlock lever, poised to open it.

"No, but you might be able to get close enough to send a tether strap to her. She's just run out of fuel. Zack, open the airlock," Kaylan said.

Zack clutched the tether gun to his side and opened the airlock. He used his suit-thrusters to leave the shuttle and homed in on Katie. Her spacesuit had dark splotches on the legs and arms. Zack held his breath, looking for some sign that she was unhurt.

Katie saw him and smiled. "Miss me, Casanova?"

Zack laughed, brought up the tether gun, and shot it toward her. "Who else is going to whip me into shape? Plus, we have unfinished business," Zack said, silently praying that the tether would reach Katie's outstretched hands. His own tether to the shuttle was almost maxed out.

The tether inched along, and Zack watched the counter on the gun close in on zero. Just as the tether reached the end, Katie was able to grab it and start pulling. Zack released the breath he'd been holding.

Katie attached the tether to her suit. "Okay, cowboy, reel me in."

Zack clicked the button and the tether started retracting. "Does this mean I'll have to do those extra pushups later?" Zack asked when Katie got closer.

Katie drew in and grabbed Zack's outstretched hand, and he pulled them both back toward the shuttle. Her ashen face was lined with worry and she drew a shaky breath.

"You're okay, I've got you," Zack said, and kept a firm hold on her until they were both inside the airlock to the shuttle.

The airlock light switched to green, and Kaylan saw Zack and Katie come through. He helped Katie to a seat and gave Kaylan the thumbs-up.

"Thanks for coming to get me. I tried to answer, but I was getting knocked around quite a bit," Katie said, and winced.

Kaylan nodded, and Brenda came between them so she could check on her.

"Athena," Kaylan said, "Zack and Katie are on board. We're heading back to you."

There were sounds of cheering coming through comms from the Athena. "Great news. Does she have any injuries?" Commander Hunsicker asked.

"Brenda is checking her now. She looks a little shaken up," Kaylan answered.

"Understood. Come on back and we'll piece together what the hell happened. Athena out," Hunsicker said.

A few minutes later, Brenda came back to the front of the shuttle and sat in the copilot's seat.

"She got banged up pretty good, but she's fine for now. I don't think she broke anything, but I want to do a more thorough check in the med bay. For now, though, it looks like she's in good hands," Brenda said.

Kaylan was nodding until the last part of what Brenda had said registered in her mind. She glanced back and saw Zack sitting by Katie's side. He was smiling, clearly relieved that she was safe. Kaylan's face registered her surprise at the way Katie was looking back at Zack. She had teased him in that manner of hers, as she did with most of the men on the ship, but Kaylan had thought it was just playful banter. Now she could see that for Zack it was something else entirely. Kaylan felt a slight squeeze at the back of her throat and turned to face forward.

"Are you all right?" Brenda asked.

"I'm fine. Just coming to grips with the moment," Kaylan said.

Brenda eyed her and glanced behind them. "Was there something between you and Zack?"

Kaylan shook her head but felt a slight blush spread across her cheeks. "I'm just glad we're all safe."

Kaylan glanced behind them again just to be sure of what she was seeing. A small part of her refused to believe it, and aside from the shock that Zack was clearly falling for someone else, she just wished he had actually followed through with the feelings he had for her. Those feelings had been there unspoken for so long that perhaps now they never would be spoken or acknowledged. Kaylan took a deep breath. Should she have said something first?

The shuttle closed in on the Athena, and Kaylan focused on safely docking the ship. Every so often, she felt a pang in her chest and wondered why she had never acknowledged her feelings for Zack. Were they there now because it might already be too late, or had they always been there?

Hicks returned to the Athena shortly after the shuttle docked. He'd been able to retrieve the payload from the Ulysses probe, which had launched away from the planet. Brenda took Katie to med bay. After removing their spacesuits, Kaylan and Zack headed toward the bridge.

Hunsicker was at the table with Emma and Efren. Before Kaylan could say anything, Hunsicker held up his hand. "You were there. I wasn't. You did what you had to do, and you were able to save a crew member's life. That's a win in my book. You both did great."

Kaylan stood a little taller. "Thank you."

Hunsicker nodded. "Efren, can you check on the container Hicks was able to retrieve?"

"Of course, Commander," Efren said, and left the bridge.

Zack glanced around the bridge. "What happened to Redford?"

Hunsicker's brows drew forward. "We had a difference of opinion."

Kaylan glanced at the swollen red knuckles on Hunsicker's right hand, and Zack followed her line of sight.

"I wish I could have been there to see his smug face," Zack said.

Hunsicker took a deep breath. "Sometimes I don't know what Jonah is thinking. It's like the compassion part of his brain doesn't work."

Hicks joined them on the bridge, followed by Brenda and Katie. Brenda insisted that Katie take a seat, which Zack brought over.

Just then Jonah Redford came on the bridge. A dark purple bruise had formed below the eye that his shaggy hair rested upon. He made a show of opening his mouth, testing that his jaw still worked. "No hard feelings, Commander. You're not the first person to end a conversation with me that way." Redford flashed a smile that didn't reach his eyes. Jonah turned in Katie's direction. "I'm glad you're all right, Miss Garcia. Please understand that my comments in no way had anything to do with you personally."

"I understand you perfectly, Dr. Redford," Katie replied frostily, and turned toward Kaylan. "I'm just glad that not everyone shares your viewpoint."

Kaylan nodded.

The door to the bridge opened, and Vitomir and Nikolai came in. The death of his wife was still evident in Vitomir's sunken red eyes.

"Apologies, Commander," Vitomir said. "It's time that Nikolai and I started to pull our own weight."

Nikolai Vitowski gave a wave around to everyone. "I would like to help in any way that I can. Vitomir told me that I'm alive thanks to all of you."

"Welcome," Hunsicker said. "Katie, can you tell us what happened?"

Katie gathered her thoughts and wrapped her arms in front of her. "I'm not sure exactly. Once I was latched onto the probe, I started feeling vibrations through the ship. I unlocked the clamps holding the probe's payload. Then ... everything went wrong. I was spinning out of control. I tried to release the probe but couldn't. I remember seeing the arm attached to the probe twist over the canopy. I couldn't eject. I knew the probe was pulling me into the atmosphere." Katie paused, taking a breath.

Astronauts train to be able to function in a spinning environment. Kaylan had seen the horrifying spin and knew their training was nothing compared to actually being stuck inside the ship, helpless. Katie Garcia was clearly shaken up by the retelling of the event, but the sheer fact that she was able to recount it was a testament to her strong will.

"I heard Kaylan through comms," Katie continued. "The probe broke free, taking the Beagle's arms with it. I ejected, and you know the rest."

"This is extraordinary," Vitomir said. "You are very lucky. Your craft was skipping along the atmosphere. Likely if you weren't able to eject, then you would have burned up."

"The Beagle was destroyed," Kaylan confirmed.

Hunsicker brought up the holodisplay. "This is the recording from the other Beagle."

He slowed the video down and they saw a dark object slam into the probe.

"It looks like the probe was struck by a large meteor that caused the crash," Kaylan said.

Katie watched the video and took in a shaky breath.

"Commander," Brenda said, "I must insist that Katie gets some rest, but she's stubborn, just like all you military types."

Hunsicker lips curved into a half smile and he looked at Katie. "Thank you. Please go get some rest."

Brenda and Katie left the bridge, and Kaylan noticed Zack's lingering stare as she left. Anger like a coiled viper sprang up from the pit of her stomach and was gone just as instantly. Kaylan reminded herself that she had no prior claim on Zack.

The door to the bridge opened, and Efren returned.

"Preliminary analysis of the contents is promising. NASA

will want to confirm our findings, but it looks like we have fuel enough for the mission," Efren said.

"Good work," Hunsicker said. "NASA will want reports from everyone of the day's events. By the time they respond, we'll be on our way."

"Commander," Vitomir said, "Nikolai and I would like clearance for a few EVAs. We need to check the Lenoy Salvage System so it will be ready to use once we get to Pluto."

"We did what repairs we could, but I'll put you into the rotation. If there isn't anything else, let's all get some rest," Hunsicker said.

No sooner had the words left Hunsicker's mouth than Zack bolted out of the bridge. Others began filing out, but Hicks came up next to her and leaned against the wall.

"I don't know about you, but I can't just rest after something like that. Would you like to join me in the rec room?" Hicks asked.

"Blowing off some steam sounds good," Kaylan said, and followed Hicks off the bridge. Navigation calculations could wait.

Chapter Nineteen

Zack raced down toward the med bay and stopped in the mess hall along the way. He wanted to check on Katie, but he didn't want to go there empty-handed or appear too eager. She had kissed him. He scanned the mess hall, looking for something to take. He just wanted to do something nice for her. He racked his brain, trying to remember if there was some type of food or a drink that she liked. He frowned at the containers and cabinets along the wall. It wasn't as if there was fresh fruit available. He walked over to the refrigerator and opened it, giving a cursory glance at the packs of yogurts. *Don't girls like yogurt?* he asked himself. This was much harder than he'd originally thought. He closed his eyes and tried to remember some type of detail or mannerism of hers that he might have picked up on. Like lightning, an idea flashed into his mind. He had it. He closed the fridge and opened the cabinets, searching for the different types of tea they had. He couldn't find it. Why hadn't he paid attention to where they kept the damn green tea?

Emma walked in and Zack straightened up, trying to play it off as if he hadn't just been doing the "flight of the bumblebee" through all the cabinets.

She was reading something on her tablet computer and looked up at him. "What are you looking for?" Emma asked.

"Do you know where the green tea is kept?" Zack asked guiltily.

"Oh, it's just down there," Emma said, gesturing toward the opposite end of the line of cabinets.

"Thanks!" Zack replied, and with as much poise as he could muster, he located the tea and took out a packet of green tea from the container.

He grabbed a coffee mug and added water, then stuck it in the microwave. Waiting for the tea to brew was worse than waiting for the light to finally change at a busy intersection. He removed the tea bag, recycled it to be used in Emma's hydroponic garden, and stared down at the cup.

"Cream and sugar are over there," Emma said, "but I don't think cream goes with green tea."

Zack carefully brought the steaming cup over to the sugar and poured some in. He stirred it up and glanced back at Emma. She gave him an approving nod and went back to reading her tablet.

Zack put a lid on the mug, left the mess hall, and approached the med bay. There were three beds and an examination table inside. All the beds were empty except one. The med bay was mostly dark except for the soft glow of ambient lighting near Brenda's workstation and by the bed Katie lay in. Her eyes were closed. Brenda looked up at his arrival.

"I just wanted to keep her company," Zack whispered.

Brenda eyed him and glanced at the cup of tea in his hand. "As long as you're quiet, you can stay. I need to step out for a few minutes anyway. Would you mind staying until I get back?"

Zack nodded and walked over to Katie's bed. Her long black hair was pulled to the side, leaving her neckline exposed, and her eyes were closed. He stopped for a second, taking in the sight of her.

You've been so concerned about the past that you never stopped to consider what was right in front of you.

Katie's words echoed in his mind. He knew he was standing there, smiling, and part of him acknowledged that he must look like a fool, but he didn't care. He placed the cup of tea on the bedside table and quietly sat in the chair next to the bed.

Katie slept and Zack stayed by her side. He brought up his tablet to check on a few things he was working on but decided he didn't much feel like working at the moment. He leaned back in the chair, resting his head against the wall, and was soon asleep.

Zack dozed for a short while before a slight movement next to him caused him to wake. He opened his eyes to see Katie looking at him. She held up the teacup.

"Thank you for bringing me tea," Katie said.

"Oh, it was nothing," Zack said. "I just wanted to see if you were all right. I can leave—"

"Stay— I mean, only if you want to," Katie said.

This was a side to her he hadn't seen before. The Katie he

knew was direct, with nothing held back, and here they were
both tiptoeing around.

"Did it just get weird? I don't want this to get weird," Zack
said, and started to rise out of his seat. "I should go. You kissed
me, and maybe you just lost a bet with Hicks or something, or
you didn't like it, but I really did—"

Katie reached out, grabbed his hand, and pulled him back.
He sat on the bed next to her. She didn't let go of his hand and
looked at him in a way that made his stomach clench. "I kissed
you because I wanted to. Because I like you. And if you stop
acting silly," she said, pulling him closer, "we can kiss each other
again."

Their lips touched softly at first, and Zack felt as if his chest
was about to explode. He reached up and gently pulled her
closer. If he was dreaming, it was a dream he didn't want to wake
from. They stopped kissing and smiled at each other, Zack
wondering what he'd done to earn Katie's attention.

"Not bad, Romeo," Katie said, and smoothed a lock of his
hair away from his eyes.

Zack leaned in and kissed her neck, working his way to
her lips.

"Mr. Quick, I do believe you're making me blush," Katie
purred.

Zack was about to say something when the door burst open
and Hicks rushed in carrying Kaylan, who was shaking in
his arms.

"Kaylan needs help. Where's Brenda?" he asked.

Kaylan's eyes were closed, but she was muttering something
like she was in some type of trance.

Zack was on his feet in an instant and cleared off the bed

across from them. Hicks came over and gently laid Kaylan upon it.

"She won't respond. We were in the rec room doing a bit of kickboxing, and the next thing I knew she was on the floor," Hicks said.

Zack frowned. There was something tugging at the edges of his thoughts. He'd seen this somewhere before.

"Did you hit her in the head?" Zack asked.

"Of course not," Hicks replied.

Katie came to his side and placed her hand on Kaylan's forehead. "She's burning up." Katie grabbed Kaylan's wrist and watched the clock on the wall. "Her heart rate is elevated."

Zack's eyes widened. "I've seen this before."

"This has happened to her before?" Hicks asked.

Zack shook his head. "No, not to her. The old videos of the viewers when they were in a trance. It's the same thing. The same symptoms as when the event occurred."

Hicks glanced down at Kaylan, his mouth open in astonishment.

"In the video they had to wait for it to pass. Brenda stepped out to go talk to Hunsicker," Zack said.

Hicks nodded and walked over to the comms panel by the door.

"Are you sure about this? Is there anything we can do?" Katie asked.

"We need to record everything she says and take her vitals. That's what they did before—"

"Need the key. The key … the key," Kaylan muttered.

Hicks called Zack over to the comms panel. A video display showed Redford's face.

"Zack, we've got a reply from the transmission we sent. We need you at the comms station," Redford said.

Zack was about to tell Redford to go to hell, that he wasn't leaving, when Hunsicker's face came on screen.

"Brenda is on her way back. She'll look after Kaylan. We need you here," Hunsicker said.

Zack swallowed what he was going to say and looked back at Kaylan on the bed, muttering incoherently.

"Go on. We'll stay with her and let you know if anything changes," Katie said.

Zack turned back to the comms panel. "I'll be right there."

With a last look back at the others, he left the med bay just as Brenda was coming in. Zack tried to remember everything he could from the old videos as he ran to the bridge. The men in the chairs were all viewers for the project. They were trained. How could Kaylan be one of those? The project had been cancelled, and the data Dux Corp provided pointed to the program having been quietly retired. There had been no further contact since the initial incident. If Kaylan was trained as a viewer, then why hadn't she said anything? She wouldn't have kept it from him, not unless … she didn't know she was trained to begin with. That didn't make any sense. Her grandfather was Bruce Matherson, one of the founders of Dux Corp, and one of the primary reasons they were here. Would he have done this to his own granddaughter?

The questions tumbled through Zack's mind. He came at the problem from different directions but kept coming back to the same place. Some of the viewers who were part of the program had ended up in the psych ward, succumbing to some type of permanent psychosis. If the same thing was happening to Kaylan

… He stopped that line of thought. He would dig into the data more to see if there was something that could help her.

Zack opened the door to the bridge and went to the planning table. Redford had the holodisplay up, showing a line to their position coming from way out in the Oort cloud.

"It's just where you thought it was," Redford said.

"What's the transmission saying?" Hunsicker asked.

Zack logged into the interface and began inputting commands. "I started writing an interpreter based on the decoded data. It might help with this."

Zack worked silently for a few minutes, bringing up different windows with bits of code streaming. Other data points popped into being across the Oort cloud that lay millions of miles past the solar system's last planet. Their positions were too precise to be anything other than intentional.

"This looks almost like a grid, except it's surrounding the entire solar system," Hunsicker said.

"That's precisely what it is. Except we don't know why they put it there," Redford said.

Zack's interpreter routine began spitting out data on a bottom window of the display.

"We're getting coordinates for whatever those things are—I'll call them beacons for now. They're checking in," Zack said.

Hunsicker pressed his lips in thought. "What did you put in your initial transmission?"

Zack shrugged. "Just simple stuff, really. Whenever I try to connect with a network I don't know much about back home, I just use an opening handshake, if you will, and provide a way for the system to talk back to me. If I'm really paranoid, I'll find a way to passively check if they are there, which is usually the case, but that wouldn't work here. I used an opening handshake, except I was flying a little bit blind. I used some of the alien data to trick their system into thinking I was one of them."

Hunsicker exchanged glances with Redford. "I'll take your word for it," Hunsicker said.

Zack scanned the holodisplay. More and more reference points populated it.

"Is there any way to tell how much data is being sent?" Hunsicker asked.

"No, we'll just have to wait until it stops. But this might help us get into the structure on Pluto," Zack said.

"How?" Hunsicker asked.

"If I can get a grasp on the protocols used by the alien system, then I can use them to communicate and gain access to their system."

Zack highlighted one of the reference points on the display, and below it both the raw data and the interpreted data showed.

"What is it?" Redford asked.

Zack entered a few commands, and three of the reference points highlighted in front of them on the holodisplay. "The word 'shroud' keeps getting referred to as part of each point. I'm not sure the interpreter is working properly."

Redford leaned closer to the display. "A shroud ... now that's clever."

Zack's eyes widened as he followed Redford's thinking. "You've got to be kidding me."

"Would one of you like to fill me in?" Hunsicker asked.

Zack minimized the windows on the display except for the mockup of the solar system. The highlighted data points in the Oort cloud still showed.

"This is the shroud," Zack said.

Hunsicker's slack-jawed expression deepened as he took in what was showing on the display. "Are you sure? What does it do? Why wouldn't we have seen it?"

"I don't know what it does, but I know it's there," Zack said.

"Zack's right," Redford said. "It's certainly there. As to why we wouldn't have seen it? That depends on certain things. If they don't reflect light and are too small to divert our view away from the Earth, then we might never have detected it."

Hunsicker circled around the table, his eyes never leaving the holodisplay. "This is so contrived. How could anyone have done this?"

"Well, we're not really sure what they've done," Zack said.

"Any species that could accomplish this is way more advanced than anything we've come up with as a species," Redford said.

"So we have an alien structure on Pluto, the signal that came during the 1980s, and now this shroud that exists so far away and is so small that we might not have been able to see it in the first place. Does that about sum this up?" Hunsicker said.

Zack nodded and Redford did the same.

"So why have the shroud? I can accept aliens building something on the farthest planet from our sun, maybe to keep an eye on us or something, but the presence of the shroud changes things," Hunsicker said.

"How?" Zack asked.

"This alien race took the time to put something between us and the rest of the galaxy, or the other way around," Hunsicker said.

"You mean to keep the rest of the galaxy from knowing we're here?" Zack asked.

"Maybe. I'm just thinking off the top of my head. The presence of the shroud suggests intentions that I don't fully understand," Hunsicker finished.

"Biases when determining the intentions of an alien entity can be a problem," Redford said.

Zack frowned. "Let's take aliens out of the equation for a second. Actually, let's take the solar system out of the equation to simplify things. You put a wrapper around something else to isolate it, maybe to protect it. What if that's what the shroud is doing?"

"It's the isolation I don't like," Hunsicker said. "I want to bring the others in on this."

"What for? This is astrophysical," Redford said.

"The functionality may be, but not the intent. We should hear the others' perspectives on this before we send any of this information back to Earth," Hunsicker said.

Zack's eyes widened. "You want me to delay sending this back to Earth?"

Hunsicker nodded. "That's exactly what I'm saying."

"I really don't see why we need to bring the others in on this," Redford said. "If you bring in someone like Hicks, with his military background, he'll see something like this as a threat."

"That's exactly what I think it is. I don't quite understand why you're so resistant to having the others' input. I thought peer review was part of the academic mantra?" Hunsicker said.

Zack's lips curved into a small smile, which he hid behind a cough.

Redford held up his hands. "I just want to avoid fear-mongering."

"Think about it, Jonah. Why put a shroud over anything? Sure, Zack's interpreter could be off and it's called something else, but that doesn't disguise the intent. You put a shroud over someone's eyes because you don't want them to see what you're doing, and that bothers me more than anything," Hunsicker said.

"The technology involved on this scale is unimaginable. We should study it," Redford replied.

The bridge comms lit up.

"Sir," Hicks said, "Kaylan's come out of it."

"Is she all right?" Zack asked.

"Yeah, but you need to come down here," Hicks said.

"We'll be right there," Hunsicker said.

Redford frowned. "What happened to Kaylan?"

Zack was about to answer, but Hunsicker cut him off.

"She's just a little sick," Hunsicker said.

Zack closed his mouth. If Hunsicker wanted to lie about what had happened to Kaylan, then he wasn't about to provide Redford with any more information.

"Oh, well I hope she feels better."

Zack had started to leave the bridge when Redford called out to him.

"We've got work to do, Zack," Redford said.

"It's still streaming in. I can monitor it from my tablet. I'm going to check on Kaylan, and then I'll be back up in a few minutes," Zack said, and left without waiting for a reply.

Chapter Twenty

Kaylan took a sip of water, which chased away the feeling of sandpaper in her mouth. Her head ached terribly. One moment she had been doing kickboxing drills with Hicks and the next she'd awakened in the med bay with a captive audience. Brenda and Hicks were speaking in hushed tones near the door. Katie was leaning against a bed and watching her with a tablet and stylus ready to go.

"Are you okay?" Katie asked.

Kaylan closed her eyes and the disorientation faded away. "I feel like I was knocked out. How did I get here?"

"I brought you," Hicks said, coming over.

Brenda came to the other side of the bed and shined a small penlight in her eyes. "How are you feeling?"

"My head hurts, bad," Kaylan said.

Brenda nodded and brought out a small handheld scanner.

She ran it from Kaylan's temple across her forehead and stopped at her other temple. Her headache lessened to barely a dull ache.

"Keep sipping the water. You might be a little dehydrated. Do you remember what happened?" Brenda asked.

"Yeah, Hicks and I were exercising and talking about what we'd find on Pluto, and then the next minute everything started spinning. I ..." Kaylan's response trailed off. She'd had another vision. She was standing before the domed entrance to the alien structure. It wasn't cold. At least she couldn't feel it this time. She remembered wanting to get inside, but she needed something. "A key," Kaylan said.

Brenda exchanged glances with the others. "You kept saying something about a key."

Kaylan's eyes widened. "Was I talking ... before?"

"You said some things. I've been writing them down," Katie said.

"What else did I say?" Kaylan asked.

"You kept talking about the nine and needing the key. You were quite insistent on the key," Katie said.

Kaylan looked away, feeling embarrassed. They must think she was crazy or cracking up. The door to the med bay opened and Zack and Commander Hunsicker came through. Hunsicker asked if she was all right. Zack kept watching her as if weighing something.

"I think I know what happened to you," Zack said.

Kaylan's heart was pounding. *He knows about the visions.*

"Kaylan," Zack said, "I think you've just experienced the same thing as the viewers did back when the event first happened in the 1980s."

Kaylan's eyes darted to all of them. They all looked concerned.

"Are you saying the aliens have reached out to her?" Hicks asked.

Zack shrugged. "I don't think so. I'm not sure, but the stronger viewers became so focused that it appeared they were in some type of a trance."

"Is there anything you want to tell us?" Hunsicker asked.

Kaylan pressed her lips together. "Something like this happened once before. Just after we left for Titus Station I was in the observatory. Zack had found some files that were locked. The clue for the passphrase was something only I would understand. The content was a video message from my grandfather. He said that I had been trained as a viewer, that I had similar traits to one of their most gifted viewers to come through the program."

Zack frowned. "Trained? You've never mentioned anything like this before."

"That's because I didn't know. The message went on to talk about the games we used to play. Like scavenger hunt. There was always a group of us, but I had a knack for finding things. But that's it. There wasn't any formal training program. I studied science, aeronautical engineering. I don't even believe in any hokey psychic stuff. The whole idea is absurd," Kaylan said.

"Games like that emphasize critical thinking. I'm not exactly sure how this ties into remote viewing, but it must be important," Brenda said.

"Why don't you tell us what you saw the first time? Just stick to the facts," Hunsicker said.

Kaylan sucked in a breath. "I keep seeing the alien structure.

I'm standing outside of it in front of the dome. It's cold, and I feel like if I don't get inside then I'm going to die."

Hunsicker frowned in thought. "What was different about today?"

"The first time I was focusing on it. This time it seemed to just come out of nowhere."

"Well, one thing for sure is that you're not crazy," Hunsicker said, a slight smile lifting the edges of his lips.

"Not crazy? How could this not be crazy?" Kaylan asked.

"It's not, and I'll tell you why," Zack said. "Science is an attempt to explain the unknown. We're standing here based upon some alien entity reaching out to us through unconventional means. I've studied the videos from Dux Corp. None of those people were crazy."

"No, they just ended up that way," Kaylan said, glaring at Zack.

"Not all of them," Zack replied.

"You don't get it. If something like this can happen at any moment, I become a liability instead of an asset on this mission," Kaylan said.

"Well then, study it. Have one of us around when you try," Zack said.

"It's not a bad idea," Brenda said. "I could monitor you. If we can learn what triggered the event, then maybe it can be overcome and controlled. Your mind is already working on this whether you want it to or not. We're all thinking about what we'll find once we get to Pluto."

Kaylan looked away from the others. She had reviewed the viewer files, and some of them had ended up in a permanent state of psychosis. She didn't want that to happen to her. At the same time, what the others were saying did make sense.

"I'll think about it," Kaylan said. She didn't like that this ability could take over. The others were right; she needed to learn what she could about it.

"We should let you get some rest, come up with a plan, and take it from there," Hunsicker said.

Brenda chased everyone out of the med bay, leaving Kaylan alone with Katie. They were both silent, each lost in their own thoughts. Kaylan knew that if she ignored the problems she faced, things would only get worse. She glanced over at Katie, who was reading something on her tablet.

"He's a good person, you know. Zack," Kaylan said.

Katie looked over at her and nodded. "I know he is," she replied.

"Don't hurt him," Kaylan said.

"I won't," Katie answered quietly.

Kaylan nodded, turned over, and closed her eyes. She didn't want to sleep, but she was tired. Her body felt as if she had run a marathon. After a few minutes Kaylan drifted off into a dreamless sleep.

A few days later, Kaylan was back in the med bay to meet with Brenda. She hadn't had any other episodes. Hicks was still nervous around her, afraid she would collapse. She'd thrown herself into her work, from checking that their approach to Pluto was optimal to running diagnostics on the Athena. She'd even lent a hand with Zack's work with the shroud network. But Brenda had kept after her until Kaylan finally relented and agreed to go and meet with her. At the gray med bay door, Kaylan hesitated before going inside.

Brenda looked up and smiled. "I'm glad you came."

"I'm here. How do you want to do this?" Kaylan asked.

"First, I know you're afraid there's something wrong with you. I've checked your medical history and there's nothing in it that points to any mental health issues. So the likelihood of permanent psychosis is remote. The people who suffered from that had also been using experimental drugs. It seems they were desperate to re-establish contact with the aliens," Brenda said, and motioned for her to sit on the nearest bed.

"That's something at least. Are you going to try to hypnotize me?"

"Goodness no. I wouldn't know how. Not all doctors with a secondary degree in psychiatry can perform hypnosis. My goal is to help you make sense of what you're seeing, if I can. In order for that to happen, you need to be conscious," Brenda said.

Kaylan nodded. Her fingers longed for something to twirl in them, which she often did without thinking about it. "I don't even know how any of this works. How could anyone communicate in such a way?"

"People have been communicating with each other nonverbally for much longer than anyone thinks. Some refer to it as a sixth sense that presents itself as a feeling or need to do something, usually involving a loved one. Some dismiss such occurrences as coincidences or observations processed by our subconscious, but that doesn't account for instances where people are separated across distances," Brenda said.

"Yeah, but the examples you've provided all have to do with emotional attachments. How can an alien be emotionally attached to people? That doesn't add up for me," Kaylan said.

"Agreed. I was merely establishing the premise. So if the

premise exists in one form, then why not another form? What if this alien race has figured out a way to communicate across vast distances that's not limited by the physical world?" Brenda said.

Kaylan pursed her lips in thought. "Maybe," she said.

"I'll give you something else to think about. People like Redford and other physicists go on about the physical world and the limitations it brings. Speed of light, for example. Einstein insisted we could not travel faster than the speed of light. A thought doesn't have physical substance other than the synapses in your brain that fire to make you aware of it. Communicating that thought across space and time isn't limited by a general theory of relativity, so perhaps there is room for another theory that hasn't been studied in as much detail."

Kaylan frowned. "What do you mean?"

"Life is all connected. On some level it interacts and we form bonds. What if there is a sentient race of beings out there that has the ability to manipulate this connection in order to send information?" Brenda said.

"And because we dabbled in this field, we just happened to receive the message. Interesting theory to be sure, but I would want to better understand how to measure something like that," Kaylan said.

"Me too," Brenda said, and finished bringing the monitors online. "What I want you to do is the same thing you did that first time where you thought about going to Pluto, only this time describe to me what you're seeing as it occurs. Don't worry about how it sounds," Brenda said.

Kaylan settled back on the bed and closed her eyes. She counted backwards from thirty, clearing her mind and building an image of the alien structure.

"The ground is icy and uneven. The air is cold. The dark, smooth walls shimmer with a deep lustrous purple that runs along the surface. There is a panel in front of me ..." Kaylan said.

"Try and focus on the structure. Is there any way to get inside?" Brenda asked.

"I don't see anything. All the walls are smooth."

"Instead of looking for a door, just picture yourself inside. Are you able to do that?"

Kaylan focused on the structure and what lay beyond the walls. There was a snap, and the next thing she knew she was inside. "I'm inside, I think. Feels warmer, but it's dark. Like everything is on standby. There are glowing panels on the far side. There is a red light emanating from one," Kaylan said. She felt her concentration begin to unravel. She wanted to get to the panel, but she couldn't move. It was like her feet had become fused to the floor, rooting her in place. Kaylan opened her eyes and saw Brenda watching her.

"How was that?" Brenda said.

Kaylan took a second to collect her thoughts. "Honestly, it was better. I didn't feel alone like the first time. Everything was overwhelming that time. This time I had a better understanding of what to expect."

"That's good, and you were better prepared for it. Imagine this is like any other muscle. You just need to strengthen it. Let's try again tomorrow. We'll keep these sessions short. Tomorrow we'll focus on going inside the structure," Brenda said.

"I'm seeing it in my mind, but what if it's my mind that's putting it there?" Kaylan asked.

"Can't say for sure until we get there. You described physically what it was like there, but were there any other impressions? Like was someone else there?"

Kaylan shook her head. "Not at all. I was alone. It's as if everything is on standby, like if we powered down the ship and left only emergency systems running."

Brenda nodded and wrote down some notes.

"Is this going to be reported back to NASA?" Kaylan asked.

"Not right now. Hunsicker wants to keep this among ourselves," Brenda replied.

"At some point we'll need to tell them," Kaylan said.

"You're absolutely right, but Hunsicker just wants to hold off for a little while until we get a better understanding of what it all means."

"Seems reasonable, I guess. Thanks for your help. I'll see you later then," Kaylan said, and left.

Chapter Twenty-One

Z ack spent much of his time on the bridge working at the comms station. It became his unofficial work area. This allowed him access to the large holodisplay over the planning table. It beat standing for hours on end in the observatory with Redford. The data dumps from the shroud network were quite large. It was as if they hadn't reported in for some time. Jonah sat next to him at the comms station. Zack still couldn't help but compare Jonah's sharp, angular facial features to that of a hawk. Sometimes he even referred to the illustrious Dr. Redford as Hawkman in his mind.

Commander Hunsicker joined them. "Are they still reporting in?"

Zack nodded. "There are a lot of them."

"How many?" Hunsicker asked.

"The projection I have puts their number in the millions," Zack said.

"And we still can't see them?"

Redford shook his head. "They could be small. The data they send back is much like that of a probe. It gives the current status of what we think are its core systems, its position, and the position of its neighbor. I think the only way to learn more is at the alien observatory or to head out into the Oort cloud and see for ourselves."

"I can tell you now that we won't be going out to the Oort cloud," Hunsicker said. "So you think the structure is an observatory?"

"That is correct. Why else build something way out here?" Redford said.

"I still say they wanted this place to be found," Zack said. "They could have put this thing anywhere. If it were on Mars, then we might have found it too quickly. Sure, they could have chosen a moon that orbits any of the planets in our solar system, but if it were me, and I wanted something to remain hidden for a particular period of time, then I would pick an obvious place that we would likely go visit."

Hunsicker shrugged. "I would go along with that."

"It does make sense, but we still don't know why they put it there or why the shroud even exists in the first place," Redford said.

Vitomir and Nikolai came onto the bridge and headed over to them.

"The LSS has been repaired. It will be fully operational for when we reach the planet," Vitomir said.

Zack glanced at the two Russians. They had a habit of being around him and Redford when Commander Hunsicker wasn't around. He guessed it could just be a coincidence that the EVA schedules worked out that way.

"Is this the shroud?" Nikolai asked, studying the holodisplay. Zack nodded.

"Remarkable, and under our very noses," Nikolai said.

"A needle in a haystack is more like it," Zack said.

Nikolai gave him a puzzled frown. "I get it. Yes."

"Were you able to apply the data from the shroud network to what we already have?" Hunsicker asked.

"I've been taking it and constructing a few keys that I'm hoping will open up communications once we get there. We tried sending a signal directly to the structure, but we didn't get any reply," Zack said.

"Could be by design, especially if we're just poking around in the dark. Or it's offline," Hunsicker said.

Zack checked the time on the screen. He was still training with Hicks and Katie, and since today it was with the latter, he was eager to get there. In spite of everything going on, he couldn't remember being happier.

"The surveyor probes are still offline, but we're less than twenty-four hours away," Redford said.

"The others will be here in a few minutes, and we'll talk about next steps," Hunsicker said.

The rest of the crew came on the bridge and gathered around the planning table. It was getting a bit more crowded with Vitomir and Nikolai added to the mix. Katie came over and stood next to Zack. It hadn't gone unnoticed that they had been spending a lot of time together. Occasionally he got weird looks from Kaylan, accompanied by her lashing out at him. At other times she was completely fine. Sometimes it annoyed him. After all, she spent much of her time with Hicks. Why should she begrudge him the time he spent with Katie?

Kaylan was last to come on the bridge.

"Thank you all for coming," Hunsicker began. "In the next twenty-four hours we will hit our objective and accomplish a major milestone in space exploration history. No human has ever come as far as we have. I'm proud to say that I get to share it with each and every one of you. You were picked for this mission because you were the best. No space agency in the world sends astronauts into space that they know couldn't make the cut. One of you had little to no training for this mission, and yet you still came. You've worked hard and we all appreciate your dedication." Hunsicker paused to nod to Zack. "Others have trained in outer space but weren't part of the core team that was slated to go to Titan. You are all part of Athena's crew now. The success of this mission will be because you are here with us. A lot will change after we achieve our objective. Our world will change based upon the discoveries we will be making. Cooperation among international space agencies is for the betterment of humankind. It's that kind of tenacity that makes this mission possible, and I just wanted to thank you all for volunteering."

Zack hadn't felt like a volunteer in the beginning. In fact, he had been preoccupied with finding the quickest exit, but now he was glad he was here. What they were doing was bigger than taking down greedy corporations, and he yearned to see this through. Hopefully they would all live through what was to come. He glanced at Katie. She was listening to Hunsicker speak. He wanted to take her on a real date—go out to dinner, perhaps drink a bit too much, and watch the sunrise over the ocean.

"The shuttle is capable of bringing all of us down to the

surface of Pluto," Hunsicker said. "However, we're not all going down. At least not at first. Some of you will remain on the Athena and monitor the away team from here."

Some of the crew sucked in a frustrated breath, and Zack couldn't blame them. They all wanted to go down there.

"Don't misunderstand me. Everyone will get a chance to go down to the surface after we've established that it's safe enough for you to do so. It's not imperative that we bring all of you down at once," Hunsicker continued. "The LSS will dock with the shuttle, and both will be going down to the surface on the first run."

Kaylan took control of the holo-interface, and the last surveyor image of the alien structure came to prominence. "We'll be landing about half a kilometer from the structure. We don't want our only means of returning to the Athena to become compromised. Depending on what happens, we've selected secondary and tertiary landing coordinates in the event of some unforeseen circumstance."

"Like if the aliens attack," Zack said before he could think to keep his big mouth shut.

Hunsicker glanced at him, but his expression was serious. "We have to account for every possibility. That's why Hicks and Garcia will be armed."

Zack's mouth opened in surprise, and he glanced around at the others.

"They've trained for space combat, and we need to take precautions to protect ourselves. None of us know for sure what we'll find once we arrive. Jonah, go ahead," Hunsicker said.

"We scanned the structure and detected traces of a heat

signature, so we believe the structure does have power. Whether someone is home is anyone's guess," Redford said.

"What do we know about the area itself?" Zack asked.

"We believe the surface is a mixture of ice and rock. The structure is located in what looks like foothills," Kaylan answered.

Hicks cleared his throat. "The ground team will split into two groups being led by myself and Garcia. If for any reason it is determined that approaching the structure is too dangerous, I expect you to comply with our orders. This is for your protection and everyone around you," Hicks said.

"Yeah, but," Zack said, "we didn't come all this way not to attempt to get inside."

"You're misunderstanding me. We're going to try to get inside, but it will be with minimal risk to the crew. We don't know for sure what happened to the rover. You said the event reminded you of a challenge, as if there is some type of lockout. If the facility decides we're a threat, then I think it's in everyone's best interests to proceed with some caution," Hicks replied.

Zack glanced at Katie.

"Zack, you're with me," Hicks said. "We'll be among those who will first approach the structure."

Zack didn't bother trying to hide his disappointment but understood the need for caution.

"Vitomir, Emma, and Efren will remain onboard the Athena," Hunsicker said. "You will observe through our suit cams and monitor."

Two of the three nodded, with the notable exception of Emma.

"But sir, I'm a xenobiologist. If you do encounter alien life forms, you'll need me," Emma said.

"You're absolutely right. That's why I want you observing and advising from the ship. You'll be able to use the ship's computers to help if we do encounter an actual alien. You'll be in the second wave. In a nutshell, if everything goes okay, then I'll make a shuttle run to retrieve the rest of the team," Hunsicker said. "Now for the part I like the least. Should the worst happen, meaning catastrophic failure on the surface, the navigation computer is already preconfigured with a flight plan that will take you back to Earth. Between that and assistance from NASA, the Athena will get the remaining crew members back to Earth safely."

Zack thought about what Hunsicker had said. He had looked down at his hands and was thinking about taking one of Katie's hands in his own when she reached out and took his hand, giving it a gentle squeeze.

"Getting into the structure is only one part of this mission. We have less than twenty-four hours until we arrive. I suggest you each get some time at the comms station and send messages back home," Hunsicker said.

Their meeting broke apart, and Katie took him by the hand and led him off the bridge. They didn't say anything as they went. She led him to the port observatory, which was a smaller lounge far enough away from the main observatory for privacy. Out of the windows, a sea of stars stretched away, too numerous to count. Katie led him to one of the couches and Zack sat down. She sat next to him, and Zack wrapped his arm around her shoulders. They quietly gazed out at the beautiful view in front of them. It was deceptively serene, but Zack had been in space long enough to know some of the dangers that lurked in the void.

"You'll do fine tomorrow," Katie said.

"I'd much rather be on your team," Zack said.

Katie let out a soft laugh. "We're all on the same team. I won't be far away."

"You know, being with you has shattered my whole macho motif I dreamed about as a kid," Zack said, and grinned.

Katie lifted her head from his shoulder and looked at him. "Just remember, when we're out there it's serious."

Zack swallowed. "I know."

She settled back down and they sat there together, each of them preparing for what was to come as best they could.

Chapter Twenty-Two

Zack uploaded some last-minute tools to the tablet computer he was taking to the surface and placed it into a specially designed case that contained its own heat source. This would prevent the subzero temperatures from destroying it. He'd spent much of the past twenty-four hours reviewing the data from the shroud network in order to improve the translation software he'd written. He had also configured portable versions to be compatible with the others' suit computers. What he had was by no means comprehensive, but at least they wouldn't be stumbling around in the dark. The aliens, whoever they truly were, had taken steps that allowed him to decipher the structure of the code they used. In the time he'd been on the Athena, he had come to appreciate how clever the aliens were. They almost reminded him of his teachers.

He just couldn't help but wonder about the parts of the alien message he still didn't understand, although he'd made real progress while on the Athena. He'd taken the different data sources recorded in the initial incident and had been able to merge the data. The keys to unlocking the secrets were buried in the headers of the packets of data. His theory for this was proven when they'd received replies from the machines that made up the shroud network.

Zack stood up and ran his fingers through his hair, taking one last look at his workstation.

"It's time to go," Kaylan said.

Besides them on Athena's bridge were Vitomir and Emma, who would remain behind.

"I know. I just want to make sure I didn't forget anything," Zack said, and took another look around. "I can't believe this is it."

"Moment of truth," Kaylan said.

Zack placed his hand on her shoulder. "Once we get inside, we'll likely have more questions than we do now, but at least we'll know whether the things you've seen are real. I, for one, believe you."

Kaylan placed her hand on his and looked as if she were about to say something else but stopped. "Let's get going. The others are waiting."

They were already in their EVA suits, so Zack followed Kaylan to the shuttle. He wondered what she'd been about to say. They hadn't spoken much in the past few days. At least he wasn't the only one with pre-mission jitters.

Most of the others had already boarded the shuttle. Kaylan headed to the pilot's seat in the front while Zack stowed his equipment and sat across from Katie. He pulled on his helmet, realizing he no longer felt the urge to check the seals on his suit every three seconds.

"See, Hicks? You owe me money." Katie grinned.

Zack gave them a puzzled look.

"I bet her that you would check your helmet at least a couple of times after you sat down," Hicks said.

Zack felt a wide smile lift his lips, and he beamed at Katie. "Well, I had an excellent teacher."

The others around them grinned and, from the front of the shuttle, Hunsicker asked what was so funny.

"We're just noticing that Zack here is becoming a full-fledged astronaut," Hicks said.

Zack grinned with the others. Physically he had never felt better in his life, although he'd had his doubts when the commander had first insisted that he be on the away team to Pluto's surface. He nodded to both Katie and Hicks. They were the ones who had worked with him the most.

The shuttle detached from the Athena and headed for the planet's surface. Uranus had been unbelievably huge compared to anything Zack had ever seen, and Pluto, in spite of being a large dwarf planet, looked to be just as interesting from his vantage point. Charon, Pluto's largest moon, was off to the side. It was half the size of the dwarf planet itself. The remaining four moons were much smaller, and Zack imagined the view from Pluto's surface would be as awe-inspiring as their view from the shuttle.

"Pluto is at a point in its orbit where it's actually closer to the sun than Neptune," Redford said.

Zack glanced out the window behind Katie and saw the sun. From the shuttle, it looked more like a distant star than what he thought of as the sun, but it was bright even at this distance, and he felt a closeness to the celestial body that allowed all life to flourish on the Earth.

A soft shudder was felt in the shuttle. When Pluto was this close to the sun, a thin atmosphere formed, but with Pluto being only a fifth the size of Earth, the gravitational pull wouldn't pose any issue with the shuttle leaving. The heads-up display showed the shuttle's trajectory as they closed in on the rocky surface that was a mix of ice-filled crevices and mountain peaks. The shuttle's approach took them over the smooth parts of the Plutonian surface, but the alien structure was nestled between some foothills ahead.

"Zack, any activity?" Hunsicker asked.

Zack glanced at the readout on his suit computer. He had coded a continuous loop to communicate with the alien structure.

"Nothing," Zack said.

The people on the shuttle craned their necks, trying to catch a first glimpse of what they had travelled millions of miles to see. Kaylan leveled off the approach, and the shuttle chased the sunrise as the landscape in front of them revealed itself in the sun's rays.

"Still nothing," Zack said.

The shuttle came to a stop and hovered a half a kilometer from the alien structure. Zack heard the landing gear deploy, and the shuttle touched gently down upon the surface. Hunsicker got up from his seat and checked that they were ready, then gave a nod to Kaylan, and the airlock door opened. They stood for a moment to take in the twilit surface, and the crew of the Athena waited for their commander to take the first step off the shuttle. Commander Michael

Hunsicker nodded to each crew member in turn as he stepped past them.

Zack watched as Hunsicker stopped at the airlock door. "I step from upon the shoulders of giants," Hunsicker said quietly.

Zack, being closest to the rear of the shuttle, exited next. The lights from the shuttle illuminated the surrounding area. Zack gazed up at the heavens, for once at a loss for words. Charon hovered in the distance. The sun, like a lonely lantern of some far-off lighthouse, shined brightly in the distance. Zack couldn't keep his mouth from hanging open. This was a sky the likes of which no human had ever set eyes upon, even with the aid of a telescope.

Small flakes of what looked like snow fell gently around them. There was a light dusting on the ground.

"It's not water. It's actually frozen nitrogen," Redford said.

The astronauts circled around the shuttle and saw the alien structure only a short distance away. Four dark spires stretched above the main structure. The outer surfaces were smooth and dark, and hints of purple reflected from the dark walls. An opal-colored dome could be seen rising above a smaller building extending from the main structure.

"It looks like no one is home," Zack said.

Hicks slapped him on the shoulder. "Well, let's go knock and see if anyone is there."

The LSS, or spider, as Zack liked to call it, detached itself from the top of the shuttle and climbed down beside them. Nikolai waved to them from inside, and they continued on. Zack glanced at Katie, who now held some type of rifle. Hicks also carried one. Zack had no idea how they worked; he just knew they were designed to operate in space.

"Still no sign of the rover," Kaylan said.

The closer they got, the bigger the structure appeared. Hunsicker waved them over to a small, rough patch of ice. The small rover from the Russian surveyor probe was sunken into the ice.

Redford squatted down for a closer look. "It looks like some kind of pocket opened up while it was sending the signal."

"Do you know what caused it?" Zack asked.

"Likely the weather," Hunsicker said. "There are temperature variations here that could have caused such an event."

"And I thought it was just cold here," Zack said.

As they closed in on the structure they spread out, looking for a way inside, but there were no discernible creases that indicated a door. Zack headed toward the side of the smaller building that jutted out from the main structure and touched the surface. It was solid, and bits of ice stretched up the sides. Zack knocked chunks of it off, and a small panel glowed on the surface. The PDA that was attached to his arm chimed. One of the programs he'd written had made a connection. A partial menu appeared, written with alien symbols. The HUD on his helmet translated what it could, and Zack selected one of the options. The panel closed, and a line of cyan light split the area in the middle, running twenty feet up the wall. Chunks of ice fell away as each section of the wall pulled inward. The doors opened twenty feet wide. Dim lights along the interior wall came on and lit a pathway that led inside.

"Good work, Mr. Quick," Redford said.

"Well done, Zack," Hunsicker said. "Let's see what's inside."

They all entered the structure. Nikolai exited the spider and joined them. *At least we didn't have to tear a hole to get inside,*

Zack thought. After they all went through, the doors closed behind them, and the lighting along the walls grew brighter.

"It's a massive airlock," Kaylan said.

Off to the side was a large vehicle. It had a rounded front and open space with benches built into it. The seats were so high that if Zack were to sit in one, his feet would dangle. Metallic crates were stacked next to it.

"Everything is so big," Zack said.

"The species that built this place must be a lot taller than us," Kaylan said. "Emma, are you seeing this?"

"We see what you're seeing, and you're right. I would estimate an average height of eight to ten feet," Emma said, her voice coming through comms.

Great, a race of giants built this place, Zack thought.

Hunsicker waved him over to a glowing panel on the internal wall. Zack came over, and the HUD on his helmet visor translated the symbols.

"It says, 'Stand by, reading life signs,'" Zack said.

Zack looked above them, but there was no sign of any instrumentation.

"I guess we …" Hunsicker's voice died as the interior door opened.

A puff of air gasped into the airlock.

"Sir," Hicks said, "my suit is detecting an atmospheric reading in here."

"Mine is as well," Kaylan said. Her eyes widened as she looked up. "Mostly comprised of nitrogen and oxygen. It's an Earth-like atmosphere."

The others confirmed the same thing, and Hunsicker asked Brenda for her input.

"It's a sanitized atmosphere just like we have on the Athena," Brenda confirmed.

"So we can take our helmets off then?" Zack asked.

They all glanced at each other, and Redford was the first to take his helmet off. His hawk-like face split into a grin as he breathed in the air.

"This is amazing," Kaylan said.

The rest of them took off their helmets.

"Does this mean they breathe air like we do, or that their systems were smart enough to detect the type of atmosphere we breathe and reproduced it?" Zack asked.

"Could be either of those," Kaylan said.

The lighting in the corridors beyond grew brighter and extended off in opposite directions.

"Let's split into two teams," Hunsicker said.

Zack became aware of Katie standing next to him. He glanced at her, but her gaze was fixed on Hunsicker.

Hunsicker gave her a small nod. "Hicks, why don't you take Kaylan and Nikolai and explore the east side of the structure. The rest will come with me and we'll head west. Check in every fifteen minutes. Judging by the state of the inside, it looks like this place is running on reserve power, or the main power system is on standby."

"Be careful," Zack called out to the others. Kaylan waved back at him.

They walked down the hall, carrying their helmets. It was warmer inside than Zack had expected. The walls were a swirling mix of dark grayish hues. Glowing cyan lines the same height as his chest ran along the wall. The soft white lighting overhead gave them plenty of light to see by. The way forward curved to the right, and further along was an open doorway.

Hunsicker stopped outside the room, and Katie reached out to hold him back.

"Let me clear the room first," Katie said, and then handed Zack her helmet. She brought up her weapon and stepped inside.

The room opened into a large, circular dome where the ceiling was more than triple the height it was out in the corridor. Spaced throughout were large, rounded workstations with couches that extended up and away from them like a small stadium.

Zack moved over to the nearest workstation and sat on the edge of the couch. He tapped the area in front of him and nothing happened. He chewed the inside of his bottom lip and glanced at his hand, then removed his gloves and tapped the area in front of him again. A holodisplay outlined in bronze sparked to life.

"I wonder if this is some kind of control room," Redford said.

The others surrounded him.

"It looks like their system is starting," Zack said.

Alien symbols started cascading across the screen in rapid succession. Zack brought up his PDA so he could try and read the information.

"Looks like you were right. They're on standby power," Zack said.

"Are you able to turn the power on from here?" Redford asked.

Zack frowned. "I'm not sure if that's such a good idea."

"Agreed," Hunsicker said. "Even if we could do it from here, we don't know what turning on the power will do."

After a few moments' consideration Redford nodded, though he looked annoyed.

"See what you can find out, but be careful. We're poking around in the dark here," Hunsicker said to Zack.

"I will," Zack said. "If this is set up like the shroud network, then I should be able to decipher the status of the systems for this place."

Hicks called them over comms.

"Sir, we've found something I think you need to take a look at," Hicks said.

"What have you found?" Hunsicker asked.

"We think it's some kind of power station for this place," Hicks said.

Redford's eyes widened with anticipation.

"All right, we'll be right there," Hunsicker said.

"I'd like to stay and see what I can learn from here," Zack said.

"I'll keep an eye on him, sir," Katie said.

Hunsicker nodded, and the others followed him out of the command center.

Zack opened the case that held his equipment. If he had to keep working off his PDA, he would claw his own eyes out. He needed something with a little more computing power. He set up his own computer and started scanning different frequencies around him based on what he had learned from the shroud network. A smile lit up his face.

"What is it?" Katie asked.

"I was hoping for this. Our alien friends are practical in the sense that the shroud network operates on similar protocols as they have here. This is going to speed things up," Zack said.

"You're cute when you get excited." Katie smiled.

"You better not start distracting me." Zack grinned.

"Keep working, smarty-pants," Katie said.

Zack focused back on the screens in front of him, relishing the challenge they posed. He always enjoyed the thrill of hacking into a new network, except in this case it would be the hack of a lifetime. He rubbed his hands together. *Let's see what you've got.*

Chapter Twenty-Three

Kaylan peered into the large room where they thought the reactor was. The components were much more complex than what they had on the Athena, but certain things were reminiscent of a fusion core. A window separated them from the large interior. Thick black cables several feet in diameter ran to a pedestal where a pitch-black orb hovered in the air. A faint purplish glow shone along the edges. The orb spun slowly on its axis and had the appearance of liquid metal.

"There's more over here," Hicks called.

Kaylan stepped away from the window and headed for one of the smaller rooms off to the side. Hicks and Nikolai found some storage rooms that were filled with dark metal containers seemingly made of the same materials as the structure itself. Hicks and Nikolai opened one of the crates and a blue glow reflected off their stunned faces.

Kaylan entered the room and gasped. Inside the container

were orbs glowing with pinpricks of light like tiny galaxies swirling around. She held up her PDA and waited for Zack's program to translate the alien symbols inside the container. After a few seconds, a lone question mark appeared on the display.

If the orbs were dangerous, would they be left out in the open in an unlocked container? She reached inside and ran her fingertips across one of the orbs. The orb grew brighter at her touch and then immediately dimmed when she pulled her hand away.

"What do you think they are?" Hicks asked.

"I'm not sure," Kaylan said, touching one of the orbs again. "It reacts to touch. I can feel it along my skin like static electricity."

"Maybe we shouldn't touch them," Hicks warned.

Kaylan withdrew her hand and they closed the case. They heard Hunsicker call them from outside the reactor room and went out to meet him.

"This is it!" Redford exclaimed. "You've found the reactor. It's radically more advanced than anything we have back on Earth, but still, the concepts should be similar enough to figure—"

"We're not turning this thing on," Hunsicker said.

Redford rolled his eyes. "Not this again. We didn't come all this way to take a catalog of what's here and then leave. We need to find out how this place works."

"You're in such a rush to turn it on you haven't stopped to consider why they turned it off to start with," Hunsicker said.

"Perhaps Efren could help determine the status of the reactor," Kaylan said.

Hunsicker sighed. "I've sent the shuttle back to the Athena. Efren and the others will be here soon."

"We found some containers in the other room," Hicks said.

Redford clapped his hands and headed for the room. Hunsicker nodded for Hicks to follow and motioned for Kaylan to wait.

"This is the happiest I've ever seen Redford," Kaylan said.

"He's being reckless," Hunsicker said. "I wanted to ask what you thought of this place. Is it anything like you thought it would be?"

Kaylan leveled her gaze at Hunsicker. "It's exactly what I saw down to the finest detail."

Hunsicker glanced at Brenda, who nodded. "If I didn't know better, I'd say she'd been here before."

"That's remarkable. Did you see anything else about this place?" Hunsicker asked.

"Remarkable? Scary is more like it. I don't even understand how it works."

"I'm sure you'll figure it out in time, and there haven't been any more occurrences like the last time," Hunsicker said.

"I've been trying to figure that out. There's no reason I should know the location of the reactor or that those two storage rooms were over there. There is another place I'd like to check out, but I don't know what would be worse—if it's there or if it's not there. I'm supposed to be your second in command for this mission, but how can I be fit for duty if I'm—"

"What," Hunsicker cut her off, "some kind of freak? What you're able to do is like any other talent."

"If I'd come into this program saying I could see a location and learn its layout without ever having been there, I wouldn't have been selected by NASA to become an astronaut, much less be on this mission," Kaylan said.

Hunsicker gave her a patient look. "You think you're the first astronaut to exhibit signs of a sixth sense? Think again. This is a tool and could be an exceptionally powerful tool in your arsenal. Don't be afraid. Test it. Collect the data and then draw your own conclusions. If it isn't reliable or it hurts you in some form, then you don't have to use it."

Kaylan pursed her lips in thought. "Sounds like you've been meaning to say that for a while."

"You're part of my crew. We look out for one another," Hunsicker said.

Redford came out of the storage room with his eyes alight like a kid in a candy store. "I'd like to take some of this back to the Athena to study. The equipment I would need can't be brought down here."

"All right," Hunsicker said. "Let's finish exploring and start taking some of these things back to the ship. One thing, though. Nothing goes back to the ship without some assessment beforehand."

Redford nodded. "We'll need to prioritize."

They spent the next few hours going through the containers and cataloging what they thought they'd found, which made it difficult for them to make any type of accurate assessment for some things. Others were tools and supplies. One small room had a large oval table, and Zack's translator returned the word *healing* in the midst of the alien symbols. They marked it as the structure's medical bay. There were very few things in the way of comforts. Some of the doors were locked, and they hadn't been able to get through them.

The more time Kaylan spent here, the more she itched to check out if this place had the small pyramid-like structure she had seen in her sessions with Brenda. She needed to confirm whether or not it was real.

———

"Hey everyone, Zack here. I just wanted to send out an update. I was able to decipher some of the logs, and the aliens refer to this place as a listening station. The station has been here for a hundred and fifty years. The shroud appears to have been here for about the same amount of time. Oh, and if that wasn't weird enough for you, they didn't run out of power. The place was shut down sixty years ago when the original message was sent to Earth. It looks like when this station is operating at full power, it's able to receive signals from wherever these aliens come from. I'm still checking on that, but there was one last thing. They shut the station down because of some type of threat. The logs don't mention the Xiiginn though," Zack finished.

The lighting in the command center dimmed and then returned to normal.

Katie frowned. "That's the fourth time that's happened. Are you sure it's not something you're doing?"

Zack shook his head. "I'm just gathering information, not playing with the lights or any other system."

Katie eyed him for a moment. "Okay. Are you making a backup? You know, copying it up to the Athena."

"That's a good idea," Zack said, and opened up a comms channel to the ship.

"Athena here," Brenda said.

"I just wanted to let you know that I'm going to be copying

some of this data up to the ship, so if you see a warning message about it, just ignore it," Zack said.

"Acknowledged."

"When did Brenda get back to the ship?" Katie asked.

"She and Nikolai went back up about an hour ago with some of the containers they found here," Zack said.

Katie nodded and glanced over to the door.

"You don't have to stay here and babysit me. If you want to go look around, I'll be fine," Zack said.

"No, we stick together, so if I want to walk around, then you'll have to come with me," Katie replied, and headed for the door.

"Oh, you mean now. I'll be right there," Zack said, and got up from the chair.

He needed to stretch his legs anyway, and they had been stuck in the command center for hours. It would be good for them to take a look around.

KAYLAN LED Hicks further into the station. They had to climb up a staircase meant for beings that were on average two feet taller than they were. They hardly had to use their suit lights because the lighting in the corridors always came on ahead of them. She hadn't seen anything like motion sensors but knew there must be something that tracked their progress.

"Do you know where you're going?" Hicks asked.

"I think so. If I'm right, then just around that corner there should be a doorway that leads to a room," Kaylan said.

"Another storage room?"

"I don't think so," Kaylan replied.

"It's strange that we haven't found any living quarters yet," Hicks said.

"Agreed. Even if this place is meant to run autonomously, I would have expected something in the way of living quarters and a kitchen or something."

"Katie and Zack found some locked doors, so it's possible they're there," Hicks said.

Hicks must have noticed the frown on Kaylan's face because he reached out to her.

"What's the matter?"

Kaylan pinched her lips together and shook her head. "It's dumb."

Hicks's eyebrows drew up, and his eyes filled with mirth that he could barely contain. "You're jealous."

"No, I'm not," Kaylan said quickly, walking faster.

"Yes, you are," Hicks replied, following her. "Don't worry. Your secret is safe with me."

Kaylan stopped in her tracks and glared at the wall. "I don't even know why. It's not like Zack and I were a thing."

"Yeah, but there is a history there. Anyone could tell that," Hicks said.

They continued down the corridor.

"I didn't even think about him until I saw him again in that hangar in North Carolina. It had been ten years since the last time I'd seen him," Kaylan said.

"So old feelings started to stir."

"I guess," Kaylan said.

"Well then, he's an idiot."

Kaylan laughed and then grew serious. "I can't even fault him for being with Katie. I like her. She's great," Kaylan said.

Hicks shrugged. "You won't get any arguments about Katie from me. We've been friends for years, but I think there's more here than just about Zack and Katie."

Kaylan shook her head. "He never told me how he felt about me. I know he had feelings for me, and I did for him too, I think, but we never talked about it."

"So tell him how you feel."

"No. I won't do that to him."

"Why not? I mean, if you have feelings for him, then you should tell him."

"That's just it. I don't know how I feel. It's like one moment something was there and the next it was gone," Kaylan said.

"Oh, I see," Hicks said.

"What's that supposed to mean?"

"You act as if you had some kind of prior claim on Zack, only neither of you knew it, and someone else stepped in."

Kaylan glared at him, searching for any excuse to yell at him, but his fiery blue eyes just calmly looked back at her. "I suppose you would have just taken the bull by the horns or clubbed her over the head to get your point across."

Hicks's lips curved into a half smile as he stepped closer to her. Kaylan stood her ground, and he stopped within inches of her face. His blue eyes had specks of brown in them. "If I was interested in someone, I would take the chance. If I was really interested in her, I would have taken some time to get to know her. Then, in the hallway of some alien outpost, I would listen to her talk about how she's hung up on some other guy, all the while wondering if I was too late to make my own intentions known."

As Hicks talked, Kaylan's back brushed up against the wall.

Hicks leaned in. "And if I couldn't find the right moment because we're facing one disaster after another, I would just kiss her," Hicks said, and kissed her.

Kaylan found herself kissing him back as if all the pent-up frustration had boiled over. Hicks pulled her closer to him, and for a few fierce moments she lost herself in his strong embrace.

Their suit comms chimed, and Hunsicker asked for their whereabouts. Hicks pulled away from her. "This isn't over," he said, and then answered Hunsicker.

"Have there been any power fluctuations going on where you are?" Hunsicker asked.

Kaylan frowned. "No, everything is fine here."

"We might need everyone to pull back until we can figure out what's going on," Hunsicker said.

"All right. We'll finish checking out the area we're in and then head back," Kaylan said.

"Acknowledged," Hunsicker said.

Hicks wore a wry grin, and Kaylan felt herself smile. "Let's go."

"After you, ma'am," Hicks replied.

They had just rounded the corner when they felt the floor shudder beneath their feet. After a moment it was gone. They shot each other quick looks and kept moving.

"There's the door," Kaylan said, and tried not to glance back at him.

He had kissed her. She had imagined kissing him sometimes. They had been working together closely since they'd first come on board the Athena. He was quite handsome, but his timing was either terrible or perfect, and she couldn't decide which.

There was a panel next to the closed door, and it lit up as they approached. Kaylan pressed her palm against it, and the door opened. Glowing cyan lights raced up the cathedral-high ceilings, coming to a central point. Crimson lines of light also came on from twin points on the floor and continued to an interior pyramid inside the room. The pyramid was made of steel-colored blocks outlined in a red glow. The door to the pyramid sank into the floor, showing an inner chamber beyond.

Kaylan stepped toward it, and Hicks reached out to stop her.

"Are you sure about this? We don't know what this place is or what's inside that thing," Hicks said.

"I've seen this place before. I feel like I was supposed to come here," Kaylan said.

Hicks glanced at the pyramid and back at Kaylan. "Just a quick look around. Then we can come back with some equipment and take some readings."

They crossed the room and stood just outside the pyramid. Across the threshold was a string of alien symbols. She held up her PDA and waited for the translation.

"It says only one may enter," Kaylan read.

Hicks sucked in a breath. "I'm not letting you go in there alone. It's not safe."

Kaylan leaned in to take a closer look. "There isn't much in there. I'm gonna take a quick look. If I see something, I'll call you in."

Hicks drew himself up, looking mulish. "Five minutes. If I don't hear from you, then I'm coming in. I don't care what it says in the doorway."

Kaylan nodded and headed inside. As she crossed the threshold, a beam of dark blue came from the ceiling to a crystal sphere rising from the central-most point in the pyramid, and the door behind her hissed shut, cutting Hicks off.

Kaylan brought up her suit comms, but the signal was cut off. The glowing sphere rose until it was eye level with her. Kaylan's eyes scanned the area, looking for a way out. A beam shot from the sphere and then she was lost, her mind spinning down an azure pathway.

Hicks slammed his fists against the metal door. It had closed so quickly that he'd barely had time to react. He backed away and placed his palm on the panel that Kaylan had used to unlock the chamber earlier, but nothing happened.

"Damn it!" Hicks swore, trying the panel several more times.

He knew he shouldn't have let her go in alone. He pushed his ear against the door but couldn't hear anything going on inside. At least she wasn't screaming in pain, or worse. For a moment his mind flashed back to Titus Station where he'd watched a man commit suicide to save him. The floor shuddered beneath his feet, stronger than it had before. Hicks backed away and started circling the perimeter of the pyramid, looking for a way inside.

Chapter Twenty-Four

Zack and Katie were running back to the command center. The quakes were getting more frequent. He racked his brain trying to go over everything he had done. He was sure he hadn't tripped anything off—at least nothing that would cause this. They rounded the corner and found Hunsicker in the command center, trying to raise the crew on suit comms.

"What do you mean trapped?" Hunsicker asked, speaking into his PDA.

"She went inside a room, and the door shut behind her. I've been trying to find a way inside, but the panel isn't working," Hicks said.

Hunsicker glanced at them as they came in.

Zack bolted to his equipment. "I'll see what I can do."

Earlier he had found a schematic of the station and was noting where the unexplored areas were. He uploaded the schematic to their own systems and used Hicks's suit telemetry to pinpoint their position.

Zack frowned at the readout. "It says it's a Mardoxian chamber. I'm not sure what that is. It might be that she needs to unlock it from the inside."

"Can you override the door controls?" Hicks asked.

"I'm working on it," Zack said.

"Commander, this is Athena," Brenda said.

"Go ahead, Athena," Hunsicker said.

"I'm getting strange energy readings from Athena's sensors," Brenda said.

"What kind of readings?" Hunsicker asked.

"They look like energy spikes, but it's coming from a point in space not far from the ship," Brenda replied.

Hunsicker glanced at Zack and Katie. "We're aborting. Is the shuttle still en route to the surface?"

"Yes. It should touch down in the next ten minutes," Brenda said.

"Okay, we're going to evacuate here. In the meantime I want you to start the preflight checklist Kaylan had ready in case we needed to leave quickly," Hunsicker said.

"Acknowledged," Brenda replied.

Hunsicker looked at Zack. "Can you get the door open in ten minutes?"

Zack looked downward, considering, and then he steeled himself. "Yes."

"Okay, get that door open and then get the hell out of here," Hunsicker said.

"Sir, where are you going?" Katie asked.

"The others haven't checked in. They were last at the reactor," Hunsicker said grimly.

"I can come with you if you think there's trouble," Katie offered.

Hunsicker shook his head. "Stay here with Zack and make sure you get yourselves out of here."

Hunsicker grabbed his helmet and ran out of the command center.

Zack focused on the alien system in front of him and got to work. There was no way he was leaving Kaylan behind.

―――――――――

THE MARDOXIAN CHAMBER on the ninth planet of the Sol system activated for the first time in sixty years. Kaylan shut her eyes against the dark blue beam of light. She felt something shift in her mind, and her perceptions were swept away along a highway made of pure light.

The light faded and Kaylan opened her eyes. She was within a pyramid, but it was outlined in a dark green glow. A tall figure was seated. Kaylan couldn't see more than an outline of it at first. The figure rose to its feet, easily eight feet tall. Its dark brown skin held roughened crags reminiscent of tree bark. It was humanoid in shape. The alien opened its eyes, and bright green irises reflected the light. Seemingly startled by Kaylan's presence, its brows drew downward in compassion, and Kaylan found herself less afraid than she thought she should have been. The entity's long features remained passive, and it gestured with one of its large hands for Kaylan to sit on the floor. It sat first, and Kaylan followed suit. Bringing its hands up as if it were holding a bowl of air, the alien closed its eyes and Kaylan felt a strange sensation in her mind, as if she were feeling someone else's emotions. The creature opened its eyes and nodded.

Human.

Kaylan stiffened and then relaxed. The word had been spoken in her mind. Kaylan nodded.

This will not be gentle, and for that I am truly sorry. Time is short, and the use of the chamber will draw unwanted attention. Come find me when you wake up. I am Ma'jasalax.

Before Kaylan could form a question, a golden glow blinded her. She felt herself thrust backward as if she were falling through the air. Images played through her mind on a thousand screens. It was too much for her to keep up with. The last of the images before Kaylan lost consciousness were of Earth, along with profound regret, but the emotions were not her own. They were the alien's.

THE DOOR to the Mardoxian chamber opened.

"It worked!" Hicks exclaimed.

"I haven't done anything yet," Zack said.

Hicks ignored Zack's reply and plunged into the chamber. Kaylan lay unconscious on the floor. *Not again,* Hicks thought. She was in a trance, like she had been before, and completely unresponsive. Hicks grabbed her helmet and placed it on her head. He put his own helmet on and lifted Kaylan in his arms.

"I've got her. I'll meet you at the shuttle."

Chapter Twenty-Five

Commander Michael Hunsicker double timed it to the reactor, cursing himself for not keeping a better eye on Jonah. Efren should have known better than to start the reactor. Jonah had been so fixated on restoring full power to the alien listening station that it was affecting his better judgment. As brilliant as Redford was, Hunsicker knew he wouldn't have been able to start the reactor without Efren's help. He hadn't thought Efren could be swayed to Jonah's thinking, but he had guessed wrong. Now the structure was becoming more and more unstable. As a space veteran, he should have kept a better eye on Redford or, better yet, not left him alone.

The floor shuddered beneath his pounding feet as he ran across the station. The quakes were getting worse. There might be time to undo the damage if they could shut down the reactor. There was a reason the aliens had shut it down. He closed in on the power station and stormed inside.

"What have you done?" Hunsicker demanded.

Efren stood up from the control panel to the reactor interface. In the room beyond, the alien reactor was booming to life. Bright flashes of light rolled off the liquid metal sphere that spun over the pedestal. Efren held up his hands and glanced back at the control panel. His wide-open gaze was confirmation enough of guilt.

"Can you turn it off?" Hunsicker asked.

"I've been trying. I'm sorry, sir," Efren said.

Redford and Vitomir came in from one of the storage rooms.

"Don't be sorry. We'll learn more about this place now that the reactor is powering up," Redford said.

"I gave an order that it wasn't to be powered on until we had studied it more," Hunsicker said.

Efren glanced at the others and then back at Hunsicker, looking confused, and then his furrowed brow drew forward angrily.

"You told me we had clearance," Efren said, stepping close to Redford.

"You unbelievable bastard!" Hunsicker said.

"Don't be ridiculous. If it were up to you, we'd never have turned the damn thing on and would still be stumbling around in the dark," Redford sneered.

Efren growled and charged. Redford dodged out of the way and slammed the nuclear scientist into the wall. Efren sagged to the floor, unconscious.

Hunsicker stepped toward them, but Vitomir pulled out a pistol.

"Not so fast, Commander," Vitomir said.

Hunsicker stopped in his tracks and held up his hands. "Are you going to shoot me?"

"It's not my first choice, Commander," Vitomir said.

There was another earthquake and the floor shuddered violently beneath their feet. Each of them grabbed onto something to brace themselves. Hunsicker stumbled to the control panel.

"Not another step, Commander. I will shoot you," Vitomir said.

Hunsicker raised his hands. "Turning the power on is causing the earthquakes. Why are you doing this?"

"I won't let the next hundred years be dominated by United States technological superiority," Vitomir said.

"What are you talking about? This was a mission where all the data we learned would be freely shared with the world," Hunsicker said, and risked a glance at the control panel.

"Commander, you are a good man. But the decision is not up to you," Vitomir said.

"It's up to all of us. Put the gun down, help me turn off the reactor, and we can sort this out," Hunsicker said.

Vitomir lowered the gun and glanced at Redford. For a moment Hunsicker believed Vitomir was experiencing a change of heart.

"No, if I do this then your military will take me into custody. Hicks and Garcia are from your military. They've been specially trained," Vitomir said, and pointed the gun back at him.

"That's right," Redford said. "They are part of the special forces partnered with Dux Corporation's contractors for the military. They were sent with us to protect the crew and to see that whatever technology was recovered made its way back to Dux Corps' hands."

"You've seen the mission specs. Nowhere does it say anything like that," Hunsicker said.

Vitomir's eyes darted to Redford and then back at Hunsicker.

"Are you going to shoot all of us?" Hunsicker said.

Redford gazed at Hunsicker, his eyes full of hate and menace. "Dux Corp wasn't the only shadow organization to act on the alien message that came to our planet sixty years ago. There were others."

Hunsicker's eyes widened and took in the sight of the two men before him. "The Russians?"

"That's right," Redford said. "I was recruited right out of Oxford, and it was then that I made sure I would be part of the Athena Mission."

Hunsicker's pulse raced, his mind catching up.

"But they knew I would need help. We needed crew members who weren't on the original manifest," Redford continued.

Hunsicker's eyes darted to Vitomir, his mouth open in horror. "You sabotaged Titus Station?"

Vitomir's hands shook and his eyes teared up. "The explosion was just supposed to cripple the station enough so that you'd have to take me and my crew with you."

Hunsicker felt bile rise up his throat. "Your wife and three of your crew died for you to be here. Is Nikolai part of this too?"

"Don't you mention my wife!" Vitomir shouted, brandishing the gun.

"Why not? She's dead because of you, because of your

actions. That kind of blood will never wash off," Hunsicker said. He'd lost his wife to cancer years ago and would have given anything for one more minute with her.

"Don't you judge me, Commander," Vitomir said.

Another quake shook the alien structure. Hunsicker seized his opportunity and charged Vitomir. He grabbed the hand with the gun and the two men struggled. A bright light flared like lightning from inside the reactor room. Redford grabbed one of the metal containers and swung it at Hunsicker, who side-stepped, and Vitomir took the brunt of the blow.

Hunsicker twisted Vitomir's wrist, and the pistol fell free from his hands. He scrambled to the floor, trying to get the pistol, but Redford beat him to it.

The gun fired. Hunsicker's eyes widened in shock as a lazy tendril of smoke licked the barrel. He felt hot liquid seep down his leg, and he looked down to see a splotch of red expand around his thigh. The nano-fiber of his underclothes constricted around the wound to slow the bleeding, but the bullet was lodged in his femur. Hunsicker stumbled to the ground.

Redford's eyes were as big as saucers as he stared at the gun and then back at Hunsicker. The station shook violently from another quake and the ceiling panels began to crash down. Vitomir pulled Redford back toward the door.

More of the ceiling collapsed, and Hunsicker covered his head with his hands. Something hit his head and his vision went blurry. He shook his head, trying to clear it. He brought up his PDA, but his suit comms was damaged. He couldn't reach the others to warn them. The pile of debris cut him off from the door. He glanced at the control panel. Efren's tablet was still connected to it. Hunsicker pulled himself along the floor, crying out as he jostled his injured leg. His suit recognized the trauma and released painkillers into his system. Hunsicker's head cleared, but he knew it would be short-lived. He opened the video recorder on the tablet and recorded a short message. Zack still had an active connection to the Athena, and Hunsicker thanked God for the young man's presence on this mission. He uploaded the file to Zack's data stream and then sagged against the floor, his vision swimming. Each blink of his eyes took longer until the darkness reached in and wouldn't let him go.

"YOU SHOT HIM," Vitomir said, and groaned as they lifted Efren Burdock's unconscious form.

"I didn't mean to. I swear it was an accident," Redford said.

"The others will never believe that," Vitomir said.

After the ceiling caved in, they'd tried to find a way through, but they were cut off from Hunsicker.

The two men struggled to carry Efren down the corridor, heading for the airlock.

"What are we going to tell the others?" Vitomir asked.

"That the ceiling collapsed and Hunsicker was trapped underneath," Redford said.

"The others won't leave the commander behind, and if his suit comms is working, it will report the trauma to his leg back up to the Athena," Vitomir said.

Redford's arms were screaming in protest, but they couldn't afford to leave Efren behind. He couldn't make himself think about Hunsicker right now.

"We'll figure it out when we get there," Redford said.

They continued on without talking. Carrying the unconscious astronaut was work enough for the two men. Redford cursed their luck. He had just wanted to restore full power to this place and unlock all its secrets. Now it might be lost to them forever.

Chapter Twenty-Six

"Come on, Zack, we need to leave now," Katie said.

Zack stood hunched over the holo-interface, inputting some last-minute commands. He grabbed his tablet and jogged to the door. The earthquakes were coming more frequently, but they made it to the airlock in no time. Zack gasped when he saw Hicks laying Kaylan's unconscious form on the ground.

"I found her unconscious in that room. She won't respond, but she doesn't appear to be injured," Hicks said as they came over.

Katie checked her PDA. "Let's get her to the shuttle. It's landing outside."

Zack moved to Kaylan's feet, and Hicks hunched over and grabbed underneath her arms. Together they lifted Kaylan up. She wasn't heavy at all, but the spacesuit added bulk and weight.

"Has anyone else reported in?" Zack asked.

Hicks shook his head. "Last I heard, the commander was checking the power station inside. Let's get Kaylan to the shuttle, then come back for the others."

The airlock doors opened, and the Plutonian surface lay beyond. Ice and pale-colored rock adorned most of it, and nitrogen snow covered the surface. There was no time to take in the majestic sight of the heavens above. They headed directly to the shuttle and carried Kaylan inside.

Zack looked around to be sure Katie was with them, and she gave him a nod.

"I've got three more on approach," Emma said from the pilot's seat.

Zack and Hicks headed back to the airlock. As the others drew in closer, they saw Redford and Vitomir carrying Efren. They brought Efren inside and secured him.

"Where's Hunsicker?" Hicks asked.

Redford sat down, gasping for breath. "The ceiling in the power station collapsed, and he was caught in it. We couldn't get him out."

Hicks grabbed the emergency salvage kit. "I'm going back for him."

"Major, he's under tons of debris. His suit is offline. You can't get to him," Redford said.

"Like hell we can't. We're not leaving without him," Zack said.

Vitomir came back from strapping Efren to a seat. "No, it is impossible. We would have gotten him out if we could."

Zack narrowed his gaze. Something about the two men roused his suspicions. He glanced at Hicks and saw that he wasn't the only one having trouble believing them.

"Seismic readings are off the charts. We can't stay here," Emma shouted from the front of the shuttle.

At the alien structure, ice and rock were blasted into the air. The dome was starting to glow brighter.

Katie grabbed Hicks's arm. "We can't go after him now. We need to get these people to safety first. It's what the commander ordered. We'll come back for him."

Hicks pressed his lips together and then nodded. He headed to the front of the shuttle, and Emma gave the pilot's seat to him. The shuttle's engines engaged, and they lifted off the surface.

Katie coaxed Zack to a seat, and he glanced out the shuttle's window. The dome of the alien station glowed brightly. It wasn't on fire, but there was definitely energy gathering there. The ground around the alien station shifted as if something underneath was twisting free.

"What's happening to it?" Zack whispered.

Katie sat down next to him, glanced out the window, and shook her head.

Twenty minutes later the shuttle closed in on the Athena. Hicks docked the shuttle and they disembarked. Brenda called them all to the bridge. They used stretchers to carry Kaylan and Efren to the med bay. Efren had a nasty gash on his head, and Katie put a healing band on him that would ease the swelling.

Kaylan appeared to be sleeping, but they couldn't wake her up. Brenda called for them to come up to the bridge with a frantic edge to her voice. They secured Efren and Kaylan to the beds and headed to the bridge.

The door to the bridge opened, and numerous alarms were flashing.

Brenda's relief at seeing them lasted only a few seconds. "Where is Hunsicker or Kaylan? Are they not with you?" Brenda asked.

"Kaylan is in the med bay and …" Hicks's voice trailed off. "Hunsicker is trapped down there."

"What?"

Hicks glanced at Redford, and Brenda's eyes narrowed.

Redford held his hands up in front of him. "The ceiling collapsed on top of him. We're not sure he's alive. His suit comms is offline. Vitomir and I carried Efren to the shuttle."

Hearing that others needed medical attention focused Brenda.

Zack went to the comms station and brought up the alarms on the holodisplay.

"What's going on here?" Hicks asked.

"Hunsicker ordered me to put the preconfigured away-point into the Nav computer for the abort. I authorized it, but the sensor array is picking up an anomaly close to the ship," Brenda said.

Redford studied the data on screen, his mouth agape. He moved over to the window and Zack got up to follow him. A blackened sphere with twisted, bending lights was forming not far from the ship. Light crested along the edges of the sphere as if it were an eclipse, only Zack knew the sun was in the opposite direction.

"The anomaly just appeared?" Redford asked.

Brenda nodded. "Shortly after you left the surface."

"What is it?" Hicks asked.

Redford glanced out the window and back at them, his eyes wide with shock. "I think it's a wormhole."

"That's impossible. Wormholes don't just appear in space," Hicks said.

"Quite the opposite. It's theorized that they do appear in space randomly; however, this doesn't appear to be random at all," Redford said.

"What are the odds that a wormhole would suddenly appear at this particular moment? There's something else going on here," Zack said.

Hicks moved to the pilot's seat. "I don't care about how it got here. We need to move the ship away from it."

"We need to study this—" Redford began.

"Don't start," Hicks cut him off. "We're moving the ship. Then we're heading back down to the surface to rescue the commander."

Redford narrowed his gaze. "Who put you in charge?"

"Are you seriously arguing with me about going to rescue Hunsicker?" Hicks asked.

Redford made a move to grab Hicks by the shoulder, and Katie was there in an instant, seizing his hand and twisting it around. Inside a second, Redford was bent over with his arm pinned against his back.

Everyone on the bridge was frozen in place. Redford struggled against Katie, but Zack knew it was hopeless. Once Katie had a person pinned, the only way that person was getting up was if she allowed it.

Hicks climbed out of the pilot's seat and nodded to Katie, who let Redford go. Redford turned around, rubbing his shoulder, his face dark with anger. Katie coolly stared him down as if daring him to try something.

"Are we done yet?" Hicks asked. "If you try something like

that again, I'll have you confined to your quarters. If that fails, I'll think of something else. Do we have an understanding?"

Redford glared at them and nodded.

"You want to study the thing, fine, but we're moving the ship and going back for Commander Hunsicker. Both you and Vitomir will be coming with us. Is that understood?" Hicks said.

"Of course," Vitomir said.

"Fine," Redford said.

Zack kept watching Vitomir. The Russian sounded sincere, but something just seemed off with him.

Hicks returned to the pilot's chair and entered a new course for the Nav computer to execute. Katie kept an eye on the others. A few seconds later, Hicks swore.

"What is it?" Zack asked.

"The engines won't respond. The reactor is fine, but it's like the Nav computer won't accept the new course," Hicks said.

Zack frowned and headed over to the comms station. Just then the engines engaged, sending them toward the wormhole.

"I can't shut the engines down. They won't respond. Neither do the maneuvering thrusters," Hicks said.

Zack's fingers flew through the interface, bringing up his own command prompt. He tried to override the Nav computer, but it rejected his attempts. "I can't either."

"I thought you said NASA couldn't override Athena's systems because you removed their lockout," Hicks said.

"I did. Unless there's someone else …" Zack's voice trailed off.

He brought up another command window and started checking connections. The only thing connected to the outside was the connection he had established from the command center at the alien station. Zack's gut clenched as he looked over at Hicks in horror.

"It's them," Zack said.

"Who?"

Zack frowned and tried to kill the connection, but it didn't work. "Holy crap! The aliens are in the system," Zack said.

"How the hell could they be in our system?" Hicks said.

"I had created an uplink and started uploading their files, but their systems were passive. I don't understand how this could be happening. They've locked us out," Zack said.

Zack and Hicks stared at each other, at a loss for words.

"Hold on to something," Katie shouted.

The Athena increased its velocity, closing in on the wormhole. The crew scrambled to a seat on the bridge and strapped themselves in. Zack reached out and grabbed Katie's hand. They watched the view of the stars out the window folding away from them as if they were riding a huge wave. The ship started to shimmy. Anything not secure crashed to the floor. The seats shook and alarms blared their warnings on the bridge. Zack closed his eyes, praying for it to end. He felt as if he were bolting down the first long drop of an extremely high rollercoaster. Lines of starlight rippled past the windows. The shaking got so bad, Zack was sure the ship would come apart and they would all die. A crushing force pinned him to the chair, and pinpoints of light pressed in on his vision. He squeezed his eyes shut and held on to Katie's hand for all he was worth.

Chapter Twenty-Seven

Zack was slumped in his chair when he finally regained consciousness. A battalion of miniature jackhammers were working overtime in his head. He groaned as he pulled himself upright and heard the others waking up around the bridge.

Zack unbuckled himself from the seat, while Katie did the same. The others on the bridge looked as haggard as he felt.

"Is everyone all right?" Zack asked.

Most of them nodded. Brenda headed for the door, saying she was going to check on Kaylan and Efren. The holodisplay showed a long list of system failures, but at least life support was working, and they still had power.

"Looks like we'll need to reset the sensor array so we can see where we are," Redford said.

Hicks nodded. "We'll need to run diagnostics on all the systems and see what shape we're in."

Zack glanced at them and appreciated the fact that while

there were still some really big questions to be answered, they needed to work together or everyone would die out here.

"We went through a wormhole. We could be light years away from Earth. How are we going to get back home?" Zack asked.

"One thing at a time," Hicks said. "We fix what we can, figure out where we are, and then take it from there."

They all nodded. Redford and Vitomir left the bridge. Emma followed soon after to check on the hydroponic garden.

Hicks came over to the comms station where Zack and Katie were.

"We need to keep an eye on Redford and Vitomir. They're hiding something," Hicks said.

"You don't need to tell me twice," Zack said.

Hicks and Katie left him alone on the bridge. There was a lot of work to do. Zack began checking the comms systems and noticed there was a message waiting from Efren's terminal. Zack opened the message and the video of Michael Hunsicker's face appeared.

"Hello, Zack. I know you'll be the first to see this. I've been shot by Redford. I'm not sure he meant to do it, but you cannot trust him or Vitomir. Perhaps Nikolai as well. The destruction of Titus Station wasn't an accident …"

Zack's mouth opened wider the more he listened. He kept glancing over his shoulder, expecting someone to sneak up on him. He couldn't believe it. He knew Redford was ruthless, but shooting someone? The door to the bridge opened, and Zack quickly exited Hunsicker's video message. Nikolai came through and nodded to Zack before going to a workstation on the other side of the bridge. Zack swallowed his growing angst, wondering if Nikolai was there to kill him. No, they wouldn't do anything now. They had to repair the ship, and that would require the skill of the entire crew, but what would happen after that? Zack took a deep breath and began making a mental list of tasks he had to do, while weighing what their next course of action would be.

MICHAEL HUNSICKER WOKE up on a table under the warm glow of an overhead light. His spacesuit had been removed. He blinked his eyes and tried to raise his head, but his muscles felt like dead weight. He worked his mouth enough to swallow, and even that was a monumental effort. His leg ached where he'd been shot. The dark gray walls of the alien station surrounded him, but he didn't recognize where he was. The table he rested on was warm and emitted an amber glow. The warmth seeped into his arms and legs until he felt his strength returning. His vision cleared and his mind became more alert. Hunsicker reached down to his thigh where the gunshot had punctured his suit. The nanofiber of his under-suit had stemmed the blood flow and kept him from bleeding out. The wound was gone.

He sat up and slowly swung his feet to the side. A slight clearing of the throat and shifting of feet off to the side drew his attention, and he froze. He wasn't alone. Across from him was the largest being he had ever seen. It had brown, roughened skin with crags that reminded him of the bark of a tree. Its head had pronounced facial features that framed large, pale, flaxen eyes. Dark hair hung down to its massive shoulders, tied off with white beads. The alien's eyes drew him in and watched him as if reserving judgment.

Hunsicker glanced down at his fully healed leg and back at

the creature. His PDA with Zack's translation program was with his spacesuit, which he didn't see anywhere in the room.

The creature began to speak, and it took a moment for Hunsicker to realize that it was trying to speak the different languages spoken on Earth.

"Thank you for healing my leg," Hunsicker said, gesturing down to his thigh.

The creature's eyes followed his movements and nodded.

"My name is Michael Hunsicker."

"I am called Chazen," the alien said in a deep voice commensurate with its great size.

"Do you know what happened to the other people who were here with me?"

Chazen watched him. "They are not here."

Hunsicker drew in a breath, trying to rein in his thoughts. He was millions of miles away from home. He didn't know where anyone was, and he was talking to an alien who looked like he could crush a small car.

"Why are you here?" Chazen asked.

"We came to investigate this place," Hunsicker said, and repeated the alien's question.

"We watched you for a long time," Chazen said.

Judging by the simplistic responses, Hunsicker assumed the alien spoke only basic English.

"Our ship was in orbit around this planet. If I could contact them they might be able to help repair the station," Hunsicker said.

Chazen still wore the look of reserved judgment, and Hunsicker didn't think the alien meant to harm him. It had healed his leg, after all.

"The ship is gone," Chazen said.

"Gone? Where did it go?" Hunsicker said, finding it hard to believe the Athena had left without him. Even if Redford had convinced them he was dead, there was no way Kaylan and the others would have left him behind.

"To home system. Why was the power restored?" Chazen asked.

Right to the crux of the matter. How was he supposed to explain what had happened? "It was an accident."

Chazen lifted his hand. "You were hurt by a weapon."

"Yes, I was," Hunsicker replied.

Chazen seemed to accept this.

"How long have you been here? Where were you?" Hunsicker asked.

Chazen took a moment, considering. "Asleep. I've been here for sixty Earth cycles. Gateway was ordered closed."

Hunsicker frowned, trying to piece the information together. "You were trapped here?"

Chazen nodded. "There was great danger. Couldn't risk opening the gateway."

"But we turned on the power," Hunsicker said. Again the warning—both from the alien message fifty years ago and just now. Since the alien had been asleep for that long, it must have used some form of suspended animation. "What happens now?"

Chazen gestured with his large hand toward the door. "We prepare."

"For what?"

"The Xiiginn."

Afterword

THANK YOU FOR READING STAR SHROUD - ASCENSION SERIES - BOOK 1.

If you loved this book, please consider leaving a review. Comments and reviews allow readers to discover authors, so if you want others to enjoy *Star Shroud* as you have, please leave a short note.

If you would like to be notified when my next book is released please visit kenlozito.com and sign up to get a heads up.

About the Author

Ken Lozito is the author of multiple science fiction and fantasy series. I've been reading both genres for a long time. Books were my way to escape everyday life from when I was a teenager to my current ripe old(?) age. What started out as a love of stories has turned into a full-blown passion for writing them. My ultimate goal for writing stories is to provide fun escapism for readers. I write stories that I would like to read and I hope you enjoy them as well.

If you have questions or comments about any of my works I would love to hear from you, even if its only to drop by to say hello at KenLozito.com

Thanks again for reading *Star Shroud.*

Don't be shy about emails, I love getting them, and try to respond to everyone.

If you would like to be notified when my next book is released, SIGN UP HERE

Connect with me at the following:
www.kenlozito.com
ken@kenlozito.com

Also by Ken Lozito

First Colony Series

GENESIS

NEMESIS

LEGACY

SANCTUARY

Ascension Series

STAR SHROUD

STAR DIVIDE

STAR ALLIANCE

INFINITY'S EDGE

RISING FORCE

ASCENSION

Safanarion Order Series

ROAD TO SHANDARA

ECHOES OF A GLORIED PAST

AMIDST THE RISING SHADOWS

HEIR OF SHANDARA

BROKEN CROWN SERIES

Haven of Shadows

Made in the USA
San Bernardino, CA
22 February 2019